THE FOWL TWINS

GET WHAT THEY DESERVE

EOIN COLFER

HarperCollins *Children's Books*

First published in the United Kingdom by
HarperCollins *Children's Books* in 2021
Published in this edition in 2022
HarperCollins *Children's Books* is a division of HarperCollins*Publishers* Ltd,
1 London Bridge Street
London SE1 9GF

www.harpercollins.co.uk

HarperCollins*Publishers*
Macken House, 39/40 Mayor Street Upper,
Dublin 1, D01 C9W8, Ireland

4

ISBN 978–0–00–847525–3

Typeset in Jenson Pro by Palimpsest Book Production Ltd, Falkirk, Stirlingshire
Printed and bound in the UK using 100% renewable electricity
at CPI Group (UK) Ltd

THE FOWL TWINS

Books by Eoin Colfer

AIRMAN
BENNY AND OMAR
BENNY AND BABE
HALF MOON
INVESTIGATIONS

THE
SUPERNATURALIST
THE WISH LIST
IRON MAN:
THE GAUNTLET

The Artemis Fowl series

ARTEMIS FOWL
THE ARCTIC INCIDENT
THE ETERNITY CODE
THE OPAL DECEPTION

THE LOST COLONY
THE TIME PARADOX
THE ATLANTIS COMPLEX
THE LAST GUARDIAN

The Fowl Twins series

THE FOWL TWINS
THE FOWL TWINS DENY ALL CHARGES
THE FOWL TWINS GET WHAT THEY DESERVE

The W.A.R.P. series

THE RELUCTANT ASSASSIN
THE HANGMAN'S REVOLUTION
THE FOREVER MAN

Graphic novels

ARTEMIS FOWL: THE GRAPHIC NOVEL
THE ARCTIC INCIDENT
THE ETERNITY CODE
THE OPAL DECEPTION

THE SUPERNATURALIST

And for younger readers

THE LEGEND OF SPUD MURPHY
THE LEGEND OF CAPTAIN CROW'S TEETH
THE LEGEND OF THE WORST BOY IN THE WORLD

To Seamus and Matt,
the internet Vikings

PROLOGUE

THERE ARE THOSE WHO BELIEVE THAT TRUE LOVE is humankind's greatest motivator.

Those people are sweet but completely wrong.

Certainly, true love is a powerful force, but the actual greatest motivator of all is undoubtedly revenge. Humans will climb the highest tower for love, but then murder everyone inside that tower for revenge.

And then possibly demolish the tower.

Once someone commits to a course of vengeance, the changes inside begin: their heart becomes petrified so that love may not enter. Their senses of reason and perspective are cauterised so that good judgement shall never prevail. And any code of decency that they may have lived by is replaced by a single commandment: *Thou shalt do whatsoever needs to be done.*

This is the story of one such revenger and the children he would cheerfully go to the ends of the earth to have his revenge upon. It is also the story of what those children were up to that summer, as these were not the kind of youngsters to simply laze around, waiting for vengeance to be visited upon them.

The man was Lord Teddy Bleedham-Drye, the Duke of Scilly, and the children, you may be less than surprised to learn, were the Fowl Twins.

It may seem unlikely that a peer of the British realm would devote his precious time to the killing of twelve-year-old Irish twins, but these particular boys had grievously wronged the duke, and Lord Teddy was determined to repay them in kind, by which he meant slay them in a convoluted and epic manner.

For decades, Lord Teddy had been consumed by two objectives:

1. Live as long as possible (one hundred and fifty years plus so far). And . . .
2. Mount a claim to the British throne. But for this he would need the Lionheart ring, which we shall come to later.

And now Teddy had developed a third obsession: killing those blasted twins.

It may also occur, if a person is at all familiar with the notorious Fowl Twins, that the duke's chances of putting one over on Myles and Beckett were slim at best. But Lord Bleedham-Drye was something of a specialist in the art of vengeance. This was not, as American humans might say, his first rodeo.

In point of fact, Lord Teddy considered the Fowl crusade to be the third epic revenge campaign in his one-hundred-and-fifty-year life. His first was hunting the border-fens fox to extinction simply because one had stolen a salmon sandwich from Queen Victoria's fingers at a picnic he was hosting, which was simply devastating for the duke, as it put the brakes on his plan to become her second husband, the most direct route to the crown.

The second quest for vengeance is quite famous in the annals of American crime history, as there was quite a gruesome spate of homicides of snake-oil salesmen in the western states during the mid-twentieth century. Lord Teddy had visited such a salesman in California and purchased a life-extending elixir. The concoction had brought on a series of catastrophic bowel movements while he was attending an opera at the governor's mansion. So outraged was the duke by this public humiliation that he did away with the entire network of salesmen over the following season.

Of course, Teddy had dealt many other swift retributions, but he did not count these as proper revenges, as the duke agreed with Charles Dickens, who wrote: *Vengeance and retribution require a long time; it is the rule.*

Lord Teddy considered the Fowls worthy of a campaign because he could honestly say that no human beings living or dead had infuriated him more than the twins. Not only had they avoided being permanently murdered, but they had also utterly ruined Lord Teddy's birth body, thus forcing the duke to have his living brain transferred into a cloned host. To cap it all, they put a rather big hole in his front lawn. And, as every royal correspondent knows, nothing matters more to a duke than his daffodils.

No, Teddy old boy, the duke told himself, *the Fowl blighters simply have to go, and that's all there is to it.*

And so Lord Teddy laid his elaborate and unnecessarily complicated plans, resolving that on this occasion he would take pains not to underestimate the Irish boys as he had in the past.

Ishi Myishi, Lord Teddy's closest friend and arms dealer to the world's criminal masterminds, had once told him, 'He who commits his life to revenge is already dead,' but this did not deter the duke from his course in the least, because his plan actually depended on him being dead.

I will be completely and undeniably deceased, thought Teddy as he reclined in the brass bathtub of electric eels where he did the lion's share of his plotting. *And that will be my advantage.*

1
CORPSE

THE SOUTHBANK CENTRE,
LONDON

MYLES FOWL HAD TRAVELLED TO LONDON TO present a lecture to the Coroners' and Pathologists' Association of Southern England, or CORPSE, in London's Southbank Centre on the river. Beckett had tagged along because he thought CORPSE was a fabulous name for a group, plus he instinctively felt that a coroners' convention in London was exactly the sort of setting where a classic Fowl Adventure might kick off, and he would be simply devastated to miss the initial stages.

Also, Myles had promised that he could wear a disguise.

Beckett was absolutely right to tag along, for a Fowl Adventure did in fact *kick off* in the Southbank Centre. However, it was not to be a classic Fowl Adventure, as those generally tended to ramp up

7

towards an explosive climax, whereas the Fowl Phantom Solution (as the affair would be named in fairy Lower Elements Police files) started with a big bang, followed by a series of smaller bangs, then another big bang.

Myles Fowl stood front and centre on the lacquered wood of the Southbank main stage in an auditorium that was packed with the cream of Europe's coroners and pathologists. For even though CORPSE was a British organisation, doctors had flown in from all over the world to hear the Fowl prodigy speak, and Myles had not disappointed. Unless one were disappointed by the fact that the pompous twelve-year-old dressed in a formal tuxedo, bow tie and gleaming patent-leather loafers had not tripped over his own inflated ego and fallen flat on his smug face. Myles had expertly covered molecular pathology, computational pathology and the clear advantages of medicological investigators being recognised as first responders, and he was finishing up with some coroner-related puns.

'And so my *examination* is over,' he said, deactivating the laser pointer in his eyeglass frames. 'And, while I am certain there will be many *postmortems* in the bar, unless there is an *inquest*, this twelve-year-old body must be released.'

Not exactly hilarious stuff, but the members of CORPSE were not expecting stand-up comedy and so, for the most part, they were content to applaud politely. But not everyone was content. A hand shot up from the clumped gloom of the audience.

'Before you go and hang out with your amazing and much more interesting brother . . .' said the short man attached to the hand. He wore thick glasses and sported a bushy moustache. 'Maybe I can ask you a question, *Master* Fowl?'

Myles appeared to fall for the bait. 'I hate to stand on ceremony,' he said, 'but I do prefer to be addressed as *Dr* Fowl when the occasion calls for it, or even *Professor* Fowl in specialist situations like this.'

The man stood, his head jutting into the beam of Myles's spotlight, and read his question from a card. 'That's just it, isn't it, *Master* Fowl? I've done a bit of digging, and you may have doctorates in other areas, but it seems that your PhD in criminal pathology does not exist. It seems very much like you are here under false pretences.'

'Oh, that,' said Myles, as though misrepresenting himself were nothing. 'I can explain that.'

This admission was met with gasps and chatter. Could it be that Myles Fowl was, in fact, a charlatan? A fake?

The questioner flicked to a second card and read the statement written there: 'I think we would all very much like to hear you try.'

Myles gave his full attention to the moustachioed man who had dared to question him. 'It is true,' he said, 'that earlier this morning I had no *official* qualification in pathology. But if you'll allow me a moment to check my email . . .' Myles switched his focus to the lenses of his graphene smart glasses and refreshed his mail feed. 'Ah yes, here we are. As promised by University College London, my doctorate was conferred several minutes ago. I think you'll find that I actually achieved an unprecedented perfect score.'

With a series of blink commands, Myles cast the email to the large screen behind him. The attendees saw a copy of Myles's latest doctorate along with an animation of a digital Myles in a cap and gown, this supplied by NANNI, the Nano Artificial Neural Network Intelligence system that lived in his spectacles.

The questioner was melodramatically aghast. 'Are you telling us that you qualified *during* your lecture?'

'That is true,' conceded Myles.

'What kind of poopy-headed move was that?'

Myles frowned. 'Poopy-headed move? Is that the question you were instructed . . . I mean, is that the question you wanted to ask?'

The moustachioed man cleared his throat and tried another question. 'So you began the lecture unqualified?'

'Technically, perhaps, but actually no,' retorted Myles. 'I began the lecture without an email from the university. That is all. There was never any doubt I would graduate – after all, I spent three whole weeks on this doctorate. Your quibble should really be addressed to the university's communications department, as I was promised my degree several hours ago.'

This was met with murmurs of sympathy from the audience members, who had been forced to deal with university communications offices themselves over the years.

'It is historically true that progress is hindered not by lack of ideas, but by the slow grind of bureaucracy,' concluded Myles. This actually won him a second round of applause, which did not surprise him, as this entire mini inquisition had been part of his plan, the supposed interrogator being, in fact, his twin, Beckett, in the promised disguise.

'Thank you, lesser academics,' said Myles. 'That concludes my lecture, but just as every killer signs his own kills, and every artist signs his own work, I will sign bound copies of my thesis in the foyer. I have instructed my AI to unblock your phones shortly so that you may tell your children that you listened excitedly to a Myles Fowl presentation.'

And indeed that would have been the most exciting moment in many of the audience members' lives had there not been a loud echoing *bang* as the roof peeled back. This was a surprising enough development in and of itself, as this particular auditorium did not have a retractable roof, but it was eclipsed by the appearance of an ultralight aircraft in the space where there had, until recently, been a ceiling. This aircraft dipped inside the theatre itself, hovering at the rear of the hall, and Myles could not help noticing that the craft's stubby wings were adorned with mini machine guns.

'Well now,' said Myles, seemingly to himself but actually to NANNI. 'That is unexpected.'

This was something Myles rarely admitted, as he prided himself on considering all the eventualities in any situation.

'What next? I wonder.'

What next was that the light aircraft opened fire with its portside machine gun, obliterating Myles with multiple rounds. Not the actual Myles, but rather the image of Myles on the screen behind him. Still, the message was clear. Myles Fowl was the target here.

Most people would have been petrified by this development, but Myles Fowl was not most people. In fact, he was not even *some* people – he was unique among twelve-year-olds and grasped the psychology of the moment. If the pilot had wished to kill him immediately, then Myles would be dead. Therefore, this attack was personal.

'Lord Teddy Bleedham-Drye, I presume,' said Myles, though it was not really a presumption. It was a deduction, if one considered the facts:

1. The pilot was an ace.
2. The duke held a grudge against the twins in general and Myles in particular.
3. The flying machine now hovering before him

was the very same Myishi Skyblade that Myles had once been suspended beneath.

In conclusion, if it flew like a duke and shot like a duke, then it was probably a duke.

Knowing Lord Teddy as I do, he will grandstand for a while, thought Myles. *And then he will kill me.*

But, if it was Teddy in that cockpit, then there were a few things his lordship was unaware of.

First, Beckett had shed his disguise and was fashioning a lasso from his shirt and trousers, probably intending to assault an aluminium fighter plane with everyday items of clothing.

And, second, the LEP Fowl liaison officer, Specialist Lazuli Heitz, had been observing the lecture from the stage gantry and had activated her suit's wing system, obviously intending to disobey the *under no circumstances involve the Lower Elements Police in human disputes* directive.

Myles should not have been able to see Specialist Heitz, as she was wearing an advanced shimmer suit, but he had developed a very sneaky workaround. (More on that situation later, as it will play a bigger part in his life than even Myles could have envisioned. For now, all we need to know is that Myles had a few more advantages in this situation than others believed him to have but not as many as he thought he had.)

Even so, Myles was a tad anxious because, after all, even Beck and Lazuli could not outrun bullets.

Yet, in spite of the grim nature of his current circumstances, Myles was also nurturing a spark of hope. He was confident that Teddy would indulge himself in a triumphant villain's rant, thus providing Myles's Regrettables teammates the seconds they would need to come to his rescue.

They have rescued me from more hazardous situations, he realised. But he had to admit, if only to himself, that his life had, in all probability, entered its final hundred heartbeats.

The audience's reaction to the jet's arrival was mixed. At the extreme ends of the behaviour spectrum, there were hysterics, who ran screaming for the exits, and deniers, who remained absolutely calm as though nothing whatsoever were awry. In between these two poles, Myles noted some interesting activity. The lighting technician helpfully trained several spotlights on the hovering aircraft. Two visiting Swedish professors engaged in a fistfight, probably believing that this would be their last chance to settle whatever score existed between them. And several eminent pathologists whipped out phones and snapped selfies with the aircraft in the background.

Come on, Your Lordship, Myles beamed at the Skyblade. *Tell me exactly why I deserve to die.*

The plane dipped its wings, its engines blasting air on the seats below, and Myles saw that the forward windscreen was fogged up.

Show me that royal face, thought Myles. *Give Laz some time to work.*

And it is a measure of Myles's stress levels that he shortened Lazuli's name, as he mostly avoided abbreviations, though he did use *Beck* on occasion to please his twin.

It seemed almost as if Lord Teddy had received Myles's thought-cast, for the glass defogged and the duke's ancient figure appeared hunched over the controls. He opened his mouth to speak, but Myles beat him to it.

'Lord Teddy,' he said, his voice still amplified over the house system, 'so kind of you to attend. Perhaps you had a question for the speaker. The speaker being myself, of course.'

Sometime later, when the twins were summoned back to London for an inquiry about the Southbank affair, a hostage negotiator who had reviewed the tapes set down his Earl Grey tea and said to Myles, 'You do know that provocation is absolutely the wrong course of action to take in these situations. It might have pushed the hostage-taker towards violent action.'

To which Myles said, 'Three things, Mr Earl Grey. First, to label Lord Teddy a hostage-taker gives him all the power in this situation and, as we subsequently found out, the duke was not the one with the power.

'Second, I am reasonably certain, given the battle plane and the dozens of shots fired, that Teddy had already been pushed irreversibly towards violent action.

'And, third, if you want to talk about the wrong course of action, perhaps you should look in a mirror and ask yourself whether that wispy moustache fluttering below your nostrils might have been the wrong course of action for you personally.'

And that was the end of the conversation.

This little flash-forward tells us that Myles survived the duke's attack, and now we shall find out just how he did it.

By the time Teddy could get a word in, he was so

incensed that he spattered spittle on the inside of the windscreen as he spoke.

'We meet again, Myles Fowl!' he wheezed through his ancient slit of a mouth, the shrunken lips drawn back from the teeth. 'Fowl by name, foul by nature!'

Myles winced. How reduced was the once magnificent duke that he would trot out such a hackneyed insult and spit on the glass while doing it?

'Is that all you can muster, Lord Teddy?' he asked. '"Fowl by name, foul by nature"? You do know this is being recorded? You could have referred to me as a *Naegleria fowleri*, which is a brain-eating amoeba. That would have been something. When are you going to realise that you can never beat me and it would be easier on your self-esteem if you simply stopped trying?'

Lord Teddy's face twisted until it was ninety per cent scowl. 'I was going to drag it out, you impertinent, ridiculous boy, but I can stomach your jabber no longer.'

And the duke's bony fingers tightened on the trigger controlling the machine guns, which really should have been the end of the great game for Myles Fowl and yet another trophy for the mighty hunter Lord Teddy Bleedham-Drye. But somehow it was not the end, as

Myles's goose was spared a cooking thanks to the Trojan efforts of his twin, Beckett, and their mutual friend Specialist Lazuli Heitz of the Lower Elements Police.

Lazuli and Beckett, being essentially creatures of action, had realised moments earlier that the immediate threat to Myles was not so much the ranting peer with his finger on the trigger, but the machine guns slung on pivots below the Myishi Skyblade's swept-back wings. And so each Regrettable targeted one of these weapons. Beckett could not actually see the shielded Lazuli, but he trusted that, since he was closer to the starboard weapon, she would take care of the port. And that is exactly what happened, though possibly not exactly as planned.

Beckett quickly stripped down to the gold-thread tie that represented his deceased goldfish, Gloop (*#firstpetsforever*), and his underpants, which were actually a sumo loincloth or mawashi. He found that the loincloth afforded him the most mobility in the event a stripped-down engagement was called for, something that happened to Beckett at a minimum of twice a week. He tied his trousers and shirt together and scanned the nearby audience members for a launchpad, settling almost immediately on the quarrelling Swedish professors, who were locked together in an accidental base-level grip of a human triangle.

Thanks, guys, thought Beckett, and he made his approach.

He skipped along a row of seatbacks, scuttled up one professor's back and springboarded from the crown of the other's head, achieving a vertical lift that could be matched only by Maasai warrior jumpers. Beckett flung his makeshift lasso upwards in what might have seemed like a last-ditch effort, given he was in mid-air when he made the throw, but it was not desperate, as Beckett Fowl was a savant in all things physical and could easily have competed in human or fairy games on an international level. In fact, Lazuli had given him maybe three lessons in the fairy martial art of *Cos T'apa*, and he had already achieved red slipper level, equalling Lazuli herself, who had been studying the art for decades and was more than a little envious of the human boy's lightning-fast progress. So Beckett's lasso-toss landed neatly over the Skyblade's starboard ski, and Beckett swung himself upwards, hooking both legs over the machine-gun barrel.

'Hello, Mr Nasty Gun,' said Beckett, who sincerely disliked guns and most of the people who wielded them.

'Let's see if I can't throw a spanner in your works.' And then he told the gun, 'That's just a figure of speech. I don't actually have a spanner.'

Lazuli, meanwhile, took a less eventful path to the gun she intended to disable. There was no cobbling-together of ad hoc tightrope equipment. Instead, Lazuli simply nudged the throttle of her shimmer suit's flight wings so that she lifted off from the stage's gantry and hovered directly in front of her target weapon. That might seem a reckless place to hover, but Specialist Heitz figured she could shield the human boy with her own fairy body armour, which she had been assured by Foaly could withstand multiple direct hits from anything the humans could throw at it, short of an armour-piercing shell.

Regarding Lazuli's aim, what she planned to aim was her oxalis pistol, which was a considerable upgrade from the previous model. Nearly all her equipment had been upgraded since the affair known in LEP files as the ACRONYM Convergence (see LEP file: *The Fowl Twins Deny All Charges*), and, in fact, the centaur Foaly had made her something of a test case for new technology, so she was equipped to the tips of her pointy ears with his latest updates, versions and breakthroughs.

There were those in the corridors of LEP Police Plaza who whispered that the tech-genius Foaly was obsessed with trumping the Fowls' technological advancements, especially since Artemis Fowl had outshone him comprehensively in previous engagements (see any of the LEP Artemis Fowl files). Foaly denied this, red-faced, but he did not help his case by wearing a lab T-shirt bearing the legend:

FOWL ME ONCE, SHAME ON YOU.

FOWL ME TWICE, SHAME ON ME.

The oxalis organic pistols had superseded the Neutrinos and were named for the weed that ejects its seeds using a ballistichoric system that operates by drying out the fruit walls and getting the layers to pull against each other. The pistols were genetically modified and grown in hydroponic racks, and they could actually be eaten in an emergency. Lazuli's pistol was third generation and shot seeds rather than bullets or rays. She had a range of seed types to choose from, and for this particular task she selected *gumshot* from her visor menu. Gumshots were similar to human rubber bullets except they splatted on impact.

The perfect way to block a machine gun, she thought, and to put a slug down Lord Teddy's port barrel without waiting for aim-assist to lock in on her visor. Her own aim was true, and her seed did not even rattle the sides on its way in. Now she could only pray that the seed had a nanosecond to splat before Lord Teddy had time to pull the trigger.

Lazuli could not know this, but Teddy had already pulled the trigger, and the electronic signal was travelling from the cockpit to the machine gun. It was now a very short race against time to see which projectile would do its work first.

And what was Myles Fowl doing while all this was going on? Surely the boy was petrified with fear and, even if he did have motor-function command, there wasn't enough time for him to actually do anything. But Myles had been in worse fixes and had trained himself to react quickly – mentally, at least. While Lord Teddy was still monologuing, Myles had sent NANNI's electronic fingers probing the Skyblade to see if he could penetrate the duke's defences. Unfortunately, they had been rebuffed by one of the famous Myishi closed systems. Simultaneously, Myles initiated Operation Trapdoor, which was a pretty self-explanatory name. Myles knew Beckett and Lazuli were on the job, but, even so, he judged it prudent to remove himself from the line of fire so that he might remain alive and be of some use to his friends.

Oddly, Operation Trapdoor was having a little trouble initiating. Myles was certain he had sent the correct blink signal into his lenses, but still the trapdoor beneath his feet obstinately refused to move, sending back a *manual only* alert.

Override, Myles blinked, and in five seconds' time he would dearly wish he hadn't blinked those blinks, because a man known by backstage crew all over the world as the Trapmeister General had been tampering with the Southbank's trapdoor, and it did not do what it had been designed to do. Quite the opposite, in fact.

Meanwhile, Beckett was examining the machine gun's swivel housing with one of his most perceptive organs, that being his left ear.

Ball bearings, he thought. *Ball bearings that are ball bearing.*

Beckett still had traces of magic in his system from the time he had been inhabited by the spirit of a long-dead fairy warrior (see LEP file: *The Last Guardian*). The magic had transformed him into a trans-species polyglot or, simply put, he could talk to anyone and anything that could speak. This extended to an uncanny ability to interpret sounds such as ball bearings grinding inside a mechanism – in this case, the swivel mount of a machine gun. The rubber seal had been eaten away by something, possibly salt water, and a tiny section of the inner workings was exposed to the worst possible person to expose workings to.

One of those ball bearings is missing, thought the Irish boy. *And if I could slide something thin in there . . .*

Beckett didn't have anything ideal for the job. However, he did have something a little less than ideal.

Something that was flapping in his face.

Beckett pulled his Gloop tie over his head and said solemnly, 'I shall never forget your sacrifice upon this day. Farewell, my dearest friend.'

Which was a little melodramatic considering there were dozens of identical Gloop ties hanging in the twins' bedroom cupboard on the nearby yacht, the *Fowl Star*.

* * *

The portside machine gun got off the first shot, which impacted on Lazuli's gumshot blockage, inflating it like a bloom of blown glass. Lazuli could actually see the gas and flame roiling inside.

This is a bad idea, Specialist, she told herself. *Get out of the way.*

But she didn't. Lazuli's visor would alert her in the unlikely event she was actually in any danger and *then* she could move, assuming there was time to move.

She had an idea, which was the most counter-intuitive idea an LEP officer could have.

I should duck my head into the line of fire.

Because her helmet was her most heavily armoured piece of equipment and could withstand any amount of direct hits from human bullets, according to Foaly. She barely had time to move her face into harm's way when the next projectile blasted through the gumshot gunge and impacted on her headplate. It did not penetrate, but it did knock out some of Lazuli's systems.

That shouldn't have happened, thought Lazuli, and she realised that perhaps positioning her head in front of a gun barrel had been a rash move.

I need to shut this weapon down, she thought, selecting an explosive seed bullet from her menu.

But Lord Teddy fired first, and the next slug breached her armoured plating, which was supposed to be impossible and might even have killed Lazuli outright had not her SPAM (**Sp**ontaneous **A**ppearance of **M**agic; see LEP file: *The Fowl Twins Deny All Charges*) blossomed in an orange corona around her head, absorbing most of the projectile's momentum so that it lodged in Lazuli's helmet.

Myles is on his own, she thought, as the initial impact sent her cartwheeling towards the rear wall.

Beckett fed his beloved Gloop tie through the break in the seal and into the machine gun's mechanism, which gobbled it up like a strand of spaghetti. The material quickly jammed the weapon's gear and set the swivel whining and smoking. It was, as Myles might say, a serious design flaw. The gun itself turned ninety degrees and shot its first projectile at its brother gun under the opposite wing.

Time to go, thought Beckett. *Farewell, dearest Gloop tie.*

And he unlocked his legs from the ski and dropped towards the auditorium below, judging his mid-air tumble perfectly so that he landed neatly in seat G6.

Over Beckett's head the port gun's self-defence programme took offence at being fired upon and swivelled to face its brother. One furious round of aerial blasting later, the machine guns had strafed each other to scrap metal and hung limply decommissioned from their housings.

Myles had not anticipated this exact turn of events and thought that, had he been in possession of either athleticism or a shimmer suit, he would have perhaps handled things differently. But, in any case, he was relieved that the Regrettables remained in the land of the living, and that his Operation Trapdoor would finally be initiated, having made him wait for an exasperating two seconds.

Myles was not the only exasperated person in the auditorium. Inside his cockpit, the ancient Lord Teddy was enraged beyond actual words. In fact, he seemed to have snapped altogether, and he set the Skyblade into a steep dive so that he might ram the Fowl boy into the next life. The aircraft's nose dipped sharply, and Myles fervently wished that the trapdoor would spring into action, metaphorically speaking.

Metaphorically or not, the trapdoor did indeed

respond to Myles's override blink of a moment before, springing into action. What Myles did not know was that the previous evening's performer on this exact stage had been the pop superstar Shoshona Biederbeck, on the fifth stop of her very first live tour. Part of Shoshona's show was her arrival on an animatronic unicorn that weighed more than a tonne. Her stage manager, the aforementioned Trapmeister General, who had rigged trapdoors from Las Vegas to Las Palmas, had performed a little illegal boosting surgery on the trapdoor's mechanism to ensure that his star and her unicorn arrived safely on to an elevated platform. The Trapmeister had been scheduled to dismantle his trapdoor supercharger on this very evening. However, that was of little use to Myles when the trapdoor panel rushed up to meet him.

Myles's *override* blinks had triggered the piezo-electrical ignition source, unleashing the combustion-launcher equivalent of a volcano under his feet. The result of all this technical jargon was that Myles Fowl was propelled vertically to a height sufficient to give him a view across the Thames to Covent Garden.

I can see the Acorn Club from here, he thought.

Thirty metres below, through a wisp of river fog, the

Skyblade took a bite-shaped chunk from the section where Myles had been standing and belched the duke's body through its windscreen and on to the stage.

That person is dead, thought Myles, zooming in with his glasses. Or so it would appear.

It did not cross his mind to worry that he himself might actually die. After all, he could already see Lazuli speeding towards him to perform a mid-air rescue, the orange corona of magic trailing behind her helmet like a comet trail.

Not that she knows I can see her, thought Myles with some satisfaction.

In the guise of straightening his bow tie, Myles raised his elbows so that Lazuli might easily grasp him beneath his arms, which she did with typical skill, matching his descent so that her intervention caused barely a jolt.

'Thank you, Specialist,' said Myles calmly. 'And, may I say, very nice rescue technique.'

Lazuli wanted to ask, 'How did you know I was here to catch you?' but she refrained. It seemed like Myles always knew what would happen right up to the moment he didn't, which was usually when the real problems began.

So instead she said, 'You're welcome, Myles. Is he dead, the duke? Can you tell?'

'It certainly looks like it,' said Myles, and then he added with some sarcasm, 'If only there were a coroner or pathologist in the house to tell us for certain.'

Far below them, the stream of coroners and pathologists filing on to the stage looked like ants scurrying towards a lump of sugar.

2
DEAD MAN'S HOLE

LAZULI DECIDED NOT TO DELIVER MYLES TO THE Southbank's green room and instead flew him to the *Fowl Star* yacht, which Myles had docked on the river. She pinged a text to Beckett so he wouldn't worry, and five minutes later the blond twin joined them on the bridge.

'Permission to come aboard?' Beckett shouted as he swung through the hatch, even though he was patently already on board.

'Do you have to ask that every time?' snapped Myles, a little testy after his ordeal. 'And I would point out that you boarded before permission was granted.'

Beckett, who was still clad only in a sumo mawashi, decided to remind Myles about the recent life-saving inside the theatre. 'Actually, I need a new Gloop tie because mine got shredded saving your life a few minutes ago. You're welcome.'

Lazuli high-fived Beckett. 'Jinx. I saved his life too.'

Beckett hugged the diminutive pixel and swung her

round the main cabin while both of them sang the Regrettables' theme song, which was an abysmal yet catchy composition:

> The Regrettables, the Regrettables,
> We're completely unforgettable,
> We love our fruits and vegetables,
> That's cos we're Regrettables.

Myles made a sound that sounded awfully like *harrumph*, then composed himself. 'Thank you both so much for your assistance with the Lord Teddy situation, though I feel quite certain I had things under control.'

Beckett dropped Lazuli and stretched out on a leather banquette, wriggling for maximum squeakage. 'I knew that, brother. I just wanted to climb my own trousers.'

The squeaking was hugely irritating when a person suffered from misophonia, which Myles did.

'If you please, brother mine,' he said, 'don some outer garments and stop your infernal wriggling. It is imperative that I concentrate. This affair is far from over.'

Beckett disagreed. 'I think it's over. It feels over. That

was like an end-of-adventure-type event. Everyone gathered together in a big room and then an explosion and the bad guy dies.'

'Teddy dead?' said Myles, switching on the built-in coffee machine. 'I'm not so sure now that I've had a moment to think about it. I will need a little more convincing on that front.'

Lazuli was examining her helmet, which had taken quite a beating from the machine gun. 'I have questions, Myles,' she said, picking at the slug embedded in the headplate.

Myles took an espresso cup from the cabinet. 'Naturally, you have questions, Specialist Heitz. I cannot realistically expect even moderately intelligent people to fathom my reasoning and actions.'

Lazuli ignored this veiled insult. 'How are your legs not broken? That trapdoor shot you thirty metres into the air.'

This was a question that did not probe into Myles's real reason for being in London, so he was happy to answer it.

'A good question, Specialist, and, since it demonstrates a rudimentary knowledge of physics, I will enlighten you. As you may know, intellectuals like myself often have misophonia, which is an irritation caused by certain sounds – squeaking on a banquette, for example – and we also suffer from migraines. One of my triggers happens to be the vibration caused by running or even walking on an unyielding surface. So I developed a viscoelastic polymer to disperse vibration energy and then printed insoles from the material. Simply put, I let my shoes do the walking and not my feet. Obviously, they were not built to withstand the level of energy released by that trapdoor, and so they overheated slightly. But overall I am pleased with their performance.'

Beckett summarised: 'Magic shoes, Laz.'

'And how did Lord Teddy have LEP armour-piercing rounds?' asked Lazuli, holding up the slug she had tugged from her helmet.

Myles examined the bullet. 'That is something that certainly warrants further investigation,' he admitted. 'I imagine the duke was consorting with rogue surface fairies, something Foaly might have a line on.'

Lazuli tried to sneak in a more penetrating question. 'And you could see me in the auditorium, right, Myles?'

'I wish that were the case,' said Myles smoothly. 'But your new shimmer suit has outfoxed my sensors. For the moment, Foaly wins, but please inform your esteemed centaur colleague that his victory will be both short-lived and hollow. I could not, in fact, see you, but logic dictated that you would be dispatched to chaperone us on our trip, *Ambassador* Heitz.'

'Hmm,' said Lazuli, unconvinced. 'You seemed awfully relaxed up there in the sky for a person without wings.'

'I trust you, Laz,' said Myles. 'Is that so difficult to believe after everything we've been through?'

Lazuli speared Myles with a look that said, *It is extremely difficult to believe.*

'Oh, sure, we trust each other,' she drawled, affecting a Booshka accent, which in the fairy city of Haven was synonymous with sarcasm. 'That's why you tell me everything all the time.'

'I never tell anyone everything all the time,' argued Myles, selecting double espresso from the coffee machine's menu. 'What kind of mastermind would do that? But in this case I'm actually telling you everything.'

'Prove it!' challenged Beckett. 'Tell us what you have planned for tonight! I know you have something planned because you're drinking coffee after four.'

Myles glared at the coffee cup as though betrayed

by the vessel. 'Very well, fellow Regrettables, I shall share my plan with you both, mostly because I will need your help carrying it out.'

Beckett stopped wriggling so that Myles's confession would not be drowned out by squeaking and, even though Lazuli didn't realise it, she was holding her breath.

It was a historic moment. Myles Fowl was about to share his plan.

Before the bespectacled twin could spill the beans, Lazuli released her breath to deliver a gentle warning.

'This plan had better be the usual ridiculously complicated and dangerous kind, or I won't believe you for a second.'

Myles put down his coffee cup and placed one foot on a handy crate in order to strike the proper heroic pose.

'Oh, it's complicated and dangerous, Specialist Heitz,' he said, hands on hips. 'For I plan to break into a secure London mortuary and examine the brain of the most famous corpse in all of England.'

Lazuli nodded, thinking that Myles Fowl had just set a new bar for Myles-y statements. 'I believe you,' she said.

'Me too,' said Beckett. 'Because that plan is so Myles that even Myles couldn't make it up if it wasn't true.'

But Myles was, in fact, lying. He'd said *examine*, but what he actually meant was *dissect*.

Lazuli had one more assurance to extract from Myles. 'And, once you're satisfied that Teddy is dead, then you'll look into my parents? Because the only thing more important to me than the future is the past.'

'Of course,' said Myles. 'As promised, I have already started. No hits yet, but I'm sure we'll turn up something soon.'

'Good,' said Lazuli. 'Well then, I suppose we're visiting a mortuary. After all, how much trouble can a dead person be?'

Which was just asking for trouble.

The Tower Bridge Mortuary
Some Hours Later

The Tower Bridge Mortuary was a building with a gruesome and yet fascinating history. Because of the river's tidal nature, any dead bodies deposited in the Thames tended to congregate at the stone steps of the bascule bridge's north tower. Historically, the bodies were stored in an alcove beneath the tower, in a small mortuary known as Dead Man's Hole. You might think that moniker would put off tourists, but it actually seemed to make the bridge more popular. The mortuary was shut down at the end of the Victorian era because of the rank odour that drifted up to the walkway, especially on summer days, and spooked the bridge's resident horses. But, in 2016, the facility was sneakily reopened by British intelligence services during a three-month refurbishment of the bridge. The mortuary was only a ten-minute water-taxi ride from Thames House, which served as HQ for both MI5 and MI6, and this meant that sensitive corpses could be conveniently stored off-site but close by if a post-mortem were needed. And, if there ever were a corpse that qualified as sensitive, it was that of Lord Teddy Bleedham-Drye, the rogue duke who had just tried to ram a visiting juvenile professor with his light aircraft.

Lazuli agreed to go along with the proposed breaking and entering, but only if she could do her actual LEPrecon job for once, which was, as the department's name suggested, reconnaissance. Or at least that had been her job before she was saddled with babysitting twin human apocalypse magnets.

Ambassador Heitz, that's me, she thought as she swooped, shielded by her shimmer suit, through the spokes of the London Eye and sped towards Tower Bridge's famous silhouette.

As a title, *ambassador* sounds pretty highfalutin, but what it really meant was that her career was on hold. While Lazuli often pretended to be ticked off about this in the LEP locker room, in actuality, the high point of any shift was spending time with the two humans she now considered her only real friends. In fact, Lazuli realised, as an orphan raised in a crowded facility, she had never sought out the company of others. The only people besides the twins she had ever actively sought out were the parents who had left her in a public square named Lazuli Heights.

For the longest time, the sole emotion she had projected towards her mysterious parents was a furious anger, but in recent years Lazuli had begun to think that maybe she hadn't been abandoned exactly. This was because she had talked to Beckett about it, and the Fowl boy had put his usual optimistic spin on the situation, saying, 'You know, Laz, your parents must have been super worried about your safety to sacrifice the joy of raising you.' To which Lazuli had responded with an eye-roll. But the idea had been planted in her head, and somehow it became her number-one theory as to why she had ended up in an orphanage.

Mum and Dad were protecting me.

And now she was protecting the Fowls.

Protecting people runs in the family.

It must, because here she was, voluntarily diving with both wings into another *Fowlscapade*.

Even though I don't exactly trust Myles.

That wasn't the whole truth. She didn't trust Myles to share facts, even facts about her own parents should he locate them, but she would one hundred per cent trust him with her life. In fact, if she were caught between a rock and a hard place, Myles was the second person she would call. The first was Beckett, whose instincts for navigating perilous landscapes somehow went beyond intelligence. NANNI had once theorised that instinct was possibly the evolution of intelligence, a suggestion Myles found difficult to debate.

But not impossible, thought Lazuli, smiling behind her visor. Myles Fowl could argue with anyone, including himself.

Lazuli set her doubledex wings to hover and brought up Myles's face on a visor window. NANNI's multiple cameras had 360-degree coverage and, when Myles was wearing the glasses, the AI could knit together a ninety per cent accurate point-of-view picture of him for the caller. Lazuli didn't have anything as sophisticated as NANNI, who was constantly upgrading herself – in fact, the pixel's communication module had taken a battering from Lord Teddy's machine gun and its cells were still regrowing. Consequently, Lazuli had no live link to Foaly in Police Plaza, though she had sent him a digital package earlier with a full report.

I'm lucky I can still fly, she thought. *And, if it wasn't for my SPAM, I'd be dead.*

Commodore Short would send her to see a counsellor when she got back to Haven: Lazuli was sure of it. Close shaves in the line of duty always meant a visit to Dr J. Argon.

But she could think about that later. Now she was on a mission.

'I'm in position,' she said into her helmet microphone. 'Ready for breach.'

Myles had changed out of his tuxedo and into a less formal black suit with Gloop tie. 'Excellent, Specialist,' he said. 'Do you perhaps see any guards?'

Lazuli blinked to an infrared filter on her smart visor and saw that, while there were thousands of human-sized heat blooms in the vicinity, there was only one under the bridge itself, seated in a small kiosk outside the mortuary's entrance.

'A single guard posted out front,' she reported.

'And no sentries inside the mortuary itself?'

Lazuli blinked again. 'No live ones,' she said.

'Very well,' said Myles. 'What I need you to do is—'

Specialist Heitz cut him off. 'Here's the plan, Myles. Have NANNI disable any alarms and put the security camera feeds on a loop so MI5 won't be alerted. I'll put the guard to sleep and open the door. You moor the yacht at the steps and come in the back way, where I will be waiting for you. Sound good?'

Myles frowned. It did sound good, but surely Specialist Heitz was aware that planning was *his* area – most specifically, announcing the plans in an authoritative manner.

'That does sound good,' he admitted. 'But in future—'

Lazuli cut him off yet again. Myles could not understand why cutting people off was fine when he did it but most irritating when someone else did it to him.

'Sorry, Myles,' she said. 'I'm the one with tactical training, so we do what I say. If I had left the Southbank situation to you, you'd be lying in that morgue instead of breaking into it.'

Lazuli makes a good point, thought Myles. *But I'm supposed to be the Regrettable who makes good points.*

He needed to keep Specialist Heitz on his side – to further study her suit, if nothing else – so he didn't chastise the pixel for overstepping her bounds. Instead, he contented himself with a muttered, 'It's called a mortuary, not a morgue.'

Beckett overheard this.

'What's the difference, brother?' he asked.

'There isn't one, Beck,' Myles admitted. 'I meant it's actually called a mortuary – Tower Bridge Mortuary.'

'Radio silence from now on,' said Lazuli. 'Message me when the alarms are down.'

She left the twins to their morgue/mortuary discussion and swooped across the muscular throb of the Thames, over the main span of Tower Bridge and down to the mortuary door set into the recessed lower-level arches. A simple NO ENTRY sign was pasted across the steel door, and a burly guard was squashed into a security booth. It was a level of security calculated to project that there couldn't possibly be anything more important than janitorial equipment in this building. Lazuli knew that the real security was electronic and state of the art for most humans, though not for Myles Fowl.

She dropped silently to the hatch's wooden ledge and was relieved to find that the guard had nodded off with a coffee cup in his right hand, which he clenched spasmodically as he dreamed. Lazuli stuck an adhesive patch to his neck just to make sure the man stayed asleep. The patch would dissolve as it released a concentrated natural sedative, and when the guard awoke he would feel rested and refreshed. There would not be so much as a smear of physical evidence except for a slight increase in melatonin levels, which would only be noticed in the unlikely event that someone thought to run a toxicology test.

The walkway was quiet at the witching hour, but still clusters of tourists dawdled by, snapping low-perspective shots of the bridge, or selfies with London's famous skyline lit up like a gigantic Christmas decoration in the background. Lazuli did not worry about the humans. They could not see her unless there was yet another child criminal mastermind in the bunch who had developed a way past fairy filters, as she suspected Myles had.

Lazuli shuddered.

She was very fond of Myles, but one child genius was enough. Two like him could very easily take over the world of humans, and the world of fairies below it.

Lazuli crept towards the door, employing the fairy martial art of Doveli, or **Do**ing **Ve**ry **Li**ttle, which should ensure that no human noticed a patch of shimmer-suit haze that could give a fairy away at such close range, even though Foaly had assured her that suit haze was a thing of the past with the new systems. Lazuli hoped the centaur would forgive her for not trusting one hundred per cent the suit's effectiveness during its first surface trial, especially since her systems had been damaged by Teddy's bullets.

If Lazuli had been visible to humans, she would have looked for all the world like a mime artist doing her best *walking against the wind* routine across the flagstones to the door set underneath the stone arch. The door was, of course, reinforced – after all, any room in London with so much as a tin of paint inside it had a reinforced steel door – but the lock was something else entirely. The manufacturers had even stamped the word UNPICKABLE on the casing, so confident were they in their product.

'Yeah, this lock is totally unpickable,' muttered Lazuli to herself in a Booshka accent. 'No one could ever pick this lock.'

She reached into a slim pocket on her forearm and withdrew a crystal tube of oil. She popped the old-fashioned cork and drew out a limply curled hair maybe six centimetres long. The LEP did issue Omnitools that could hack most electronic locks, but, for an old-fashioned tumbler job like this, there was nothing like a quasi-legal dwarf hair, which no LEP officers were supposed to carry, but most did. In fact, it had been Commodore Short who'd gifted Lazuli the dwarf hair, with a laser-etched message on the crystal tube that read:

DONATED BY AN EXASPERATING

BUT INVALUABLE FRIEND. I BELIEVE

YOU KNOW THE TYPE.

I do indeed, thought Lazuli now and, shielding the hair with her body, she slipped the tip into the keyhole. The hair seemed to know what was required of it and wriggled eagerly into the tiny space, tracing the grooves with its own length and stiffening in sections until it had formed an ad hoc key.

It is probably inaccurate to refer to dwarf hairs as hairs. The jury is out as to whether they are tiny organs or digits, but, either way, a dwarf can manipulate them at will. And, if a dwarf has spent his or her life breaking into buildings, that hair will continue to act as a pick even after it is shed, as long as it's stored in balsam oil. This particular hair, which had originally been on the forearm of Mulch Diggums, the most notorious thief ever to crack a safe, made short work of the secret-service lock, as it actually made closer contact with the pins than any real key would.

Lazuli checked her message box and found a convoluted missive from Myles, which began with these sentences:

Dear Specialist Heitz, I have neutralised the mortuary alarm and security cameras. There were also motion sensors and pressure pads, which I took the liberty of recalibrating with NANNI's assistance. Be assured it would take the introduction of three very large and active elephants before these sensors could alert anyone to our presence. Motion sensors were actually invented by a man with the unlikely name of Bango, who applied the basics of radar to ultrasonic waves . . .

At this point, Lazuli stopped reading and opened the door, just the tiny amount necessary for her to slip her slight blue frame inside the Tower Bridge Mortuary, which, as Myles had foretold, was occupied by a single dead body. But what Myles Fowl, the great self-proclaimed genius, had not predicted was that the Dead Man's Hole would also be occupied by several live fairy ones.

THE *FOWL STAR*

London may be known as one of the cities that never sleeps, but it seemed as though the Thames was at the very least having a little snooze as the *Fowl Star* sliced through water so dark in places it seemed almost gelatinous. Nothing much moved on the river except the Irish superyacht running silently on its batteries, and Myles had suggested to Beckett that he allow NANNI to pilot the craft, since the city lights were barely illuminating the tidal water. Beckett made a counter-suggestion that he should steer with his eyes closed to test out his other senses, which led to Myles withdrawing his initial suggestion and instead dealing with a late-night/early-morning video call from his mother. Angeline Fowl had heard from one of her friends in the Kremlin, who'd herself heard it from a mole in Westminster, that there'd been an incident of some kind in the Southbank Centre, where Myles had been speaking.

Myles kept the video box on his lenses and did not alert Beckett, who had a problem with lying to his parents, whereas Myles had no problem whatsoever with bending or even breaking the truth if the good of humankind were at stake. And, as far as Myles Fowl was concerned, anything that benefited him also benefited humankind, as he was destined to improve life on Earth.

'And so, in conclusion, Mother,' Myles was saying, 'nothing of note happened in the Southbank Centre. If something had happened, surely there would be footage. The internet would be in a veritable fizz of excitement. No video, no happening. As you can see, Beckett is messing around on the bridge and we will be home in the morning.'

'No, Myles,' said Angeline Fowl. 'I want you to go to Uncle Foxworth's in Norfolk in the morning. He is considerably closer, and you can dock in Great Yarmouth.'

Myles fought the urge to smile. Uncle Foxy had been in his pocket for years and would cover for them for a price. Still, Myles protested once for appearances' sake.

'Mother, this is ridiculous. We don't need Uncle Foxy to babysit us. NANNI reports our every move to Father, and Specialist Heitz showed up to keep a close fairy eye on us.'

'My Russian source seems to think you're in danger, and she is not often mistaken,' said Angeline Fowl, who was using her tablet in bed next to a sleeping Artemis Fowl Senior.

'Perhaps she is a bot,' said Myles drily. Then, realising that now was not the time for his trademark withering wit, he added: 'Lazuli says hello.'

Angeline's face softened. 'Please tell Lazuli I say hello right back, and do ask the dear girl if perhaps she might have time for tea when you do eventually arrive home.'

'I will, Mother,' promised Myles. 'Just as soon as she gets back from checking the perimeter, which is a complete waste of time, as NANNI's sensors are far more sophisticated than anything the deluded LEP could ever—'

His mother cut across him. 'Myles, stop lecturing and go to bed. It's the middle of the night, for heaven's sake.'

'Of course, Mother. One story for Beck and then we shall turn in.'

'And to Foxworth's first thing in the morning?'

If I have nothing more important to do, thought Myles, but aloud he said, 'Absolutely, Mother.'

'Goodnight, my clever boy,' said Angeline. 'I do so love you both.'

Myles bowed. 'Thank you, Mother. As always, your feelings of emotional attachment are reciprocated.'

Angeline sighed. 'Myles, I really wish that for once you could—'

But she was speaking to the ether, for her son had ended the call.

Myles glanced out of a brass-ringed porthole and saw the span of Tower Bridge ahead. 'Brother mine,' he said, 'perhaps we should allow NANNI to autopilot us from here?'

Even as he put this suggestion forward for the

second time, Myles knew it was folly to expect Beckett to relinquish control of any vehicle. And why should he? Beckett had a kind of adeptness when it came to the physical world. Something almost superhuman. Perhaps he was actually a magical creature. His gift of tongues had been granted to him by the fairy spirit – maybe his other skills were also wishes come true.

No magic for me, thought Myles, who had also been possessed, by the Berserker warrior Gobdaw. If there even were such a thing as magic.

Rather than answer Myles's spoken question, Beckett seemed to read his mind. 'I wonder when your fairy-magic superpower will show up, brother.'

'Not that fairy-magic-superpower thing again, Beck,' spluttered Myles. 'That is still, and will always be, ridiculous. Everything is science-based. Your so-called superpower is simply an equation that I have not yet solved.'

Beckett gave Myles his full attention, which should have worried the bespectacled twin. 'If everything is science, then I must be smarter than you.'

Don't take the bait, Myles ordered himself. *Do not take the bait – we are on a mission.*

But he said, 'Smarter than me? I really would like to hear the logic behind that outrageous statement.'

'It's simple,' said Beckett, turning his gaze back to the river now that Myles was hooked. 'One of the smarty-pants that you like, that Tolkien guy—'

'Tolkien was more than a smarty-pants, brother,' said Myles chidingly. 'And so much more than a writer of fairy stories. I would consider J. R. R.'s intellect equal to my own.'

'Exactly,' said Beckett, mounting the instrument panel so he could steer with his feet, a favourite trick of his. 'And he could only speak thirty-five languages. I can speak all the languages and understand most of the noises. Like ball bearings, which I learned today. So, if there's no magic, then I must be smarter than J. R. and you.'

'J. R. R.,' corrected Myles, but he had to concede that Beckett made an infuriatingly clever point. Luckily, he was spared further debate by the fast-approaching riverside steps of the bridge.

'Beck,' he said a trifle nervously, 'we really do seem to be moving at a rate of knots.'

Beckett responded with a statement that immediately

threw Myles into a state of quiet desperation. 'You're going to love what I do next, brother.'

No, thought Myles, gripping a handy rail. *No, I shall not.*

As was so often the case, Myles was correct.

Beckett wrapped his big toe round the throttle and pulled back hard, instantly sending the left-hand propeller rotating clockwise and the right-hand propeller rotating counterclockwise to provide reverse thrust. Once the yacht had slowed to a gentle drift, Beckett flipped the gear to neutral and skipped sideways on the six-handle steering wheel, swinging the stern round so that they coasted into the bridge's stone dock with barely a nudge against the rope strung through brass rings on the quay wall.

'Don't!' said Myles when it was way too late. 'We will crash!' Also too late.

'Perfect spin park,' said Beckett. 'You're not supposed to do that with yachts, but the dolphins back home told me it would work.'

Myles held his tongue on the matter but silently added dolphins to the list of creatures he did not trust.

* * *

Lazuli was waiting at the top of the steps. Myles knew this because he could see her, thanks to his tricky secret workaround that, though he couldn't have predicted it, was about to literally come back to haunt him. Beckett knew Lazuli was there because he went up the steps so fast that he bumped into his shielded friend.

'Oops,' he said. 'Sorry, Laz.'

Lazuli backed into the mortuary, then deactivated her shield. 'No problem, Beck. I forget how fast you are.'

Beckett ran in circles round the small room. 'We might as well make conversation or play a game of crunchball. You know how long it takes Myles to climb steps.'

It was true. Myles was famously uncoordinated. And he had once declared in frustration, 'If I do develop a fairy superpower, I really hope it turns out to be climbing stairs.'

Myles had fallen up stairs so much that he had developed *climacophobia*, which he dealt with by counting each step out loud as he progressed. This was a very effective coping mechanism, as it forced him to pay attention to where he was going, but it did slow him down somewhat.

Lazuli buzzed up her visor, then nodded towards the mortuary fridges sunk into the wall. 'I don't think playing crunchball here would be appropriate,' she said. 'Do you?'

Beckett skidded to a halt. 'I suppose not,' he said. 'And, anyway, here comes the tortoise.'

This was not a gibe, but a reference to 'The Tortoise and the Hare', a story that Myles often quoted when he eventually arrived somewhere, as he did now.

'Slow and steady wins the race,' he said, closing the door behind him and flicking on the strip lights. 'Those steps are frightfully uneven. It's almost as though they were designed specifically to trip a person. Deathtraps. With a rock climb, one expects an uneven ascent, but surely the whole point of hewn steps is some semblance of regularity.'

Beckett knew that phobias were no joke, so he appealed to Lazuli. 'Can't you do something about Myles's problem with steps, Laz? It's really slowing us down. You healed him when he was blasted with that shotgun, after all.'

Lazuli opened her visor. 'That healing was an accident. And, to be honest, Myles was fortunate I didn't kill him. The internal scar tissue could have led to fibrosis. Luckily, our gnome warlock was able to undo what I did. Only a warlock can override a healing.'

'I'm standing right here,' said Myles. 'There's no need to spout exposition about me in the third person. Anyway, I am planning to undergo a programme of self-hypnosis to overcome my climacophobia. So can we please get down to business?'

Beckett and Lazuli nodded, and it was entirely possible that the whole conversation had been conducted expressly to avoid getting down to business, as the business of the evening was undeniably of the grim sort.

Beckett distracted himself further with a question. 'Why are the walls white?'

'Ah,' said Myles. 'Excellent question, brother. Mortuary walls were often covered in white tiles for two reasons. One, they provide a reflective glow, which effectively increased the wattage during examinations.'

Beckett stage-whispered to Lazuli, 'I hope reason two is less boring than one.'

It was.

'And two,' continued Myles, 'due to a lack of air conditioning in Victorian London, corpse gas would often expand and cause violent rupturings, and the white tiles were easier to wipe down.'

Lazuli may have turned a little green. It was difficult to tell, considering her face was blue.

Beckett, however, seemed more excited than queasy. 'Are you saying that this room was the site of countless fartsplosions?'

Myles frowned. 'Hardly countless, brother, but dozens certainly. And I presume you know that *fartsplosions* is not an official word, though I have to admit it certainly is evocative.'

As he spoke, Myles strolled along the wall of refrigerators until he arrived at one marked with the day's date.

'Here lieth the Duke of Scilly,' he said. 'Come to an ignoble end. Perhaps.'

And without further ado Myles tugged on the handle, rolling out the refrigerated remains of Lord Teddy Bleedham-Drye. The duke looked exactly what he was: a dead old man, in no way as threatening or awesome as he had been in life.

'"Death makes meat of us all,"' said Lazuli, and then explained. 'That's a line from a nursery rhyme I learned in preschool.'

'Your preschool sounds amazing,' said Beckett sincerely.

Myles did not take part in the poetry appreciation,

for he was a Fowl in his element now – the recently qualified pathologist Dr Fowl conducting a secret examination of a duke's corpse in MI5's private mortuary.

Artemis would be livid with envy, he realised, resisting the urge to cackle, which even Myles, with his limited social skills, guessed would be unseemly.

Teddy's battered and emaciated remains lay on a bed of chemical-infused ice crystals shrouded by a blue gaseous cloud. The whole scene was undeniably creepy and, now that she was actually here, Lazuli was beginning to think this entire mission was a big mistake.

Myles must have noticed her expression for he said, 'It is perfectly normal to experience a sense of foreboding in the presence of a corpse. Bodies tend to remind one of one's own mortality. Most especially the body of an acquaintance, even one who tried so very hard to kill us all.'

Perhaps Myles is right, Lazuli thought. *Teddy continues to give me the creeps even after his death.*

Myles switched his attention to his AI. 'NANNI, let us perform a DNA test. I presume physical contact is preferred for optimum results?'

'Correct, Myles,' said NANNI. 'Get me in there good and deep. At least two samples.'

'Of course,' said Myles. 'We cannot risk a false positive.'

He removed the eyeglasses from his face and twisted one spectacle arm up the ancient duke's left nostril.

Lazuli swallowed. 'DNA?'

'Naturally,' said Myles. 'Although a clone would possibly have the same DNA. But there could be a discrepancy in the mitochondria.'

'I don't care about any of that,' said Beckett, tucking both hands under his armpits so he would not succumb to the almost overwhelming temptation to move Teddy's jaw up and down while doing a funny voice. 'I just care that you get to stick your glasses inside Teddy. Can I do that?'

'Not unless you have a doctorate,' said Myles, removing the spectacles. 'Now for sample number two.'

Beckett's eyes widened. 'You're going to sample his number two?'

Myles rubbed the bridge of his nose. 'I was referring to my second sample site, which will be this gash in Lord Teddy's chest.'

Myles folded out the right arm of his glasses and levered the tip under the reddish scab that had formed over the wound.

'Wounds often continue to heal post-mortem,' explained Myles. 'But not as efficiently as they would on a live host.' He twisted the glasses' arm perhaps three centimetres into the wound and then swished it around inside Teddy's body.

Beckett was more fascinated than he'd ever been in his life. 'You should have told me that doctors have such amazing jobs! Are you going to taste anything?'

'Good question, brother,' said Myles seriously. 'I had considered performing the fingertip taste test on Lord Teddy's blood, to make sure it was actual human blood and not synthetic, but NANNI can run those while she's inserted. I can taste diabetes in pee, but I'm not sure I could tell synthetic blood from real blood.'

Beckett thought he might faint from excitement. 'You've been drinking pee?'

Lazuli was not in the least excited by this latest revelation. 'Myles. Do not tell me you've been drinking pee.'

Myles was not the type to be embarrassed by scientific endeavours and so answered, 'Only my own. And it had been screened by NANNI. A true scientist must follow every trail, no matter how salty. Surely you are not surprised that I would go to any length for science?'

'I'm surprised you would use the word *pee*,' said Lazuli.

Beckett agreed. 'Me too. You won't even call Mum *Mum*.'

'*Pee* is an acronym,' explained Myles. 'The letters stand for *personal effluent excretion*. You can't possibly think that I would simply use the word *pee* without good reason?'

'No,' said Lazuli. 'What kind of animal would just say *pee*?'

The pee discussion was cut off by a beep from NANNI. She was confirming the cadaver samples had been analysed. Myles withdrew his glasses from Teddy's wound with a squelching sound that Lazuli would never forget but that Beckett imitated with a remarkably similar raspberry.

'This is great,' Beckett said. 'I think I might study to become a doctor.'

Myles disinfected his spectacles with a quick spray from a travel bottle, then popped them back on his face.

'Report,' he said brusquely.

'That's Lord Teddy's body,' said NANNI. 'No doubt about it.'

'You're positive?' snapped Myles, surprised.

'I just said "no doubt about it", which is another way of saying I am positive. Why don't you have a glass of pee and calm down?'

Myles pounded Teddy's shelf with a fist. 'I was so sure it was a ruse! That Lord Teddy had faked his own death somehow.'

Myles's weak pounding should not really have had any effect on the corpse, but the sliding drawer was somewhat unsteady, so even the smallest impact was enough to jostle Teddy's remains, resulting in the top of his skull plopping off and spinning on the aluminium headrest.

'This day just keeps getting better,' said Beckett, who had to take a few breaths to stop himself from getting too emotional.

Myles peered into the cranium and he, too, felt a jolt of emotion. 'Where's the brain? Of course – the coroner must have performed an encephalectomy. Lord Teddy's brain would certainly have been worth studying. We must find it.'

Lazuli moaned. 'Myles, do you still need to examine the brain? Your own AI identified the body.'

'I need to be certain,' said Myles sharply. 'Don't you understand? This man survived for over a hundred and fifty years! If this specimen actually is Lord Teddy, so much can be learned about longevity from the condition of his brain, and now it has disappeared. I would be willing to bet that those secret-service animals hacked it up and tossed that most unique organ into one of their deep, dark spy holes.' Myles's eyes seemed to glitter. 'But knowledge cannot be hidden from Myles Fowl. Rest assured I will find that brain, even if I have to scour the corners of the Earth. My gaze will be as a keen sword of light illuminating the darkest corners of this planet.'

It gave Lazuli great pleasure to interrupt. 'Actually, Myles, there's a refrigerator here that says "organ fridge" on the front.'

Myles maintained his heroic tone. 'And that very refrigerator is the first place I shall search.'

There was only one tray in the small fridge, and on it were what looked like vacuum-packed slices of jaundiced cauliflower with a complete wedge of uncut section at the back. Myles removed the tray gingerly and made no attempt to suppress a shriek of horror.

'Those brutes!' he exclaimed. 'They sliced it like a

loaf of bread. Don't they understand? This man lived more than a hundred and fifty years and was sharp as a tack till the very end. I could have confirmed so many of my theories on neurodegenerative disorders with a properly dissected brain.'

He let out another shriek as he selected a shrink-wrapped slice. 'And these segments are barely three millimetres thick. Five millimetres is the accepted optimum thickness for brain slivers. Any fool knows that. Even Artemis would know that.'

'You should have seen him work,' said a voice. 'That surgeon was a proper butcher.'

'I don't doubt it,' said Myles.

'You don't doubt what?' asked Lazuli.

'What you said about the surgeon being a butcher.'

'I didn't say anything.'

'What Beckett said, then. I can't be expected to keep track of who says what in times of crisis. Especially if you are using silly voices.'

'I didn't say nothing neither, partner,' said Beckett in a silly cowboy voice.

Myles's frustration with the mutilated brain spilled over to his fellow Regrettables and he rounded on them, intending to say, 'I really wish you two would take this seriously. In case you've forgotten, we broke into a secret spy mortuary to confirm the identity of a person who recently tried to kill us all, and our time here is extremely limited.'

But he did not say any of this because he saw someone else in the room. Or at least someone half in the room. Obviously, Myles had seen people 'half in the room' before – this normally meant that the person was in the process of coming through a doorway or open window. But this man was coming through the wall. Passing unhindered right through it.

'Fascinating,' said Myles.

And it *was* fascinating, made even more so by the fact that the man's clothing was of Victorian vintage, with a high, stiff collar, waistcoat and top hat. Also, there was the fact that the man's chest had a fist-sized hole in it.

Myles was on the point of having NANNI scan the apparition when the person spoke again, but this time Myles was looking directly into his face when he did it. The man's mouth opened and out came words that were harmless enough – something along the lines of . . .

'Oh, you wouldn't believe the goings-on I've seen in

here over the years. And you was absolutely right about the white tiles. It were quite a job cleaning those . . .'

And on he went, but Myles could no longer focus on the words because the man's eyes . . . They were larger than normal, like holes torn in his face, and behind those holes revolved whirlpools that emitted something – half a raw screaming sound, half concentrated columns of jumbled memories. The pain in these emanations was quite at odds with the words spoken by the man, and Myles fell back against the wall as he vainly attempted to slap away the vision. But it was not a vision. This man absolutely existed, just on another plane.

As a scientist, Myles should have been delighted with this discovery – that so-called ghosts did indeed exist. But, as a twelve-year-old boy, he was completely traumatised and could do nothing but flap at his own face and recite the periodic table from hydrogen onwards to comfort himself.

Beckett knew immediately that something was seriously wrong because Myles did not include the recent atomic weight updates in his recitation, which he had been doing since 2018, usually adding *I knew it* after each element.

'What's going on, Beck?' Lazuli asked him. 'Is this a seizure? Has it happened before?'

Beckett knelt before his frantic twin. 'What is it, brother? Can I help you?'

But Myles was beyond responding to questions. He could only react to the apparition, who was completely out of the wall now and still chatting even as the ghost beams pulsed from his eye sockets.

'You can see me, can't you, lad?' asked the spirit genially. 'That's nice. You ain't got some tobacco to spare, I suppose? I haven't filled me pipe in over a century.'

The beams shattered across Myles's brow, showering him with memory fragments:

A childhood in the London slums.

Rats with red discs of light in their eyes.

Babies crying. More than crying – howling.

Scrabbling for potato skins in the market gutters.

Too much grog one Christmas.

An argument over a top hat with a sailor in a cobbled lane.

The man pulling a small kindling axe.

Horrible chest pain.

The scenes and emotions were beamed directly into Myles's brain. The ghost's memories became his. The ghost's opinions tainted his own. The spirit's decision-making parameters temporarily dulled the twin's frontal lobe by perhaps fifteen per cent, which would have serious consequences going forward. It was too much.

The revenant squatted before Myles, poking his head through Beckett's chest.

'Are you poorly, boy? Is it me eyeholes that distress you so? They're the windows to the soul, see? Shakespeare had it right. I reckon he seen a few spirits himself. And Dickens too.'

Myles moaned. He could hear the words now, but they didn't matter. All that mattered was the stream of horrific memories and how to cut it off.

Perhaps he could scare away the ghost with a laser. Myles was not familiar with the science of the spirit realm, even though he had trespassed in it, but surely a laser was worth a try.

He blinked a command into his spectacles and NANNI fired a concentrated laser at the ghost's head. The beam passed directly through and snipped off one of Beckett's blond curls before heating up one of the cadaver fridge doors.

None of this registered with Myles because he was in deep shock due to the seemingly never-ending stream of horrific episodes from the ghost's life. They shotgunned into the boy's hippocampus, merging with his own episodic memories until it seemed as though he himself had lived through ghoulish times in Victorian London.

Parents dead from consumption.

Years of hacking through meat in the Leadenhall Skin Market (which was an even more horrific place than the name suggests).

Dying slowly in a gutter, watching a lattice of his own blood fill up the cobble canals.

Shut it down, was all that Myles could manage to think.

Shut it down!

And he mumbled it aloud. 'Shut down.'

'Shut down and erase all settings?' asked a voice that had apparently understood Myles's command in spite of his mumbling, and the moment Myles automatically gave the blink command the process of erasing and shutting down began. This was to cause even more problems going forward than the brain-dulling.

But, whatever it was that he had shut down, Myles's nightmare did not end. The ghost never so much as flickered but continued with its chatter.

'Percival's the name, and I lived a criminal life, no mistake,' it confessed to Myles, looming over the boy. 'Took up the knife and pistol for the Battering Rams once I got done with the army and meat business. Sent many a cove to the very place I can't seem to go – the Great Beyond.'

'Go away,' said Myles. 'Leave me be.'

'Now *you* I would murder with me little axe,' said Percival, drawing an axe from the air. 'Little cove like you I would chop up neat as you like. Then into the offal barrel at Leadenhall with you.'

Myles saw or imagined his own reflection in the axe blade and screamed his way through the next section of the periodic table.

Back in the real world, Lazuli said, 'That's it. I'm putting him out.'

Beckett's instinct was to argue, but the scar on the outside of his palm was tingling. Myles had a matching scar on his palm from where they were connected in the womb as the world's only documented set of conjoined dizygotic twins. These scars were more than pinkish welts – they functioned as an organic GPS system and also mood monitors, which Myles hypothesised was due to the shared brain effect of their mother's amniotic fluid. Obviously, a boy who was prepared to gargle pee in the name of science had no problems discussing his mother's womb, which was only right and correct.

At this moment, Beckett's scar was tingling almost as much as the time he'd licked an electric cattle fence.

I don't know what to do, he thought. *And I can't ask Myles.*

'Put him out,' he said to Lazuli. 'But don't hurt him.'

'Never,' said the fairy specialist, sticking an adhesive sedative patch on Myles's neck. In seconds, the boy's agitated features had calmed and the periodic-table recitation petered out at mercury.

Beckett was suddenly like a different boy. Gone was the freewheeling chaos typhoon, and in his place was a very serious-looking young fellow.

'Can you heal him, Laz?' he asked.

Lazuli shook her small blue head. 'Absolutely not. This is a mental issue. He could be stuck in this state forever if I go messing around in his mind, even if I could activate my SPAM. Myles is the only one of us qualified to poke about in a brain, and I don't think he's in a fit state for anything right now.'

'Then we need to get him back to the *Fowl Star*,' said

Beckett. 'Once we're away from here, I can contact Artemis.'

'Artemis?' asked Lazuli.

This was not the best news. Her mentor, Commodore Short, had warned her to stay well clear of Artemis Fowl. Apparently, he made Myles look like a Boy Scout . . . although, when she had mentioned that comparison to Myles, he had taken great offence.

'Artemis makes me look like a Boy Scout, indeed. He is the Boy Scout! A mere Cub Scout compared to me in any arena you care to mention.'

'Artemis will know what to do,' said Beckett. 'He's bound to have an underworld contact who can help us.'

This just gets better and better, thought Lazuli, and she said, 'Let's just get to the boat. One step at a time.'

'Do you have a Moonbelt?' Beckett asked. 'I read that Holly used to have a Moonbelt.'

'Moonbelts were banned,' said Lazuli. 'Their ectoplasmic power sources were interfering with magnetic fields.'

'I only ask because Myles is heavier than he looks.'

Beckett took hold of Myles's belt with one hand, his brother's right wrist in the other, and, using a variation of a weightlifter's power snatch, he yanked Myles straight overhead, then dropped him on to his own shoulders.

'I think you'll manage,' said Lazuli.

And they would have made it to the *Fowl Star* without issue were it not for the laser beam that Myles had loosed mere seconds earlier. The beam had heated the refrigerator door, which transferred the heat to the goblin who was hiding inside and whose head was touching the aluminium. The goblin thought he was being cremated and popped out with his blaster drawn, which prompted his hit-team-mates to do the same.

3
GOBLIN HERPETOLOGY

THERE HAVE BEEN MANY UNINTENTIONAL scientific discoveries throughout recorded history, including recorded history itself, which Thomas Edison claimed was accidental, at least with regard to his own invention, the phonograph. And, while Edison's remark possibly stemmed more from modesty than anything else, it is nevertheless true that the world would have a lot more dead people composting in its graveyards today were it not for fumbles, mistakes and misfortunes. One example is the stumbling-across of the antimalarial properties of quinine, when a thirsty South American man drank water from a pool gathered in the roots of a cinchona tree and found that his symptoms rapidly subsided. Another chance discovery was penicillin, which was happened upon by Dr Alexander Fleming, who found it growing on an unwashed Petri dish in his laboratory.

In the fairy world, there is the case of the technical-genius centaur Foaly, who was hoping to get a peek into other realms when he set up a camera network around the warlock known as N°1 just before one of the little demon's interdimensional jaunts. But, instead of getting a look at something, Foaly got a look at nothing, as just before dematerialising, N°1 became completely invisible when his atoms separated. The warlock was obviously still there, because he continued to speak, and it occurred to Foaly that he could incorporate that invisible moment into the LEP's shimmer suits so that not even one of the infuriating Fowl children would be able to see officers of the fairy police force. Foaly should have perhaps run a few more tests before handing the prototype to Specialist Lazuli Heitz, but she was on babysitting duty, so the centaur took a chance that nothing would go wrong.

He really should have known better, considering the pedigree of the humans being watched over.

So now Lazuli's cloak of invisibility had an inter-dimensional element, which had challenged Myles for a while until he eventually decided to press pause on all his other projects while he worked on a solution.

'No more horsing around!' he'd declared, enjoying his little centaur joke, and then set his mind fully to the task of cracking Foaly's latest tech. It took Myles three solid days of experimentation and one hack of the LEP drive, but eventually he discovered that he could continue to see Specialist Heitz's shimmer suit in its new spectrum with the aid of an intravitreal ectoplasmic injection. Or, more simply put, a liquid filter injected by micro-needles directly into his own eyeballs.

When Myles realised this, he nodded several times and thought, *I've already partaken of my own waste liquids, so why not inject myself in the eyes with an ectoplasmic derivative, which is essentially just another waste product?* And so he built a delivery system into a pair of spectacles, which would enable him to inject himself outside the laboratory. And, if the initial tests were successful, he could incorporate the system, which he called **S**pectacle-mounted **O**cular **O**bservation **K**it, or SPOOK, into all his glasses.

London was his first real-world test of SPOOK.

I can figure out what else is visible in that spectrum later, once we get home from London.

But later was too late. The side effects were happening now.

Myles was seeing dead people. All one had to do was look at the quite forced acronym SPOOK to guess that Myles's subconscious already knew what the side effects would be, even if his conscious brain hadn't yet figured it out.

That's right – Myles hadn't been in London just to deliver a lecture to CORPSE. He knew that Lazuli would be assigned to shadow the Fowl Twins on any excursions, so he was also testing his fancy injections.

More on these strands once the pesky goblin hit squad is dealt with.

Specialist Lazuli Heitz had often grumbled to Foaly how ironic it was that Myles Fowl should continually land the so-called Regrettables in adventure-type scenarios when he himself was little more than dead weight. In fact, Foaly had gone so far as to review previous Fowl-related conflict videos and concluded that, mathematically, a group gained an advantage from the human boy fighting on the opposite side in a skirmish, as he would often accidentally sabotage any efforts his own team might make.

In this particular fight, Myles was not exactly dead weight, but he was unconscious weight, which was worse. At least if he had been deadweight, rigor mortis would have set in and his person could have been used as a battering ram – not that it ever would have crossed

Beckett's mind to use his brother's head to break down a door. It might have crossed Lazuli's mind, but, to give her credit, she most likely would have dismissed the idea almost immediately. At any rate, there was no call for a battering ram right now, as the river door was not locked. The problem wasn't the door but rather the increasing number of goblins clustering in front of it. There was certainly a moment when Beck and Laz could have made their move, but their surprise was so complete that the normally quick-witted pair were temporarily transfixed.

'Are those goblins?' asked Beckett, who was wearing his brother across his shoulders like a scarf.

'Affirmative,' said Lazuli, drawing her oxalis pistol.

Beckett had never seen a goblin in the flesh, and Lazuli had never been this close to one. In fact, she had only recently begun the first module of an in-service diploma in goblin herpetology, which would both earn her credit towards a master's degree and familiarise her with the species. She had a special interest because her SPAM often manifested as fire, which was a goblin trick – not that goblins needed magic to throw a fireball – so there was a chance some of her DNA nucleotides were goblin.

But, as she watched the goblin squad assemble before her, nervously licking their own eyeballs, Lazuli was glad that she had eyelids, at least. She was not repulsed by the goblin way of moistening their eyeballs, but she was a little worried that Beckett would find it distracting.

'That's amazing,' said Beckett, immediately attempting to lick his own eyeballs.

Distracted? Absolutely.

Goblins had emerged from every freezer, talking in rising hisses of alarm while swinging from the doors and clambering down the walls to the ground. The creatures had some limited sticking power, due to the tiny hairs on the pads of their feet and hands, but most of these fellows were wearing boots and gloves because of the cold, which was certainly not a goblin's preferred environment, and therefore were forced to climb like a human would.

Appearance-wise, the goblins might have seemed a little comical, with their darting eyes and jerking limbs, but Lazuli knew that this crew were probably muscle for hire and any one of them could cough up a fireball should they feel the need. Lazuli also knew she was fireproof when it came to her own elusive magic, but she was none too keen to find out whether that invulnerability extended to goblin flames, which Foaly had told her could get up to three thousand degrees, double the temperature required to evaporate fairy bone.

Lazuli could not for the life of her figure out why a team of goblin mercenaries would be concealed in a human mortuary, and was it just coincidence that it was this particular mortuary? Once she might have told herself to worry about these questions later, when things weren't quite so tense, but, if there was one thing she had learned from Myles, it was that information is power, no matter how or when it's acquired.

At the moment, the goblins were clustered by both doors, chattering in a rapid-fire language with so many forked-tongue sibilants involved that it seemed mostly liquid-based. Lazuli couldn't understand what they were saying apart from the occasional universal fairy word, but she knew Beckett would pick the language up in a matter of seconds. That was one of his many talents.

Lazuli caught Beckett's eye and raised an eyebrow, which said, *Are you getting this?*

Beckett nodded. He was getting it.

There were eight goblins in all. Four on each side,

all armed with what seemed to be pistols that were shaped, oddly enough, like small songbirds – budgies or perhaps canaries – with glowing red eyes that operated as laser sights. Beckett could not decide if this was bizarre or amazing, but he was leaning towards amazing.

He did understand the language, but the problem was that everyone was talking at the same time, which made it very difficult to pick out a single strand. Beckett listened hard and caught snatches like:

We should kill them.

You idiot, why did you emerge?

We were told to stay hidden unless the smart one found something.

I thought they were burning me.

I wish they had burned you.

It smells like your aunt's house in here.

You smell like my aunt's house.

No need to lay an egg.

We kill the LEP officer and the idiot, but the client wants the weakling alive at all costs.

I need a toilet.

After not so many seconds, Beckett lost patience.

'Can you please be quiet so I can catch up?' he asked

the goblins in their own tongue. 'I've only just learned this language.'

The goblins froze, some with their tongues pasted to one eyeball or the other.

Had the human boy just spoken goblin words?

And how could his pronunciation be so perfect with a tongue that wasn't split?

'Thank you,' said Beckett to the kill squad. 'Now, if I'm getting this right, some person called the "client" sent you goblins here to kill us, but only if my sleeping brother discovered something fishy. And you came out of those fridges because this little fellow overheated. How am I doing so far?'

One goblin sloped forward, and he was fascinating to watch. Beckett could not stop staring. It was rude, he knew, but what he did not know was that in goblin culture *the long stare* was the greatest compliment a person could receive, as it implied admiration and wonder, which was exactly how Beckett was feeling. In fact, he augmented his long stare with a dropped jaw, and the goblin chief could not help but preen.

Beckett was absolutely correct to be impressed. From a purely physical point of view, the goblin was undeniably a beautiful creature. He stood perhaps three feet tall with a bullet-shaped head encrusted with intricate interlocking metallic scales that seemed almost like jewelled armour. His side-mounted eyes were a bright orange with keyhole pupils that dilated as he swiped a tongue across them. The goblins wore a tactical uniform that was transparent so the goblin's own skin could take care of camouflage duties. Myles would doubtless have explained that this was accomplished by altering the layer depth of the crystals beneath their skin, thus changing the light frequency, which in turn changed the skin colour. If Foaly had been there, he might have added that goblin crystals were often smarter than the goblins themselves.

'I accept your compliment, human boy,' said the goblin chief, and Beckett thought that Goblin was surely the most difficult language he'd ever tried to wrap his head round, even with the gift of tongues stimulating the neurons in his brain. The language incorporated not just what might be called the standard word sounds, but also a variety of chirps, clicks, squeaks and hisses, which were often accompanied by an inflated throat. The most difficult part, though Beckett was unaware of this, was that goblins also produced sounds that were inaudible to humans. This meant that his sub-conscious had to fill in the blanks from context, which worked most of the time but not all, as the next sentence proved.

'But even so,' continued the goblin boss, 'I will give the order to kiss you.'

Unexpected, thought Beckett, who had missed a silent syllable in the middle of the word. *And inappropriate.*

'No kissing,' he said. 'That's a new rule I just made up.'

The chief took a moment to lick his eyeballs. 'Kissing? No one is kissing here today. I said we were going to *kill* you.'

Beckett slumped in relief, causing Myles's loafer heels to click together. 'Murder. Oh, thank goodness. People try to murder me every day, so I know how to handle that. Kissing is unusual, and every species has different customs. For example, killer whales like to swallow entire people and hawk them up again, which can be alarming.'

While Beckett was spouting all this, he was actually thinking, *I wish I'd brought Whistle Blower to the mortuary.* Of course, he wasn't supposed to have brought his warrior toy troll with him on the London trip at all, which was why he'd hidden the little fellow inside a crisp packet made of foil, which would fool

Myles's scans. Said packet was stashed in the yacht's pantry not a hundred metres away, but that was of zero use to Beckett right now.

Whistle Blower would tear these goblins apart, Beckett felt sure.

'I am glad we got that straight about the kissing,' said the goblin chief, and then he had to ask, 'How is it that you speak our language? Most fairies, even those with the gift of tongues, have lost that power.'

Beckett was delighted to have a question he could answer. 'Oh,' he said. 'I know that one. My brain got taken over by an old fairy. Really old. So I can speak what he could speak. Can I ask a question now? Fair is fair.'

The goblin shrugged and a flash of gold rippled across his body. 'One question. But it must be quick before we murder you, as we are on a schedule.'

Beckett had so many questions he would love to ask, like:

How do you sleep without eyelids?

How long are your tongues?

Did you get born in an egg?

Do your skins shed? And, if they do, may I have one for a superhero costume?

(On a side note, someone else less than four hundred miles away had already stolen one of these skins. We'll get back to this later, but remember it, as it's important to our story.)

As Beckett considered which question to ask, the goblins watched, rapt with fascination. Their heads followed him as he moved and gestured. They were like spectators at a sporting event with money on the outcome. And, while they observed Beckett, Lazuli studied *them*, diverting some concentration to the search of her own being. Where was this magical fire hiding? Why couldn't she summon it at will? She knew that imminent death was her trigger, but after that the magic ran on autopilot. Perhaps it would save her, but it certainly wouldn't save the boys. It might even kill them.

Where are you? she asked the SPAM. *I need you.*

The SPAM, as usual, declined to comment.

'I have a question!' blurted Beckett, startling everyone except Myles.

'Ask, human,' said the goblin chief. 'I grow weary of this game.'

But the chief was lying. He was fascinated by this boy and would've loved to keep him as an oversized pet.

'Okay,' said Beckett. 'Your bird-shaped guns. Do they shoot bullets or beams? And do the beams melt walls and metal?'

'That is two questions, but I shall answer as it suits me. The Blast Directional Guns, or BDGs, fire what we wish them to fire.'

Beckett fought to control his excitement but was not completely successful, which was evidenced by the fact that one of Myles's loafers jittered off his heel and dangled from the unconscious boy's big toe.

'Are you telling me that your bird-shaped guns are called Budgies?'

'That's what we call them. It's an in-joke. And right now our Budgies are dialled to discharge solar beams. You will find out shortly that they are tuned to a frequency that will not harm property – in fact, they bounce right off reflective surfaces. Very eco-friendly. We're all on Budgies except young Kimodo over there, who is quite handy with a Bluster. It will melt just about anything you care to mention, won't it, Kimodo?'

The only female in the group nodded eagerly. 'Anything, Dad – I mean Chief. Especially humans.'

Beckett snuck in another question. 'So, if you were

to shoot at that freezer door, the beam would just ricochet right off?'

The goblin chief, who was, after all, a tiny soldier, answered automatically. 'At which freezer?' he asked, pointing his gun. 'That one?'

Beckett took a micro-moment to scan everyone in the room, noting their positions.

'No, the one above,' said Beckett.

As the goblin corrected his aim, Lazuli was amazed at Beck's ability to draw his enemies into conversation.

'That freezer door?' asked the chief.

'Yes, but anyone could hit a door,' said Beckett, slyly shifting the goalposts, and suddenly this had become a challenge. 'I bet you couldn't hit the handle, right on the corner.'

The chief flapped his lips. 'Are you kidding? I could hit that while licking my eyeballs. I do not miss, boy. And, to prove it, I won't miss you in a moment.'

'You're aiming at the door handle?' asked Beckett, just to confirm.

The chief's only answer was a long stare. Then again, without eyelids, goblins were on full-time stare duty.

'I'm pretty fast, you know?' said Beckett. 'I could make it to you before you had time to shoot.'

'It doesn't matter, idiot human,' said the chief, adding a sneer to the insult. 'Like all of my warriors, I'm on a dead-fairy's trigger.'

'Are we doing dead-fairy's triggers, Chief Jeffluent?' said the goblin with the scalded head. 'I didn't know that.'

Jeffluent rolled his eyes, which in the case of goblins is quite mesmerising to watch. 'Yes, Garn,' he said. 'We were told that this human is extremely fast, remember? So switch your weapon to DFT.'

Garn flicked a dial on his Budgie gun. 'Okay, Chief. All set. DFT.'

And suddenly Lazuli understood what was happening. Myles had pulled off a variation of the same stunt with a dwarf in a Dalkey village basement.

That's ridiculous, she thought. *There's so many of us and we're all in here together.*

Ridiculous or not, Beckett would make his move soon. He had to. And she would be ready when he did.

And what a move it turned out to be. Ambitious even by Beckett's standards and ridiculous by anyone else's. Later the goblins would claim that the whole thing had been a fluke, but Lazuli knew even as it was happening that it went exactly as the Fowl boy had intended. In the beginning, at least. He probably hadn't anticipated the internal inferno, but neither had Lazuli and it was her doing.

Picture the scene if you will: the Tower Bridge Mortuary, which is basically a reflective box, stuffed with two living humans, a pixel, several goblins, one corpse and a ghost. (We can discount the two dead people for the moment. They are not unimportant in the mortuary Fowlscapade, but they play no part in this particular episode, though the ghost did enjoy the fireworks.) The goblins are a gang of soldiers for hire and will do anything for gold as long as those things are nasty and will enhance their reputations as outlaws. In fact, they were once offered a small fortune to rescue a princess with hair extensions from a tower, but they turned it down because they felt it would damage their bad name. The pixel, Specialist Lazuli Heitz, had three ridiculously monikered Budgies aimed at her, and Beckett Fowl still had his tranquillised brother draped over his shoulders.

Beckett calculated that he could carry Myles for about a million years without growing weary of the burden, but in spite of that he said, 'Myles is really heavy. I might collapse any second now.'

Which seemed like an obvious set-up to Lazuli, but the goblins seemed to buy it.

'Don't worry about that, Fowl boy,' said Jeffluent. 'Because, as I said, we're going to kill you.'

Garn raised a hand. 'Ooh, can I do it? I'm next on the rotation.'

'No,' snapped the chief goblin. 'You *were* next on the rota until you caused all this trouble. I'll do it myself.'

Now or never, thought Beckett. *Before Jeffluent adjusts his aim.*

'We should do the parting ritual,' Beckett said to Lazuli. 'You know, the one where you stand on one foot? Your right foot.'

Lazuli caught on immediately and raised her left foot, at which point Beckett shrugged his shoulders violently, sending the loafer that dangled on Myles's toe spinning through the air.

The shoe spun towards Jeffluent and, before the goblin chief could react, the heel thumped into his head, leaving an imprint that the upcoming fiery shenanigans would sear into his forehead for life. Jeffluent's brain sent a lightning relax impulse to his digits, including his trigger finger, which unclenched just enough to release the dead-fairy's trigger. A concentrated purple solar beam sped from the nozzle of his Budgie and almost instantly proved that the goblin chief was as good as his word when it came to the standard of his aim. The beam twinkled briefly on the freezer handle and ricocheted off on the next leg of its journey, which was directly towards Garn, who had barely time to open his mouth in surprise before the beam landed just above his right kneecap, administering as a result a fiery version of the non-lethal paralysing blow known as the cluster punch, which had been mastered by perhaps a dozen martial arts supremos. Beckett was one of those supremos, and he had just demonstrated that not only could he land the punch in person, but he could use a beam of solar power to administer it by proxy.

Cluster-punch victims had enough time for a quick spasm before keeling over, paralysed, and Garn's spasm released his trigger, sending another purple beam pulsing in a downward trajectory. It passed beneath Lazuli's raised foot, where it bounced off the tile floor and was trapped underneath the open freezer shelf for a dozen bounces before it sped into the open and, in quick succession, followed the five points of an M pattern, which were:

1. A goblin outlaw's metal toecap.
2. The chin guard of the same goblin.
3. A metal toecap on the adjacent goblin.
4. The adjacent goblin's extended Budgie.
5. That goblin's left boot, which was missing its toecap and absorbed the beam.

Both goblins fired. The first goblin's beam bounced directly back at himself, slamming him into the wall, and the second goblin outlaw's beam clipped the top of Beckett's ear before ending its journey on Kimodo's shoulder.

Kimodo, if you remember, was armed with a Bluster and, when she released her trigger, a beam of what looked like sewage spiralled from the barrel, passed through the strategically placed crook of Beckett's arm, and blew a section of the rear door all the way into the middle of the Thames.

This all took perhaps five seconds at most, and from above it would have seemed like a fiery game of pinball.

Beckett ducked out from under his sleeping brother and caught him on the way down, pressing a nerve in his twin's right glute, which would have pained Myles had he been awake but simply stiffened him while he was unconscious. Then, gripping Myles by the belt and Gloop tie, he seesawed his brother to build up momentum. On the third swing, he released his grip so that Myles threaded the funnel of space in the crowd of goblins, passed through the glowing hole in the steel door, and touched down on the rear stairway overlooking the Thames.

Myles is safe, thought Beckett. *Now to save Lazuli.*

But he would not save Lazuli.

For even though Beckett was extremely gifted when it came to instinctive physicality, he would be the first to admit that he was not exactly a scholar, and certain facts could be effectively hidden from him simply by writing them down. In fact, if you wanted to be absolutely certain that Beckett Fowl would not find out about something, all you had to do was hand him the information on a printout and ask him to read it.

In this case, the pertinent information was freely available to Beckett in Artemis's own fairy files, which on several occasions Myles had instructed Beckett to familiarise himself with, considering their ongoing relationship with the Fairy People. Beckett, who never appreciated being instructed to do anything, had cheerfully ignored his twin. Consequently, he had an appalling ignorance on the subject and was blissfully unaware that:

1. His ancestor the pirate Red Peg Fowl had once ridden a kraken across the Atlantic.
2. His Uncle Foxy regularly sheltered bands of outlaw dwarves on his estate.

And, most importantly in this case . . .

3. Artemis had been involved in a goblin-related episode some years previously, during which he had learned and recorded that goblins were by and large fireproof.

So, even though Beckett had stunned the goblins momentarily by pinging them with their own solar rays, he had not incapacitated them and, in fact, he had unwittingly performed a kind of bio-induction on Jeffluent and his crew so that they were actually more powerful now than they had been mere moments before.

And, though Beckett did not know any of this, he realised pretty quickly that none of the goblins were as unconscious as he'd hoped when he saw that the entire crew had opened their mouths and sparked up fireballs in their throats. What's more, his famous instincts were not suggesting a solution. There was no way for him to cartwheel his way out of this one.

Lazuli noticed the sudden desperation in Beckett's face and knew immediately that the baton had been passed to her. It was her responsibility to save the team. After all, she was the Fowl ambassador.

Beckett turned to Lazuli with his mouth open and eyes wide. The message was clear: *I'm sorry, Laz. You're my best friend and I got you killed.*

And it was at this point that Lazuli shot him in the chest.

There was, of course, a good reason for this shot. It would have been very out of character for Specialist Heitz to use the time before the goblins unloaded to maliciously shoot one of her charges. She did it to propel Beckett to safety through the same hole his brother had exited. She had time for one shot and used it to blast Beckett with a concussive seed from her oxalis, which struck him like an invisible fist, cracking three of his ribs and sending him across the room and through the opening. He did not go through the dripping ring as cleanly as Myles had. He lost the top of the ear that had previously been burned by solar fire, and also the edge of his right trainer, which, unfortunately, had a toe inside it, but Beckett was clear of immediate danger. As for herself, Lazuli would try to stay alive, but in all honesty it wasn't looking good. This mortuary might well become, perhaps fittingly, her final resting place.

Beckett did not stay conscious for long, but, before he passed out completely, his mind threw up something that he'd been puzzling over.

'Jeffluent,' he muttered. 'Sounds like *effluent*, which means *poop*. Funny.'

And then he passed out on top of Myles. Nose to nose with his twin.

The goblin crew were beyond giving or taking orders. Indeed, they seemed to be beyond speech itself, but that might have been because their mouths were full of roiling, hypnotic fire. Lazuli made herself look away, because it was a goblin hunting trick to mesmerise prey with the spinning fireball before letting it fly at a target that was not moving and would never move again unless its corpse were dragged to a cold rock shelf where the meat would keep.

The goblins circled Lazuli, their heads jutting forward in the old way, some dropping to all fours. So strong was their fire after Beckett's tune-up that their chests glowed orange and the colour spread out across their leathery skin and head scales. Pack mentality had taken over and there was only one imperative in the goblin troop now: kill the non-goblin.

Lazuli knew that all her fancy martial-arts moves would be of no use and, even if she did get off another shot, she didn't have Beckett's uncanny ability to pick a trajectory that would somehow incapacitate several targets at once. Her mentor, Commodore Holly Short, had once told her: 'There will come a day, possibly sooner rather than later, considering the company you keep, when the odds are so overwhelming that all your equipment and training will count for nothing. When that day comes, you'd better pray there is a Fowl somewhere nearby.'

There were two Fowls nearby, which was not nearly enough, and at the moment there were too many goblin limbs in the way even to see the twins.

All I can do is hope that my SPAM kicks in, she realised. *Imminent death is my trigger, and death seems pretty imminent at this moment.*

But how much magic could one fairy have inside them? Surely she must be scraping the bottom of the charm barrel by now?

I am about to find out, she thought, and suddenly the planets aligned, so to speak, and there was a small sliver of open space through which Lazuli could see the Fowl Twins. Beckett had landed on top of Myles.

Myles won't be happy about getting his suit wrinkled.

But both boys were moving a little, so they were alive, at least.

I wouldn't change it, thought Lazuli. *I wouldn't change a thing.*

Which was a comfort.

The goblins opened their reptilian jaws to widths of up to one hundred and twenty degrees and vomited forth fireballs. Often a goblin will transfer the ball of fire to his or her palm and launch it from there, as a direct throat-launch does mean a momentary loss of sight lines to the victim. But the goblins were not inclined to fool around with flame transfers and so swivelled their keyhole-shaped pupils and hawked fiery missiles at Specialist Lazuli Heitz.

If we might once again take advantage of a bird's-eye perspective and slow the action down to one hundredth of its actual speed, we could see that to call the goblins' projectiles *fireballs* was something of a misnomer, as they were more of a stream of dense flame, ash and acrid smoke, the precise smell of which depended on the spewer's diet. Suffice it to say, goblin fireballs are rarely evocative of spring flowers, except for those of one famous deep-tunnel goblin who credited his aromatic fireballs to sports massages and a diet of prison soap. But, though this story is fascinating, it can be found elsewhere, in epic-poem form, in his auto-biography, *My Life in Ashes* by Pú-Rí the Aromatic.

Returning to the mortuary situation, which is playing out in super slo-mo, we can see the seemingly doomed LEP Specialist Lazuli Heitz at the centre of a wheel of fire with the flaming spokes roiling her way and her hands outstretched in a futile and pathetic attempt to ward them off. The expected outcome would be for the goblin flames to consume the unfortunate pixel until she was little more than a smear on the mortuary floor. There would not even be enough left for a pathologist to examine.

This was not how the incident played out. Rather than be consumed, Specialist Heitz seemed to welcome the flames as they flowed through her, doing no apparent damage to her person. There was no scorching of flesh and no liquefying of organs. Even Lazuli's corn-blonde hair refused to frizz, though it did stand out in a spiky halo round her head, having partially dislodged her helmet. Her uniform popped and crackled as the goblin fire traced its cables and sensors, but the skin below was unaffected. And, though Lazuli's face was grim with what might pass for determination and purpose, in truth she was operating on autopilot.

There was no amazement on the faces of the goblins, as their point of view was obstructed by their own fire, but, even if every keyhole pupil in the mortuary had been focused on Lazuli, her response to their fireball attack was simply too lightning fast and overwhelming to be processed until much later, when they regained consciousness. And even then most of Jeffluent's crew would be left scratching their head scales for the rest of their days.

What happened was this: when the goblins spat

their fire at her, Lazuli's SPAM responded in kind, but her fire was threaded with strands of magic, something to which even goblins were not immune.

During previous manifestations, Lazuli's magic had been spontaneous and wild, but on this occasion the power seemed to have focus and intent. Where that intent came from Lazuli did not know precisely, but it made sense that she was the source. Some part of her brain knew what she was doing, but her conscious mind had not yet found the key.

Lazuli absorbed all the fireballs, and just about the only obvious change in the pixel was her personality. Her fine features, which had been bunched with stress and fear, smoothed out considerably as though the specialist had not a care in the world. So Zen was Lazuli, in fact, that she actually levitated perhaps fifteen centimetres from the ground and, before her heart monitor frazzled, it recorded her heartbeat as twenty-two BPM, which is yogi-level calm, and an incredible decrease in such a short span of time. When she had taken all the goblin fire, she returned it to them in precise bursts from her flaming eyes, spinning as she slammed her reptile assailants into the wall, tiles cracking with the force of their impact. This alone would have been astounding, but the power inside Lazuli was not done yet.

Once the goblins were pinned, squirming, to the wall, the magic-laced fire lassoed them together and ejected the entire bunch through the hole in the doorway, over the *Fowl Star* yacht and into the river. It was only then that the fire retreated into Lazuli, some of it remaining visible as twin coronas round her fists.

Anyone with even a passing knowledge of enchantment will know that none of this is normal. Fiery lassos and levitation are not pages from the usual magic playbook, even among late-blooming hybrids. What was happening here was, according to all the top magic tomes, virtually impossible. In his recent bestseller *When the Magic Happens*, Dr J. Argon postulated that there is a viable path to power for unique beings that might allow them to perform special feats, e.g. harnessing fire while levitating. But this was such a long shot that it remained a theory, and no amount of computer modelling could convince the scientific community that such a thing was possible. Maybe it had happened before, but no living fairy had ever witnessed it.

Until now.

But more on fanciful theories later. For the time being, we must concern ourselves with the fate of the Regrettables, or what was left of them.

The being who floated across the mortuary floor towards the rear door was Lazuli, no doubt about that, but she was something else too. Something extra. Her late-blooming hybrid magic had well and truly blossomed and was flowing through every cell in her body. In a way, Lazuli was like a toddler in a toyshop – awestruck by the wonders – so she was half dazed even as her LEP training reared its head and reminded her to protect the team.

'Team,' she said dully. 'Protect the team.'

Percival the ghost agreed wholeheartedly. 'Protect the team,' he said. 'Capital. I happen to believe that a fellow can commit all sorts of transgressions, but, so long as he looks after his mates, his soul ain't completely forfeit.'

Lazuli, who was unperturbed by the spirit's spinning-memory-hole eyes, gave the man a fiery gaze and then melted her way through the riverside door.

'You can see me too, fairy?' said Percival. 'Everyone can see me today. I've not been noticed in an age and all of a sudden it's like I'm prancing across the stage at the Orient Theatre.'

But then, as Lazuli drifted down the stone dock, Percival seemed to fade. For it is the way of spirits that sometimes, if there isn't a soul to see them, the ghost begins to wonder if they're really there.

Either that or he was exhausted after all the chatter.

The toes of Lazuli's boots were a few centimetres off the ground as she approached the twins, and yet sparks leaped from the near-contact as though flints were being struck.

Lazuli was thinking like herself but much more slowly than usual. This was not because the magic had decelerated her thought process, but because she had a new perspective. So many things seemed unimportant now.

But not love.

She did love this infuriating pair, and they would not like to be laid out here like this. Especially Myles, with his distaste for embarrassment.

Embarrassment – one of the things that no longer seemed important. Nevertheless, if it was important to Myles, she was prepared to go along.

Lazuli descended to grasp an ankle of each twin, and then, with no apparent effort, she held them both aloft, rising again so their heads would not bash against the stone. She carried the boys to the *Fowl Star* and dropped them on the foredeck.

And now I need to sleep, she thought.

This was not unusual. Magic had a way of sapping the wielder's energy, especially if that wielder was a novice and not accustomed to such concentrated displays of power.

Lazuli was beyond doubt a novice and could feel the utter exhaustion weighing upon her like a leaden blanket.

I must rest.

But not in the open. Even in a combined state of exhaustion and magical bliss, Lazuli knew better than to lie on a deck on the Thames with the police already on their way. So she glared fiercely at the bowline, which was enough to burn through its strands, and then, with her last seconds of consciousness, she floated belowdecks and squirrelled herself away in a storage locker among the life jackets.

Lazuli had a couple of final thoughts before an ink-black, dreamless unconsciousness claimed her. The first was: *I hope the magic doesn't set the foam in these life jackets on fire and sink the yacht.*

And the second: *The last time I touched someone during one of my episodes, I accidentally healed them. I bet that happened again.*

And indeed it had happened again to both twins.

One of them was not only healed but activated.

Let's just say that Lazuli had not been the only one with a dormant magic issue.

4
TINY NAIL SCALES

A FEW HOURS LATER, AS THE SUMMER SUN BACKLIT the London Eye, throwing watery light on the observation carriages, Myles Fowl awoke. As was his custom, he did not emerge fully into consciousness but suspended himself in a hypnopompic state of threshold consciousness, in which he could think in a superfast mode without alerting anyone to the fact that he was not asleep.

Of course, if Beckett happened to be awake, his twin was not fooled by his playing possum, as their heartbeats were usually in sync and he could feel Myles emerging through layers of sleep. So, even though he had not yet opened his eyes, Myles knew that Beckett still slumbered. This was not unusual, as his brother often slept in until one of their parents shook him awake or one of his seagull mates tapped a beak on the window. Myles envied his brother's ability to drool-slumber his way through the night with over sixty per cent of his sleep being deep or REM, while he himself was lucky to get a nine per cent score on NANNI's sleep monitor. Plus, he usually woke with a headache brewing.

I will ask Beckett for a slap, he thought now.

This may sound like an unusual request, but, when Beckett had demonstrated that the cluster punch was based on an ancient African system that theorised that the body's twelve principal meridian lines all intersected in a cluster just above the right kneecap, Myles extrapolated that a similarly pinpoint-accurate slap just below the left cheek would reset the diameter of the blood vessels in his brain and thereby prevent a migraine. Myles had recently been halfway through explaining this to Beckett with the aid of a holographic model when his brother had slapped him in the face. Immediately, Myles's headache had disappeared. It was not a therapy that could be administered every day, due to the brain-rattling effects, but Myles treated himself to a clear head a couple of times a week if he had a lot of thinking to do.

As the evening's events slowly returned to him, he had a feeling that an especially clear head would be called for on this day, as he would have quite a lot of explaining to do to the authorities or, at the very least, his parents.

Except that I do not appear to have a headache.

Myles thought he might extend his hypnopompic state to mull over this development when he remembered he had seen a ghost and, as is quite common among the living who have seen the dead, he shot upright, barking the exclamation, 'I saw a ghost!'

He was immediately disappointed in himself that he should blurt such a cliché, as it was his duty as a visionary genius to inspire others with his every utterance.

"'I saw a ghost,'" he muttered in disgust. 'Really, Myles. Imagine if Artemis had overheard. The shame.'

Nevertheless, he *had* seen a ghost, and a quite unsavoury one at that, and it didn't take a genius to realise that his dabbling in ectoplasmic intravitreal injections had more than likely revealed that spectre to him.

'No more injections outside a laboratory,' he decided on the spot. He would gladly accept not seeing a shielded Lazuli for a while if it also meant not seeing Percival's horrible memory visions.

Myles shuddered at the recollection. The spectre's eyes had been twin nightmares, plunging him into a sordid past that he had no wish to revisit, even though it was possible he would have learned something from the experience. There were places that even a scientist could not go until he figured out the proper dosage.

It occurred to Myles then that there might even now be a ghost somewhere in the vicinity. But a quick glance at his smartwatch calmed his racing pulse. In previous tests, the injections had worn off after eight hours, so his vision should have returned to normal by now.

I will find another way to spy on the living and investigate the dead, he said to himself, and then he said loudly, 'Myles Fowl always finds a way.' Which he thought would be inspiring if someone were eavesdropping.

Myles felt wooden slats digging into his bottom and realised he was not in bed. Also, he felt wind on his face and so deduced he was not in an MI6 black site being prepped for interrogation. Somehow they had escaped the Dead Man's Hole and remained, as the police would say, at large.

Myles looked around and was unsurprised to find himself on the *Fowl Star*'s foredeck, as he had calculated by clenching his butt cheeks that the wooden slats had a one-centimetre-wide drainage groove between them, which would be consistent with the building plans for the family yacht. Beckett lay on the deck beside him, snoring peacefully, and Myles decided to let him rest for a few minutes more while he himself took stock of their situation. He was also discouraged from waking his twin by a baleful stare from the toy troll Whistle Blower, who was gnawing on Beckett's ear for some reason.

Whistle Blower and Myles had a frosty relationship at best – Myles always felt that, if he weren't Beckett's twin, the little troll would have attacked him months ago. Whistle Blower raised a shaky, caterpillar-sized eyebrow at Myles as if to say, *What do you want?*

At that precise moment, Myles did not want anything from the troll, especially attitude. Until recently, he would have said that all he wanted from Whistle Blower was his indefinite absence, but the toy troll had proved himself invaluable in combat situations where Myles himself had not exactly shone, and so the boy was prepared to tolerate the troll's presence. It did irk him that Beckett had managed to smuggle Whistle Blower aboard somehow, but the mystery was quickly solved when he noticed crisp flakes in Whistle Blower's fur.

'A crisp packet,' he said approvingly. 'Well played, brother mine.'

When Myles thought about it, he realised that having Whistle Blower on board was a good thing. There was something going on in the Fowl orbit, he was sure of it. No way would a squad of goblins just happen to show up at the bridge. And, since Teddy was most certainly a little too dead for scheming, it stood to reason that someone else was up to something. Myles needed to find out what that something was before the Regrettables ended up on slabs with their brains vacuum-packed in a refrigerator.

Myles rested on a brass railing and checked their surroundings. The yacht had drifted across the Thames and lay nestled between, and effectively hidden by, two restaurant barges that were deserted except for a row of gulls that peered down from the gunwales at the *Fowl Star* decks, undoubtedly hoping for a chat with Beckett. Wherever they went, the birds somehow knew that this Beckett was *the* Beckett who loved nothing more than a chinwag with seagulls.

Beckett, thought Myles. What had happened to Beckett?

He was not overly worried about his brother because, even without examining his sleeping form, Myles's scar told him that Beckett was calm. But something had happened – he was fuzzily aware of that – and Myles detested not knowing specifics.

Did Lazuli sedate me? Is that why I don't know exactly what transpired last night?

Investigation was called for.

As was his habit, Myles brushed himself down. He found his suit to be quite severely wrinkled, which was annoying, and, not only that, one of his loafers was missing.

This is intolerable, he thought. *What if Artemis were to return from his Mars mission at this moment? He would certainly hold me responsible for the ear-nibbling troll. Not to mention the fact that I am both dishevelled and suffering from an embarrassing deficit in the footwear department.*

Myles would remedy these sartorial shortfalls momentarily, as his cabin wardrobe was fully stocked with all the clothing an aspiring mastermind would require for any climate or cocktail party, but right now he needed to inspect the yacht and then find out just what had gone on the previous night.

Something momentous had happened, Myles was certain. Because, for the first time in over a year, he felt anxiety-free. He had minor worries, yes, but the cloud of anxiety that generally hovered over him, most especially in the mornings, seemed to have evaporated.

Myles did a circuit of the deck, just to ensure there were no hostiles on board, or bobbing alongside, for that matter. For most people, this would take two minutes max, but Myles, already hobbled by his natural two-left-footedness, was now missing a shoe and on the deck of a boat that rose and dipped with the ebb and flow of the Thames, and so the revolution took almost fifteen minutes, by which time Beckett was awake and sobbing.

Myles was surprised. His scar had informed him that his brother was awake, but he had not detected any telltale throbs of negative emotion.

'Beck!' he said, hurrying to his brother's side. 'Whatever is the matter?'

Beckett lay on his back and had pulled one foot closer to his face than most people were capable of. 'My toe is missing!' he said between sobs.

Myles saw that the edge of his twin's trainer had been sliced away and the canvas was stained with blood.

Something shimmered in the space where Beckett's little toe should have been and, when Myles tapped the arm of his glasses for a closer look, he saw that in place of a normal toe there was what looked bizarrely like a . . .

'Is that . . . ?' asked Myles in surprise. 'Beck, could that be . . . ?'

Beckett shoved his foot into his twin's personal space. 'Yes, brother,' he said, and Myles saw now that his tears were of the joyful kind, which explained why his scar had not detected sadness. 'It's a Gloop toe. I've never been so happy.'

It *was* a Gloop toe. Not a living goldfish, thankfully, but an accurate golden representation, complete with freckles for the eyes and tiny nail scales. It was somehow simultaneously adorable and utterly gross, and Myles didn't know what he felt about it.

What he did know was that Lazuli must be responsible for this magical aberration.

'The top of my ear was lasered off,' said Beckett, and Myles noticed that his brother was wearing Whistle Blower on his head like a fur cap. 'But it grew back. Whistle Blower says there's barely a mark. He noticed it after he swam over from Ireland, which I had told him not to do, and found the yacht.'

This was not a serious attempt at a fib. Beckett knew that Myles would already have figured out the crisp-packet dodge.

'I'm delighted to hear your ear is fine, and I suppose you're delighted to hear it too. Please thank Mr Walker for me.'

'I will,' said Beckett, realising that he was busted.

Normally, Myles would deliver a lecture on the futility of trying to hoodwink the great Myles Fowl, but at this moment finding Lazuli was the priority. 'We need to speak to Specialist Heitz with all urgency,' he said.

'Do you want a slap first?' asked Beckett. 'I bet you need a clear head this morning.'

Myles was reminded that his head was already crystal clear. 'No, thank you, brother mine,' he said. 'I am fully functioning this morning, and I suspect it is because Specialist Heitz's magic has evolved. She has removed my anxieties, the intensity of which correlates somewhat to the levels of headache I experience. To be honest, I find it troubling that fairy magic sees anxiety as a weakness or imperfection, as some of my best ideas were born of it. So I urgently need to speak with Lazuli before she randomly cures me of something else that is not an illness.'

Whistle Blower had been around the twins enough to pick up a few non-Trollish words, and one of those words was *Lazuli*. When he heard Myles mention the pixel, he muttered something and pointed a hairy finger towards a line of scorch marks on the deck. Myles didn't need an interpreter to figure out that they would find the specialist by following this trail.

'We must follow the scorch marks on the deck,' he said quickly, hijacking the idea. 'Where the trail ends, we shall find Specialist Heitz.'

Whistle Blower muttered one of the few Trollish terms that Myles understood. It was the insult *rodent meat*, usually reserved for squirrels, which are tough to digest, but Whistle Blower often used it to disparage Myles, as he found him difficult to digest in another way. Myles was not insulted by this – in fact, he found it fascinating that trolls' thought processes were not always literal.

The three Regrettables trooped down the wooden steps, through the small galley and into the hold to the life-jacket storage bin, where the trail of scorch marks ran up the slotted doors, cracking the varnish and blackening the wood underneath.

'Aha,' said Myles. 'I deduce that when we open this

door we shall find our very own life jacket, or life preserver as our American friends might say. In this instance, the term *life preserver* has a double application, which means, I think you will find, that I have just made a hilarious joke.' By which time Beckett had opened the doors. They found Lazuli inside, curled up in a nest of plastic foam life jackets that had melted to form a mould of her body.

Myles tapped the arm of his eyeglasses. He could have awakened NANNI some minutes previously, but he preferred not to rely on the AI too much. 'NANNI,' he said, 'scan Specialist Heitz for injuries.'

NANNI neither complied nor replied, and Beckett was able to tell Myles why.

'Don't bother, brother. You deleted NANNI last night.'

Myles felt ill. 'I did *what?*'

Beckett knelt and peeled plastic blobs away from Lazuli's person. 'During your episode. You ordered a full delete. I was surprised, to be honest. It felt a little irresponsible, which is supposed to be *my* speciality.'

Myles cast his mind back. It was possible that during the panic of his immersion into the ghost world he had inadvertently shut down NANNI. In the long term, that was not an issue, as he kept a version of the artificial intelligence safe and sound in a good old independent hard drive, but right now it meant that there would be no input from NANNI until they got back to Dalkey Island, where he had zero intention of going until this goblin-ambush mystery was solved.

I will not lead killer goblins back to my parents' door, he resolved, although this was false nobility. Myles simply wanted to give his conscience an excuse to go off on another grand adventure.

'No matter,' he said brightly now. 'I functioned for several years without NANNI's help and I can do so now.'

Beckett lifted Lazuli from the storage bin and carried her gently to one of the forward cabins, where he laid her on Myles's bunk, the quilt of which, unsurprisingly, displayed a print of the periodic table of elements. Whistle Blower squatted on Lazuli's chest and felt her heartbeat through his hindquarters.

'She has a strong heart,' he told Beckett. 'Stronger than before.'

Beckett passed on the message. 'Whistle Blower says that Lazuli's heart is stronger than before.'

'And how would a troll know that?' Myles wondered.

Beckett gently removed Lazuli's helmet. 'He has incredible hearing.'

'I see,' said Myles. 'I'd speculated that he was using his gluteal vein as a type of organic monitor, which would have been amazing.'

'And that too,' said Beckett. 'But I thought you might not be in the mood to hear about butt monitors.'

'I am always in the mood for science,' said Myles.

The pixel seemed tiny and fragile on the human-sized bed, even though the twins knew that though tiny she may be, fragile she was not. There was a power inside their friend that was formidable indeed when it decided to come out. Unfortunately, she had no conscious control over her magic, and it seemed to be getting more unpredictable with each passing crisis.

Myles was not a medical GP, but he used his pathologist's training to check Lazuli's bones for breaks and was relieved to find that there were no obvious ones, though a person could never rule out fractures without equipment. Myles then used his scientific training to run a quick check on her LEP gear to find that, while her suit's filaments were completely blown and possibly beyond repair, Lazuli's wings seemed mechanically okay, and her oxalis, which was protected from energy surges including fire, was resting on standby, pretty much like the specialist herself.

'I pronounce Lazuli reasonably fit and well, though judging by her skin tone I would say possibly dehydrated.'

At this moment, Lazuli's eyes flickered open and she spoke as though she were involved in the conversation instead of being its subject. 'And you, Myles. How are you?'

Myles thought about it. 'Good morning to you, Specialist Heitz. I'm surprisingly well. I'm not anxious in the least, which does worry me somewhat.'

Lazuli propped herself up on her elbows. 'The magic healed you both. I remember that much, but not much else.'

Beckett sat on the bed beside her. 'Morning, Laz. Whistle Blower was on social media. He says hashtag FlamingFairy is trending. Apparently, something – probably you – was seen hovering over the river all lit up. A couple of blurry photos were snapped, but nothing detailed.'

There was a lot in this casually delivered statement to digest, not least the fact that Whistle Blower had been on social media.

'Whistle Blower is scrolling the internet now?' said Myles.

'Yep. His handle is HedgeHogEntrails, which is his troll name. Five thousand followers since yesterday. Ten photos posted already.'

Beckett did not add that the troll's most popular photo was one of Myles asleep on the boat with a line of drool between his mouth and the decking.

'I suppose we can discuss troll-scrolling and the associated risks later,' said Myles. 'Right now I need to know what's going on with your magic, Specialist Heitz.'

Lazuli swung her legs off the bed, and, thanks to the low-slung mounting of yacht bunks, her feet were actually able to reach the floor. 'And I need to know what happened to you in that mortuary,' she said. 'What's really going on here, Myles? I want the whole truth or so help me I'm calling Artemis and telling him that you accidentally discovered something.'

'Wow,' said Beckett. 'Hardball.'

Myles's hand flew to his mouth. 'You wouldn't.'

And Whistle Blower growled a growl that everyone in the berth knew was Trollish for *rodent meat*.

And so the Regrettables brought each other up to speed. Myles confessed that he'd been using the London trip to lure Lazuli into activating her shimmer suit so he could try out his intravitreal ectoplasmic injections in the field. The SPOOK injections had enabled him to see a ghost, which had been a terrifying experience he did not plan to repeat outside a laboratory. He'd had no idea that Lord Teddy would show up and was very suspicious that the duke should be so easily dispatched.

Lazuli admitted that she, too, found this suspicious, which was the main reason she'd agreed to go along on the Tower Bridge mission. But, now that Teddy was indisputably dead, Lazuli's job was to submit an urgent report to Police Plaza so they could decide what to do about rounding up Jeffluent and his band of rogue goblins.

'Jeffluent,' echoed Beckett, and he chuckled. To Whistle Blower, he said, 'I'll tell you later.'

'And your magic, Specialist? I have my own theories, but what do you think is going on there?'

'I don't know, Myles,' admitted Lazuli. 'It's definitely changing. Magic is not supposed to work like this. Without rules.'

'Unless . . .' said Myles, leaving it hanging.

'Unless what?' asked Lazuli.

Beckett filled in the blanks. 'I know this one. When Myles says, "Unless *dot dot dot*," that means my brother has a theory but won't tell us about it yet in case he's wrong.' He clawed dramatically at his own cheeks. 'Which would be mortifying for a scientist.'

Whistle Blower imitated Beckett's cheek-clawing and made a mangled attempt at repeating *mortifying*.

Myles was not amused. 'There is also the matter of the goblin and his band of merry murderers. Why would they be staking out the corpse of a dead duke?'

'Unless they were there for something else,' noted Lazuli.

'Unlikely,' said Myles.

Lazuli licked her dry lips. 'Unlikely? That's one of those words that loses its meaning around the Fowl Twins. Like *unbelievable* or *absurd*. I think, after the Southbank Centre and the mortuary, we're way beyond unlikely.'

Lazuli tried to take a sip from her suit's hydration tube and was unsurprised to find it as dry as a bleached bone. Even Foaly's tubes weren't insulated enough to resist fairy fire.

'Could I have some water, please? My suit has dried up.'

Whistle Blower got the message and scooted to fetch Lazuli a drink, eager for any excuse to get out of a meeting.

Myles used the dry-suit issue as a handy segue. 'I imagine your suit was not built for assault from the inside?'

'No,' said Lazuli. 'It was already damaged at the Southbank.' She shrugged inside her LEP jumpsuit and its micro scales rippled, reminding Myles of the goblins they had recently faced. 'It feels different. More rigid. But that's just an impression. I'll have to run a full diagnostic to see exactly how much damage I've done. Foaly will be livid. This is an experimental model. He spent half his budget just on the buttons, according to him.'

Myles tried to present an innocent, childlike face. 'I could, if you like, take a look, just to help out. As a favour to our friends in the LEP.'

Lazuli was not fooled for a microsecond. 'Oh, sure. I'm going to hand Myles Fowl an experimental LEP suit to plug into and maybe *accidentally* download the schematics. No, thanks, Myles. I need to check in. There's a locker on the London Eye. I'll pick up some new gear there and log into the LEP net.'

'At least drink some water first, Specialist,' Myles advised. 'You are not yet your usual self.'

'Where's Whistle Blower?' Beckett wondered aloud. 'He knows where the water is.'

At that moment, the tiny troll appeared in the doorway, holding a full pitcher of water in front of him. 'There's a boat coming,' he said, his face magnified and misshapen by the curve of the glass container. 'It's got a blue light on top.'

'Police,' said Beckett. 'There's a police boat coming.'

Lazuli stood. 'That's my cue. If they have a search warrant, I don't want to end up as hashtag FlamingFairy. I'll fly over to the London Eye and meet you back here.'

Myles was not concerned. 'Not to worry. I'm sure this is just a follow-up after yesterday.'

'I'll keep an eye on you from the top of the London Eye and we can rendezvous when you're clear.'

'It shouldn't take long,' said Myles. 'Bamboozling the police is something of an area of expertise in our family.'

Lazuli strapped on her helmet, which looked like it had spent the night in a volcano. 'Tell me about it,' she said.

'Usually we protest our innocence,' continued Myles. 'And on this occasion we actually *are* innocent.'

'Enjoy the feeling while it lasts,' said Lazuli. 'Which it probably won't.'

She was right. It wouldn't.

5
CAPSULE THIRTEEN

THE LONDON EYE, or Millennium Wheel, is a cantilevered observation wheel with thirty-two capsules numbered from one to thirty-three. Ostensibly, there is no capsule thirteen because humans would consider it unlucky. Fairies hold no such superstitious beliefs about that particular number, but they are not fond of eighteen because, in Gnommish numerals, an eighteen resembles the howling face of a bull troll, which is not a sight many fairies survive. So it was with some sense of patronising smugness towards the human race that the LEP had named their observation hideout – which was clipped on to the wheel by magnetic levitation ring – Capsule Thirteen.

The LEP had such hideouts, lockers and dead letter boxes in population centres all over the world. Some were manned for observation, but most were safe spaces for agents caught out in the cold, or pick-up points for field equipment. The London Eye location made sense, because it was hard for humans to access and could be seen from almost anywhere in central London, making it a beacon for lost fairies. Capsule Thirteen's projection system made it effectively invisible, except for one notorious incident some years ago, when LEP consultant centaur Foaly mixed up his AVs and broadcast his own irritated face on the capsule's surface for a good thirty seconds. Luckily, the episode occurred during the opening ceremony of the London Olympics and so eyes were mostly elsewhere.

Lazuli approached the capsule from below, taking it nice and slow, careful not to push her wings, which were making periodic grating noises that they definitely should not have been making.

Another thirty metres and I can retire my equipment and pick up some new gear.

By *new gear* Lazuli meant new to *her*. Whatever equipment she managed to scavenge from the capsule would certainly not have as many bells and whistles as the suit she wore now. Unfortunately, most of her bells and whistles were shot, blown or busted and, if she didn't get a change of shimmer suit, she would shortly be floating out here for the entire human population of London to see.

Nothing is easy with the Fowl Twins, she thought for

perhaps the millionth time. *Myles can't even give a lecture without one of his enemies taking a potshot at him.*

And even Myles's potshots were more bombastic than the usual potshot. Most scientists were burned by scathing articles in the *New Scientist* – Myles's attempted burning came when his enemy tried to ram him with a plane.

Lazuli activated the filter on her visor that enabled her to see past the capsule's projected camouflage, and it shimmered into view before her. On any other day, she might have paused even for a second to appreciate the view of London from this altitude. You could say what you wanted about human infestation of the Earth's surface, but, with the rows of iconic buildings rising like a kraken's teeth through the morning mist, it had to be admitted that their structures could be impressive. However, Lazuli did not pause to appreciate the sights today, for a couple of very good reasons:

1. Her wings were on the point of giving out, and . . .
2. There was a figure climbing into Capsule Thirteen.

Lazuli pulled out her oxalis pistol and primed a concussive round. It was possible that the mysterious figure was another stranded LEP officer, but the way this mission was going it seemed more likely that whoever was accessing Capsule Thirteen had come to kill her.

This is Myles's fault, she said to herself. Lazuli had no real evidence to back up this opinion, but she'd voiced it several times over the past months and hadn't been wrong yet.

Lazuli watched the figure disappear into the capsule, waited half a minute for the intruder to get set up and distracted, then silently glided to the doorway and let herself be scanned by the retina sensor. A few seconds later, she was inside and watching a familiar goblin log into the capsule system.

This was puzzling. Why would this particular person be here, making herself at home with LEP systems?

While Lazuli mulled over this latest mystery, her wings gave out, which meant that if she wanted to fly out of there, she would either have to source new wings or activate the epicyclic gears that fed directly into a motor in her wing mounts and cycle away.

Option one was infinitely preferable. Lazuli dropped

to the capsule floor with a double *thunk*, which almost made the interloper jump out of her skin.

'D'Arvit!' swore Kimodo, recently seen armed with a Bluster at the Tower Bridge Mortuary. 'Don't shoot! I didn't break in. I have an access code.'

Suddenly it made sense to Lazuli. Kimodo was an LEP source. A snitch for Police Plaza.

'Turn round slowly,' said Lazuli. 'Hands in the air, please. If I see so much as a pilot light, you will wake up in Howler's Peak.'

Kimodo turned slowly as requested. The goblin gang member wore an MK4 shimmer suit that had seen better days and would be useless against a weapon at close range. Her bullet-shaped head darted left and right and her long tongue swished over her eyes.

'You!' she said. 'Don't burn me. I barely survived the last time.'

'You look fine to me,' said Lazuli. 'In fact, you shouldn't look quite so fine. How did you make it out of there intact?'

Kimodo shrugged. 'Fire isn't so bad, even magic fire. You scalded me good, but Daddy bought a pot of salve from a healer in Scotland a few seasons back. Works pretty well, though my armour was a pile of slop.'

'Everyone made it out?'

Kimodo nodded. 'We haven't found Garn yet, but he goes missing regularly. He'll turn up.'

Lazuli cocked her gun. It was for show, really, as there was no need to cock an oxalis once it had been primed. 'So tell me, Kimodo. What are you doing here?'

As is the goblin custom, Kimodo tried a lie first. 'I was just climbing this big wheel for exercise, and I found an invisible capsule, and I said to myself, *Kimodo, you should check this out.*'

'So you hacked the door? And how did you manage to crack the retina scanner without setting off alarms?'

'Lucky, I guess. I have one of those eyeballs. Always opening doors. Dad says my eyeball is better than a thousand keys. I'm a real asset to the team.'

Enough is enough, thought Lazuli, and she said, 'Kimodo, the only way you can breach this capsule is if you're authorised. And, if you're authorised, it's because you're a confidential informant. And, if you're a CI, then you have a handler. And all I want to know is who that is. Once I check that out, you can submit your report, I can submit mine and we can part friends. How does that sound?'

Kimodo ran through this in her head and finally

came up with a question. 'And, if we part friends, does that mean you won't shoot me?'

Lazuli nodded. 'Either way, I won't shoot you, but if everything checks out I won't arrest you, even though I should after last night.'

'I was just maintaining my cover,' said Kimodo, tacitly admitting that she did, in fact, have a handler.

'Now we're getting somewhere,' said Lazuli, motioning with her oxalis. 'Step away from the terminal, and let's check your credentials.'

Kimodo did as she was told, making room for Lazuli on a sensor pad on the capsule floor. As soon as Lazuli pulled off her battered helmet and stepped on to the pad, the system logged her in and a holographic menu popped up in the air between her and Kimodo.

Lazuli selected *personnel*. 'Give me the name,' she said to Kimodo. This was a test, because handlers didn't use their real names.

'The only name I have is Crunchmag Supreme, which I suspect might be an alias.'

Lazuli knew immediately who the handler might be. A bulky gnome named Shaskell Parp, who was forever going on about his college crunchball team, and how his prowess was a magnet for the ladies, ergo Crunchmag Supreme.

'Heavens help us,' Lazuli muttered, and she v-typed his name into the system. Sure enough, Kimodo was listed as a confidential informant. 'Okay. You're telling the truth.'

Kimodo seemed to notice Lazuli's face for the first time and was suddenly eager to be on her way. 'I told you. Now, if you don't mind, I'll go out the way I came in, and I'd appreciate not getting my tail blown off. I need all the balance I can get climbing down this thing.'

Kimodo was kicking off her boots for the climb when Lazuli asked, 'Don't you want to file your report? That's what you're here for, isn't it?'

'I did come for that,' said Kimodo, 'only I don't really feel like it right now. It's probably not important.'

Lazuli was immediately suspicious. Could Kimodo's sudden reluctance have something to do with her own presence? Could the goblin's report relate to last night's event somehow?

'Who sent you to that mortuary last night, anyway?'

Kimodo hung her boots round her neck. 'We had a deal, officer. If I checked out, then I checked out, if you know what I mean.'

'I'm changing the deal,' said Lazuli. 'There's something not right here. You're a snitch who doesn't want to snitch.'

Kimodo scowled. 'I'm not *your* snitch.'

'You were happy to be my snitch until I took off the helmet. You don't like my face, Kimodo?'

The goblin hugged her boots. 'I like your face. I mean, it's fine, I suppose. It's just . . .'

Lazuli tried bad cop. 'Just answer the question, Kimodo. Who sent you to the mortuary?'

'It's not that simple,' protested the goblin, who probably wished she had her Bluster under her arm.

'*Make* it simple!' shouted Lazuli. 'Or, so help me, you're going in a containment cube until Retrieval gets here. Unless my magic gets riled up first, and we all know what happens then.'

Kimodo backed herself against the curved wall. 'Okay, all right. Calm down. No need to get riled up. I'll tell you, all right?'

'Make it quick, Kimodo. I'm still a little sore about you taking potshots at me.'

Kimodo composed her thoughts. 'Okay. Fine. You'll pass it on to Crunchmag, I guess.'

'Of course I will,' confirmed Lazuli. 'Standard procedure.'

'Right. You probably know this, but there are a lot of

surface fairies like me all over the world who are off the grid. The LEP turns a blind eye to us so long as we keep our heads down and don't steal anything too big.'

Lazuli did know this. One of her colleagues was setting up an investigation into a group of surface fairies in New Orleans who had apparently got hold of a chute pod, which was a big piece of fairy equipment to have floating around.

'Yeah, so? What's that got to do with the mortuary?'

'A lot of surface fairies have been showing up lately. Fairies hired by humans through an intermediary to do big jobs. Crunchmag wanted me to find that intermediary. So, when we were hired to stake out the mortuary, I thought the client might be the fairy he was after.'

So far, so credible, Lazuli thought. Collaring this intermediary would be a career-maker for Crunchmag, especially if it led back to the human doing the hiring.

'Do you know who this go-between is?'

Kimodo shook her head and licked an eyeball nervously. 'Not exactly. I just know Jeffluent is supposed to meet her in the Sozzled Parrot today. And, let me tell you, after the roasting you gave Dad, he ain't going to make it to that meeting.'

The Sozzled Parrot was a notorious surface-fairy

joint in Miami famous for burning down twenty-four times in the past century. It was half a world away, but this distance was no big deal for most fairy craft.

'So what's your problem?' said Lazuli. 'That's a solid lead. I can pass it on and, whatever Crunchmag promised you, he'll deliver.'

Kimodo got that shifty look again. 'Maybe. *If* you pass it on.'

Lazuli had had a hard night, and she was getting tired of this runaround. 'And why wouldn't I? You're talking in riddles, Kimodo. You know what? I don't have time for this play-acting. You can just sit here in a containment field until a squad gets here and, after last night's devastation, I wouldn't be surprised if they took you back to Haven with them.'

'No!' said Kimodo. 'I'll tell you. Let me tell you.'

'Talk,' ordered Lazuli.

'You're part elf, right? Amazonian?'

'I'm not in the mood for chitchat, Kimodo.'

'You've got those yellow markings on your neck. Those are unique, passed down through the generations?'

Lazuli did not want to talk genetics with a criminal, and so she impatiently swiped through the holo-menu looking for a containment field.

'I took a sneaky photograph of the employer when Dad was online discussing the payment,' said Kimodo, holding out a communicator. 'I used this old human phone so the scanners wouldn't pick it up. That's my evidence.'

Lazuli took the phone and looked at the screen. What she was seeing there didn't fully register for a moment, but then its full implications lit up her neurons and set her hands shaking so much that she almost dropped the device.

'Is that real?' she asked Kimodo, even though every LEP instinct in her body told her it was.

'Yeah,' said the goblin. 'I risked my life taking that shot, but Crunchmag promised me a clean record if the tip is good.'

'Okay,' said Lazuli, tapping the phone to the capsule wall to save the photograph. 'I'll pass it up the chain when I'm done with it. But now you need to go, Kimodo. Go back to your band of outlaws, and we'll be in touch.'

A little of Kimodo's natural belligerence reasserted itself, now that she saw how rattled Lazuli was. 'A second ago, you wanted me to stay, and now you want me to go. Which is it, officer?'

141

Lazuli turned to the main interface and began typing in a workaround bypass that would force the capsule to accept a command it surely would not want to accept. 'Stay here if you like, Kimodo, but I'm about to steal an LEP ship, and I don't know if being an accessory to that is covered in your deal.'

Kimodo decided that all in all it was probably better for her immediate and distant future if she got herself out of this unpredictable elf's orbit as fast as she could.

And so she did, scrambling through the hatch without a backward glance.

Once the CI was gone, Lazuli sealed the door behind her, winched a jump seat up from the floor, uncoupled the car from its maglev ring and cut Capsule Thirteen loose from its moorings.

This is crazy, she thought, as she prepared to launch. *Taking off in broad daylight.*

Her career was more than likely over, if she didn't end up in prison.

But there were perhaps three things she could think of off the top of her head that were more important than her career. A quick glance east along the river told her that two of those things were safe on a yacht that was being boarded by the police. And, if that photo was the real deal, then the third thing was in Miami for one day only.

So that is where I'm going, resolved Lazuli.

6
PROCTOR JUVENALIS

MYLES MADE A QUICK VIDEO CALL TO UNCLE Foxworth 'Foxy' Fowl from the yacht's lounge while the Metropolitan Police Marine response boat tied off alongside the *Fowl Star*.

Uncle Foxy was the twins' only uncle and, while he was definitely a criminal and possibly a mastermind, he preferred to roll through life playing his piano and stealing a few quid from the rich along the way when funds ran low. Foxy often joked that he was a little like Robin Hood in that he liked to rob from the rich, but where he and the thief of Sherwood parted ways was that Foxy preferred to keep his loot for himself rather than pass it on to the poor.

'So, if Mother calls, all you need to do is say everything is fine,' said Myles to his uncle, who was sporting his usual uniform of silk lounge jacket and fluffed cravat.

'And dear Angeline will believe me?' asked Foxy, tinkling on his piano as he spoke. '*I* certainly wouldn't believe me.'

Myles sighed. They had been through this already, and he could hear boots on the deck above his head. 'Mother will believe you because I have sent digital avatars of Beckett and myself to your phone,' he explained for the second time. 'As far as Mother is concerned, we will be right there in the room with you.'

'That sounds infernally clever,' said Foxy. 'You must teach me how to do that, Myles, my boy.'

'I will,' said Myles. 'But for now you will have to trust me that it will work.'

'Trust costs money, nephew,' said Foxy with a sly wink. 'Ten thousand pounds to be precise.'

Myles would've haggled over the cost of Foxy's collaboration on principle if he'd had time, but he did not. 'Fine, Uncle. Ten thousand it is.'

Foxy must have realised that Myles was under pressure, for he added, 'Ten thousand *per twin*, that is.'

'Ten thousand per twin,' said Myles through gritted teeth, transferring the sterling with a phone app. A *ping!* on Foxy's phone signalled the fee's arrival.

'Capital,' said Foxy. 'We have a deal, and I will see you later. Or rather I won't, but your mother will.'

Myles, annoyed by his uncle hiking up his usual fee, ended the call without a farewell.

Ripped off by my own relative, he fumed.

It was not surprising that a Fowl would make his money through extortion, but usually family members were out of bounds.

There really is no honour among thieves, Myles realised now as he heard footsteps on the wooden stairs.

Myles slid out from his seat in the lounge booth and stood to receive guests. He took a few breaths to calm down after the Foxy blackmail call, and glanced at himself in a wall mirror to ensure that his fresh Gloop tie was falling into the centre of the vee of his flash-cleaned suit jacket.

Looking sharp, Dr Myles, he told himself, then pasted on his *always happy to see the police* face, which he had learned from his father, who had learned it from his mother, and on and on back to the original mastermind, Red Peg Fowl.

Myles's fake happy face was very convincing. He had, out of necessity, spent many hours perfecting it, as he was rarely happy to see anyone. Even members of his own immediate family were unwelcome in the lab if Myles was on a roll invention-wise. Only Beckett and, lately, Specialist Heitz were spared this fake happy face and got to see the real thing, but they also had to put up with the scowls, frowns and incredulous eye-rolls that were Myles Fowl's go-to expressions.

So, face prepared, Myles turned to greet the first person descending the short flight of steps into the lounge and, even though Myles considered himself a professional smile-faker, that smile instantly turned into a frown when he saw who stood in the varnished wooden doorway. It was apparently his arch-enemy, Lord Teddy Bleedham-Drye.

The duke held up his hands and said, 'Now, my dear boy, I know what you're thinking . . .'

'I was thinking you were dead,' said Myles. 'But now I am not so sure.'

Ten minutes later, Myles was feeling a little less hostile towards the visitor, but he was far from smiling, which was not surprising considering the duke's recent attempted murder on his person. This individual claimed not to be the duke, but the resemblance was undeniably uncanny.

The company was seated in booth-style banquette seating, Fowls opposite the Lord Teddy lookalike, who had given his name as Proctor Juvenalis. Except for his head, which had all the Bleedham-Drye hallmarks –

dark mane of hair, glacial blue eyes and a nose so sharp it could administer paper cuts – Proctor Juvenalis presented as a very different creature to his deceased grand-uncle.

'We all went into hiding,' Proctor declared. 'Mother, Father and myself, because Uncle Ted was notorious for bumping off family members. Anything to squeeze the whereabouts of the legendary Lionheart ring out of us and get him one step closer to the crown. Mother didn't care about titles and so took us off to New Zealand. We changed our names and made a life for ourselves. Of course, clever Mama kept a paper trail alive with solicitors, and so as soon as the duke passed away I was notified in my Chelsea flat – I'd snuck back to old England, you see. Since Teddy has no heir, the title passes to me, and I'm embarrassed to admit that I've dreamed of this moment.'

Myles wasn't surprised. 'Don't be embarrassed. You'd be surprised how many people dream of meeting me.'

The man who called himself Proctor Juvenalis laughed delightedly, as though someone had told a joke.

Myles did not laugh, and Beckett helped Proctor out. 'But people *do* dream of meeting Myles all the time, because of his big brain.'

'Of course they do,' said Proctor hurriedly. 'The great genius, Myles Fowl, and his intrepid brother, Beckett. But I also dreamed of being Duke of the Scilly Isles.'

'But mostly meeting me,' Myles pressed.

'Absolutely,' said Proctor graciously. 'That was certainly my number-one dream.'

'Very well,' said Myles, satisfied. 'Continue.'

Proctor Juvenalis took an envelope from his messenger bag and slid it across the table towards Myles.

'This is why I'm here, Myles, if I may call you Myles.'

Myles opened the envelope, removing a sheaf of documents. 'No, you may not. But no need for formalities outside an academic setting, so rather than Professor Fowl you may refer to me as Dr Fowl.'

Proctor was taken aback, even though he'd heard the stories about the precocious twelve-year-old. 'Of course, Dr Fowl. Apologies.'

Myles had a quick read and, while he did, Beckett studied the visitor.

Proctor Juvenalis was a very different kettle of fish from his grand-uncle. For one thing, Teddy would be appalled at the lack of beardage on Proctor's chin. The younger man sported a small arrowhead goatee that pointed towards his navel, and his dark hair was coffee-hipster long and tucked behind his ears. Wardrobe-wise, he favoured a simple linen smock, which could have meant he liked Korean culture, Star Wars films or had just discovered an amazing designer.

But still, Beckett thought, it could be Teddy wearing a magic cloak of morphing jellyfish.

Kra-kark, one of his cormorant mates from home, swore that morphing jellyfish existed and were working with the seals to hide entire shoals of fish. Beckett had his doubts about that claim, as the cormorant's brother swore that Kra-kark liked to tell stories and was just a poor fisherbird.

But Beckett had no doubt that this Proctor person was not Teddy. Not because he trusted his own senses, but because he trusted Whistle Blower's nose.

The toy troll was concealed in the storage area under the bench seating, and if he had smelled Teddy in the room he would have scythed his way out of there and torn the duke limb from limb. After all, Teddy had once hooked up the troll to a venom-draining machine in an attempt to extend his own life. No attack from Whistle Blower meant that this person did not smell like Teddy, and as Whistle Blower had once told

Beckett: 'You can change a lot of things about yourself, but you can't change your scent.'

At this point, the toy troll had passed wind violently to make his point. 'What are we getting here? There are notes of rabbit and asparagus, certainly, but the core is pure warrior troll, no matter what I eat.'

Whistle Blower was right. A person could not change their core scent. No scent, no Teddy.

While Beckett was reminiscing about nuggets of troll wisdom, Myles was speed-reading Proctor's document, blinking more rapidly than he usually might, as this was a memory trick he used to store information in his brain.

After several seconds, he tapped the sheaf on the table, newsreader-style, and passed it back to Proctor. 'I can see why you were anxious to find me,' he said. 'Your window is very tight.'

Proctor swept the document into his bag. 'Extremely. When your yacht was not at its mooring, I was worried you might have returned to Ireland. Luckily, as the future duke, I was able to avail myself of SO14's services.'

'Of course,' said Myles. 'The Royalty Protection Group branch of the Met. I imagine the cruiser alongside is under their command.'

'It is,' said Proctor. 'They have been most accommodating. Apparently, the palace is eager to have a more amenable duke in Childerblaine House. Uncle Ted was forever murdering people so that he might stage a royal coup. I am more interested in attending royal weddings and possibly having my own podcast.'

'I see,' said Myles. 'And would I be right in saying that there is a seaplane en route as we speak?'

Proctor confirmed it. 'You would, Myles . . . er, Dr Fowl. One of my uncle's Skyblades, which is coming here on something called auto-fly. Of course you are not obliged to accompany me to St George, but I would be ever so grateful if you did. I can have you back here by breakfast tomorrow.'

Myles still felt that he was being set up somehow, but the lure of what he had been offered was overpowering.

A treasure trove of knowledge. Over a hundred and fifty years of research.

Teddy had never been the greatest scientist, perhaps on a level with Artemis, but he had nonetheless had some spectacular results, especially in the field of longevity, using unorthodox methods and taking short cuts that no ethical scientist would.

I wonder, Myles thought. *Would an ethical scientist take advantage of unethically sourced research?*

This, he decided, was a question for later. For now, it was imperative that he at least take a look at this research before he decided whether or not to scan it into his own databases.

'Would it be possible to see a sample of the duke's research?' he asked Proctor.

'I'm afraid not,' said the next duke. 'Everything is handwritten. More than five hundred notebooks, I'm told. All meticulously detailed and dated.'

Myles didn't doubt it. Teddy had been nothing if not meticulous, until he'd lost his temper right there at the end.

'I need to confer with my twin,' said Myles, swivelling to face Beckett.

'Here is the situation,' he whispered to Beckett. 'Lord Teddy has willed his entire estate and title to his legal successor, if one can be found, providing his research is turned over to me and only me. Obviously, the duke rightly believed that I was the only one who could appreciate it. If I do not go to the island before nightfall tonight, then his estate goes into probate and, knowing English courts as I do, I feel certain we will all be long dead before it comes out. Now, there is a lot to consider here, Beck. Is this man genuine? Is the legacy real? Would it traumatise us to return to an island where we were very nearly killed? We are impressionable children, after all.'

Beckett had a question, which he whispered back. 'His name sounds made up. I'm not great at Latin, but I think it means *young teacher*. Does it have any other meanings?'

Myles was surprised to find that he was a little hazy on Latin at this precise moment, even though he had been fluent yesterday. He could not have realised that he was suffering a little from the mind-dulling influences of the Tower Bridge Mortuary spectre.

'I'm sure it's made up,' he said irritably. 'To conceal Mr Juvenalis and his family from Teddy.'

'I'll go on one condition,' announced Beckett.

Myles had been expecting this. 'You get to fly the plane?'

'Exactly,' said Beckett. 'And I'm bringing my *wink wink* action figure in my pocket.'

'You're not supposed to say *wink wink*, brother mine. You simply wink.'

'Got it,' said Beckett. 'But I'm still bringing my action figure, which is just an action figure.'

Myles turned back to Proctor and repeated his brother's demand, because he wished to ascertain exactly how much this visitor wanted the family title.

'As long as you can fly the plane?' Proctor asked.

'Exactly,' Myles said. 'That's our condition. We will go as long as Beckett can fly the seaplane. And we do need to be back here by morning, as we are expecting a friend.'

'Our very best friend,' added Beckett.

Proctor Juvenalis seemed a little bemused by the blond twin's demand. 'When you say "fly the plane", is that twin code, or are you being allegorical perhaps?'

Beckett did not like the sound of that. 'I don't do allegoricals about flying planes,' he said severely.

Proctor took a deep, shaky breath. 'Very well, Master Beckett. You may fly the plane.'

'Both ways,' pressed Beckett.

'Both ways,' agreed Proctor.

'And I can steer with my feet?'

Proctor looked to Myles. 'With his feet, for heaven's sake?'

Myles nodded. 'My brother has excellent foot-eye coordination.'

Proctor Juvenalis must have really coveted the title

of duke, because, after turning perhaps two shades paler and wringing his hands for a moment, which people rarely did outside adventure novels, he nodded rapidly, perhaps a dozen times, and said, 'It's agreed then. Master Beckett flies the entire round trip, navigating with his feet.'

'I hope that seaplane has sick bags,' said Beckett.

'Why?' asked Proctor. 'Do you have a weak stomach?'

And then Beckett made an unusually ominous statement for such a cheery fellow. 'Oh no. The sick bags are not for me.'

THERE FOLLOWS NOT ONE BUT TWO SEPARATE aerial journeys for the Regrettables, for, as the twins were boarding the Skyblade, Lazuli was already several hundred miles into her journey across the Atlantic en route to the Sozzled Parrot in Miami. The twins' flight time would be less than thirty minutes, with most of that being used for going up and coming down, and Lazuli's flight time was about to be far less than she had anticipated.

Also, at this stage, it will be revealed to Lazuli exactly what was really happening to the Regrettables. Many of these same revelations will shortly be repeated by the same person to the twins, but, rather than force the reader to cover the same ground twice, we will refer the reader back to this section, and the reader may consider the twins all caught up.

Lazuli realised, as the capsule flashed through the air – invisible to all except cats and badgers for some reason – that she had severed ties in more ways than one. Three ways, to be precise:

1. She had literally severed the capsule's ties with the London Eye without instructions or consultation.
2. She had left the twins to their own devices, which was rarely a good idea, though they did seem to be under police protection. To assuage her guilt over this, Lazuli shot Myles a quick text: *Side mission. Will be back tomorrow. Stay put!* And . . .
3. She had severed ties with the LEP by zooming off on an unauthorised flight to the USA and was very possibly a fugitive by now.

Lazuli considered disabling the capsule's communication system, but there was no point. Foaly would have a dozen different methods of tracking this craft, and it was entirely possible the local agents would be waiting for her when she landed in Miami. Lazuli knew that a colleague of hers, Specialist Rubi Slyce, was working undercover in Orange County, and she wondered whether contacting Rubi for some local intel would be a good or a bad idea.

Bad, she decided. *There's no need to destroy Rubi's career too.*

If Lazuli were being honest with herself, career destruction was probably the least of her problems. That she would be booted out of the LEP was a given, but there was definitely the possibility of prosecution for auto theft, and perhaps treason too.

And suddenly Lazuli felt more tired than she'd ever been in her life. It was probably the combination of trauma, magic and her situation, but nevertheless she would not turn back. She could not let this opportunity pass her by. She would not.

The flight would take three and a half hours, so she could afford an hour's sleep before touchdown. She chose a green jumpsuit from the locker, switched the pilot's chair to recliner mode, and watched the sky flash by through the transparent hull. In one of those *wouldn't you know it* type of situations, it seemed that even though she had been exhausted mere seconds ago, now that she was lying down, her mind was racing.

I will never be able to sleep, she thought, and she was about to abandon the idea when a face flashed into her mind. It was the face in the picture Kimodo had shown her.

Could this person be real?

Was there a chance after all these years?

All the things they would have to talk about. She had so many questions.

Lazuli opened a holo-menu between her and the ceiling and projected the image on the transparent hull with the sky flowing past behind it.

The markings were the same. Down to the number of spikes and whorls. Of course it was possible – unlikely, but possible – that it was a coincidence, but some chance was better than none.

Could that be my mother? she wondered, and she stared at the image until sleep crept over her like a warm blanket.

Lazuli woke up two hours later, coming out of sleep all of a sudden, as though reality had fallen on her from a height. She knew who she was and where she was going and just how deep in the trouble hole she was, but still the face in the picture hovered over her and she had no regrets.

Something had woken her, and Lazuli realised it was a text alert on her suit's communication system. It was from Beckett, telling her about their visitor, Proctor Juvenalis, and how they were going to St George to claim an inheritance. This all sounded a little fishy, but Teddy was definitely dead, so they should be safe for a day.

Seeing as she was already lying down, which made it easier for the sensors, Lazuli instructed the computer to run a full Magical Resonance Imaging scan to find out if there was anything to be learned about the current state of her magic and well-being. The last time Foaly had run an MRI on her, less than a year ago, she had been forced to climb inside a claustrophobic tube, but technology moved quickly when Foaly was involved, and now the MRI was just another function of LEP multisensors.

She was bathed in invisible rays and, barely a minute later, the scanner beeped and began listing its results on the ceiling.

Everything seemed well within parameters, except for her very species classification, which should have said *Pixel*, but instead read *Undetermined*. That might have been a glitch. Her magic levels were also unusual in that they did not even register a one out of ten.

'Immediate Ritual recommended,' said the computer.

Lazuli cranked up the chair. She was not surprised in the least that she was bone dry on the magic front and required an immediate Ritual. Once upon a time, she would have had to find a fresh acorn and bury it by the bend in a river during a full moon to restore her magic. But those days were gone since N°1 had returned from Hybras. The demon warlock had unlocked a lot of the old magical hexes and spells, making life a lot easier for fairies who ran out of magic. Now all a person had to do was snap and shake a moon tube, allowing the frozen nut particles to mix with the river sludge in the vial of moonlight. It was a little like a glowstick but with magical ingredients.

As a late bloomer on the magic front, Lazuli had never used a moon tube before. She selected one now from the capsule dispenser in the armrest, snapped it and shook.

Nothing happened.

Well, that wasn't quite accurate. The tube did what it was supposed to do, but her internal magic was not interested. Her colleagues often described their magical warps as jitters or electric shocks, or even bone-shaking spasms, but Lazuli felt nothing aside from a raised heart rate, which was probably due to nerves.

She tried a couple more tubes but without result.

It's probably me, she thought. I'm *malfunctioning, not the tubes.*

She needed answers as to her exact make-up. There was more to being a hybrid fairy than skin colouring. Magical species had certain trademark powers, and different species blends meant different and sometimes unpredictable abilities. There was an actual recorded case of an elf who could make dormant volcanoes erupt, and another of a psychokinetic cenxie who could make people's elbow skin crawl so they got really itchy, which admittedly was not dangerous but quite uncomfortable for those afflicted.

I hope I didn't get the elbow thing, Lazuli thought now. In fact, at that precise moment, she would have been happy to have no magic at all, since the only thing her brand of fiery power seemed to bring was death or unasked-for healings.

She looked up at the face still displayed on the ceiling and tried to find a resemblance.

Maybe there is, she thought. *Or am I seeing things*

that aren't there? Am I simply trying to manifest my dearest wish?

A thought occurred. She could say something now to the photograph . . . Words she had dreamed of uttering but had never said aloud.

She needed to say these words, but she hesitated, not wanting to jinx the possibility . . . But, now that the idea had her in its thrall, the greeting came out almost before she knew it.

'Hello, Mother.'

Saying the word *Mother* aloud was incredibly emotional for an orphan, and Lazuli's vision blurred with tears, which, she thought, was probably why it seemed as though the picture were moving, which it could not be. Photographs were not animated . . . unless this was a live file. Did human phones have the ability to generate live files?

Even if they did, live files did not speak.

'Hello, Lazuli,' said the woman in the photo – a pixel who looked an awful lot like an older version of Specialist Heitz, right down to the markings on her shoulders and neck.

'I . . .' said Lazuli. 'How . . . ?'

It didn't make any sense. There was no logic to this.

Even Myles Fowl would have been baffled by such a development.

'I imagine you have many questions,' said the woman, smiling down at her from the ceiling screen.

This is not real, Lazuli told herself, although she wished with all her heart that it could be.

'Is it *Lahz*-uli or Laz-*ooli*?' asked the screen pixel. 'You hear different pronunciations.'

'Either,' said Lazuli, relieved to have an easy question to answer. 'Both. It doesn't matter.'

'I'm your mother, dear,' said the pixel. 'I would like to get it right.'

Lazuli felt as though she had been gut-punched. *Why did you leave me?* she wanted to ask this woman who could not be her mother.

'You can't be my mother,' she said, though her trembling voice belied the words. 'It doesn't make sense.'

'You know something?' said the talking picture. 'I don't like the name Lazuli. Would you like to know what your true name is?'

'No, I wouldn't,' said Lazuli. 'If you are my mother, I would like to know the reason you left me.'

Her mother laughed as if that were a silly little question. 'Oh, that? I can answer that one. You were loud, you see. I had a lot going on in the home office and you were such a lively baby. So I dropped you off in Haven. You seem much more relaxed now, and I hear you have developed certain skills, so perhaps you could be of use to me in the rent-a-goblin business.'

'You're the go-between. You kill humans for gold.'

Photo-Mum was not repentant. 'Yes, but it is such a lot of gold, dear. And you can share it.'

'I would rather die,' said Lazuli with feeling.

Her mother sighed. 'Very well. Death it is, Laz-*ooli*. Anyway, I have a lot going on today, so I must be off. Enjoy the last minute of your life.'

Lazuli had imagined this reunion so many times, and never had her mother's motivations for her abandonment included *I was too busy and you were too loud*.

'Wait!' she said. 'Mother!'

'*Mother*,' echoed Photo-Mum. 'I don't think I deserve that title, do you? In fact, I'm a fake mother. A deepfake.'

And this, for some reason, made Fake-Mum laugh. She laughed until her blond hair shook and the yellow markings on her blue skin rippled like elegant fish, and strangely everything she said from that moment on was in a British upper-crust accent.

'Deepfake. That's rather funny. You should see your

face – it's a picture. This little stunt was expensive and completely unnecessary but worth every penny, by Jove, just to see that expression.'

And as the face laughed it changed, morphing a little more with every chortle until the visage on the screen was no longer a pixel but a human, and no longer female but male. And no longer a stranger but Sir Teddy Bleedham-Drye. Much younger than the last time Lazuli had seen him, but unmistakably him.

'The software has come so far,' said Teddy, 'you really can't tell the difference. I can be anyone I want to be on a screen. Even the translation is instant, more or less, and that includes mouth manipulation, in case you were inclined to lip-read.'

'Lord Teddy?' asked Lazuli, though she already knew in her gut that this was the duke.

Not that I can trust my gut, she thought. *My gut told me that Kimodo's picture was my mother.*

She cursed herself for being a fool. Kimodo had set her up by posing as a CI, and she'd fallen for it because she wanted to.

I can be disappointed later, when I'm still alive.

'Yes, it is I,' confirmed Teddy. 'My brain, at least. This body was grown in a sac – can you believe that? Cloning is the future, Specialist. I am a living example of what humans and fairies can achieve together. My dear friend Myishi and the recently deceased dwarf Gveld Horteknut both contributed to my resurrection, and, between us, I have taken the technology so much further on St George. For example, should this body be damaged, all I need to do is double-click the first knuckle of my middle finger and the cranium pops open, allowing my brain to be easily transferred into a new clone.'

Keep talking, thought Lazuli. Myles always says that criminal masterminds often snatch defeat from the jaws of victory by gloating to their nemeses.

Teddy did keep talking, and what he said chilled Lazuli to her very marrow. (At this point, it is worth reminding the reader that the following passages contain vital exposition and so it might be a good idea to highlight them for easy reference.)

'You're probably wondering why I'm letting you in on all my secrets in direct violation of criminal-mastermind rule number one: no monologuing before killing your nemesis,' said Teddy. 'Two reasons. One, no offence, Specialist, but you are hardly my nemesis – you are a supporting character at best. And two, while I've been rabbiting on, the capsule's induction system has drained every last drop of power from your weapon and suit.'

Lazuli turned a slightly lighter shade of blue, which was her version of going pale. She had been counting on whatever systems were not already down to get her out of this.

'Kimodo and her father have been invaluable,' continued Lord Teddy, eager to share just how brilliant he'd been. 'Gveld, may she rest in peace, put us in touch with the goblin squad at the Acorn Club. And, for a reasonable fee, they hacked the London Eye capsule and staked out the mortuary, in case Myles was suspicious of my death. Kimodo set you racing to Miami looking for your mother. A goblin was stationed at every local LEP safe site, by the way. That cost me a pretty penny, but I knew Myles would survive the Southbank – and the mortuary, for that matter. And I know all about you, too, Lazuli. Jeffluent has contacts in the LEP, so I read your file and found your weak spot. Mummy issues. How predictably pathetic.'

Lazuli's anger flared. 'And all this for revenge? *That's* not pathetic?'

Teddy actually considered this. 'No, Specialist,' he

said. 'A failed attempt at revenge may indeed be classified as pathetic, but a successful campaign is glorious.'

Lazuli realised that the duke was talking as though she were already dead. 'You haven't won yet, Teddy,' she said belligerently.

'Oho!' said the duke. 'Still a spark of defiance. Let me extinguish that for you. In a couple of minutes, you will be dead and, when you are, I will reveal my true plan to the twins. Not only that, I will show them the video of your death so that before he dies Beckett will be desolate for all of five minutes. Myles I will not kill, but he'll wish that I had. I plan to keep him around – his brain, at least – so he may serve me for all eternity. Revengers will write books about this campaign. It will become the new gold standard. It ticks every box. Petty, convoluted and satisfying.'

Lazuli felt her spark of belligerence dim. It did indeed appear hopeless, but she tried to rattle the duke with one final gibe. 'I know all about you too, Teddy. Didn't you want to be king? Shouldn't you be searching for the Lionheart ring instead of murdering children?'

A shadow crossed Teddy's face. 'The Lionheart ring? Its whereabouts were taken to the grave by a silly child, can you believe it? She was so small they had to stick a blob of silver to the band just so it would stay on her finger when she wanted to wear it. But she didn't have it on when she died. The things I could have done with that ring. King George taught her a little rhyme: *Twist the ring, become the king.*'

Teddy realised that he was becoming sidetracked and quickly forced a smile. 'No, Specialist. You shall not ruin this moment for me. It is true that one cannot have everything, but at least I shall have more than you do. For you, the outlook is bleak. No family, no friends . . . no life.'

This was ominous, to say the least, and even more so was the extended supervillain laugh that Teddy delivered before finishing his call.

'You'll have no life too!' Lazuli blurted when Teddy had already hung up, which was just as well, really, because, as banter went, blurting *You'll have no life too* was not only grammatically dodgy but also a little pitiful.

I wonder how he intends to kill me? thought Lazuli. Then the engines failed and the capsule began its thirty-seven-thousand-foot descent to earth, which answered that question.

8
RECLAIMING THE FRONTAL LOBE

MYLES FOWL STOOD AT THE WINDOW OF THE Childerblaine House guest room and gazed out over St George. It felt strange to be on the island again when on a previous visit the duke had been quite uncivil, to the point of attempted murder. It felt strange and a little foolhardy now that he was actually here.

The duke is dead, Myles told himself to quiet his nerves. *Otherwise he would never let me near his research. It would be madness on his part, given how smart I am.*

There was also the DNA evidence of Teddy's demise. Whatever the curious circumstances in the Southbank Centre and afterwards in the Tower Bridge Mortuary actually meant, they did not change the fact that DNA did not lie. The duke was dead.

I would have preferred to have waited for Specialist Heitz as she requested, thought Myles, but this offer from beyond the grave was time-sensitive and so he would have to trust that Lazuli would find them and they could investigate the goblin problem together.

Myles wondered briefly if Specialist Heitz had gone in search of her mother. After all, that quest was the only thing that consumed the pixel as much as her Fowl-ambassador posting. If so, he wished her luck, and he geo-pinned their position for her to find on her return.

The flight over from the mainland had been as uneventful as any flight manned by Beckett would ever be, Myles suspected. His brother had insisted on flying through each concentric ring of the ethereal fog that shrouded St George all year round. This blind flying had terrified Proctor Juvenalis to such an extent that he did indeed reach for a sick bag, though, mercifully, he did not have to use it for anything other than calming his hyperventilation.

Once on the island, Beckett had enjoyed a brief chat with a seagull, then there had been a perfectly acceptable light lunch delivered from the mainland, followed by some freshening-up time in one of the Childerblaine House guest rooms. This chamber must have been occupied by a young lady a long time ago, as the wardrobe was stuffed with Georgian gowns, and there was even a wig propped on a mannequin's head in the corner.

Myles turned from the window. He should follow Beckett upstairs for the official handing-over ceremony before his brother broke something valuable in the laboratory. He fervently hoped that Whistle Blower would stay hidden in his crisp packet in Beckett's cargo shorts pocket as promised, only to be unsealed in case of emergency.

What a shock that would be for Proctor, should he pop out of a hidden doorway somewhere and force us to unleash our secret weapon.

Myles noticed sheets of steam emanating from underneath the bathroom door and was pleased. He'd hung his jacket from the door hook and turned the shower to maximum heat to steam out the creases. It was an old traveller's trick that worked in a pinch when a fellow didn't have an iron handy, and Myles did like to look his most dapper, especially for a legal ceremony. The only disadvantage to this trick was that the steam would also cloud the mirror, so he would have to trust to science that his jacket was crease-free.

Everyone should trust in science all the time, he

thought, stepping on a handy squat toilet so he might take down his jacket. It was immediately clear that one wrinkle stubbornly remained. Actually, it was less a wrinkle than a sandwich-sized lump.

Perhaps the lining has ripped, thought Myles.

Even though the garment was perfectly clean, thanks to its revolutionary self-cleaning fibres, it had been through two attacks in the past thirty-six hours, and so perhaps some wear and tear was to be expected. But a quick pat test revealed that there was, in fact, something in the pocket, which bothered Myles because he was very particular about where he stored his belongings, and he rarely put anything in the left pocket of his jacket. That pocket was specially lined and sealed so it could function as an envelope for samples. Now he would have to sterilise it, because no doubt Beckett had run out of room in his cargo shorts pockets and stuffed some half-eaten meal in there. In fairness, Beckett was storing the crisp packet in one oversized pocket, and Myles himself had asked him to keep the SPOOK glasses in the other pocket so they wouldn't get mixed up with his regular spectacles. Even so, Myles was dramatically annoyed.

'Oh, for heaven's sake, this is an absolute and

unmitigated disaster,' said Myles, rather overstating the situation. He reached into the pocket and pulled out a vacuum-packed slice of something pale that most people might assume was a cauliflower steak. But, as previously stated, Myles Fowl was not most people. He was not even some people.

'A section of brain,' Myles realised.

And not just any brain. It was the section of Lord Teddy's brain he'd been examining when the ghost had shown up in the mortuary. In his delirium, Myles must have stuffed it into his jacket pocket. His annoyance vanished as he realised how valuable this brain section could be.

I will dissect Teddy's brain in his own laboratory.

This was a macabre thought, but also it was somehow fitting that the duke's remains should end up at Childerblaine.

Myles's subconscious threw up a sentence that he himself had spoken during his Southbank lecture:

Every killer signs his own kills, and every artist signs his work.

'Hmmm,' said Myles thoughtfully. He was a firm believer in the subconscious always being a few steps ahead of the conscious brain.

Every artist signs his own work.

What was his own mind trying to tell him about this slice of Lord Teddy's brain?

It *was* Teddy's brain, was it not? NANNI had run a DNA test on it.

On the *body*.

Every artist signs his own work.

Myles removed his normal glasses, which were normal for him, but not *normal* normal, if there were such a thing.

One arm detached at the hinge, and inside the graphite sleeve was a titanium scalpel. Myles replaced the spectacles on his face and magnified his view. He might not have NANNI available to him at the moment, but he was not a complete caveman – the spectacles still had some functions.

I cannot believe I am going to do this here, he thought. *In an en suite bathroom when there is a laboratory not two flights of stairs away.*

He fervently hoped that Artemis would never hear of this.

I am simply taking a precaution. Making doubly certain.

Myles placed the packet in the marble sink and,

having sliced through the packaging, carefully peeled the glistening folds aside. Myles pressed the brain gently to test the spring-back or squish effect and was satisfied by the seepage that the brain had not begun to deteriorate and might yet be useful.

If I don't cut it to ribbons first looking for whatever it is I'm looking for.

But Myles knew what he was looking for. Unfortunately, if it was not there upon initial examination, he would have to destroy the brain to make sure. Even slivers could be useful, though, so not all would be lost.

But Myles did not have to destroy the section. In fact, he found what he'd suspected he might on the very first cut. He toppled the sliver on its side and magnified the cross section, and there, concealed in the meat, was a darker patch in the shape of a *W*.

Every artist signs his own work.

You couldn't help yourself, could you, Ishi? Myles thought. He nudged the sliver one hundred and eighty degrees till the *W* became an *M*. And not just any *M*. The trademark *M* of the Myishi Corporation.

'This brain was grown in a laboratory!' Myles declared to the tiled walls.

Which meant that, while Lord Teddy's body might have died, his brain certainly hadn't. It had found a new vessel, inside the no-doubt cloned body of Proctor Juvenalis. Myles had been so blinded by Proctor's flattery that he hadn't seen it.

Myles felt the last vestiges of mist lift as the mortuary spirit's dulling influence finally cleared and his frontal lobe became purely his own once more – something even Lazuli's magic had not been able to heal, as it was not an illness, exactly.

Then he felt his blood run cold as his Latin studies came back to him.

Proctor Juvenalis could mean many things. A young teacher or poet. Or a society of students. But, in this instance, Myles felt the most appropriate meaning was the one he was shouting to the ceiling:

'Proctor Juvenalis, the punisher of immature birds. Otherwise known as young Fowl!'

It was all so impressively dastardly, and Myles felt certain that, sometime in the future, he would look back on this and feel a grudging admiration for the layers of unnecessary complication the duke's plan contained. But he fervently hoped as he raced to the door – inasmuch as Myles Fowl could race anywhere –

that he and Beckett would not do their looking back from the afterlife.

CAPSULE THIRTEEN

Lazuli Heitz was up to her neck in physical turmoil, and from the neck up she was steeped in emotional turmoil, so, all in all, it was a full-body-turmoil experience.

The physical aspect of the turmoil had been initiated by the transparent capsule's engines cutting out, which had sent the craft plummeting earthward, shaking Lazuli like a bead in a rattle. The emotional distress had two main components: first, her mother/not-mother was trying to kill her and, second, the instrument of her death was whirling up to meet her through a transparent floor – or maybe a transparent ceiling: it was hard to tell with all the whirling.

Lazuli found herself without any weapons in her arsenal, and this included her wits, which were usually her finest asset. Her eyes were blurred with tears and her mind was fuzzy with the anguish caused by abandonment, which had been a constant lodger in the back of her head but was now pushing through to the front.

I'll never know my parents, she thought now.

And then the old Lazuli asserted herself. *No. I refuse to accept that. I've been through worse and come out the other end.*

Amazingly, this was actually true. In the past two years, shepherding Myles and Beckett through two major incidents, she'd recently calculated that she'd survived eight near-death experiences. And that number was probably a little on the low side.

The capsule's dive was stabilised by the air resistance and plummeted nose down. Lazuli found herself pinned to the aft section, her rear end jammed into the access hatch. She knew that shortly she would be little more than paste on the ocean's surface. At this speed, and from this height, the capsule would barely penetrate the surface.

I have to get out, she realised.

There was only one way out and, coincidentally, that exit, like all aircraft exits, had a backup manual lever.

Lazuli found the vulcanised handle and tugged, popping the hatch and allowing the equalisation rush to tug her out into open sky.

Not that she had much choice in the matter.

It was a measure of Myles Fowl's panic that he ran up fourteen uneven rickety wooden steps and twelve metal ones without once falling over. When Myles had time to consider this later, he realised that he had forgotten all about his climacophobia, because he'd been so worried about what Teddy might do to Beckett. And in fact Myles eventually presented a paper to the *New Scientist* entitled 'The Terror Treatment', which proposed frightening patients half to death before immediately confronting them with their phobias. One suggested therapy was to throw arachnophobes from a high tower into a pool of spiders. The paper was never published, but Myles would go on to host several pop-up clinics, until his secretary (Beckett) mixed up *arachnophobia* with *acrophobia* and they accidentally threw someone who was terrified of heights from the top of a tower. Fowl, Inc. settled the inevitable lawsuit out of court.

In Myles's own mind, he hurtled through the laboratory door to confront Proctor Juvenalis, while in actuality his entrance resembled a prolonged stumble punctuated by a breathless gasp for air. While his head was down between his knees, Myles heard these words:

'I'm so glad you're here, brother. You are not going to believe this!'

Oh, I will, Myles thought. *I will believe it.*

But, when Myles raised his gaze, he found that he could not in fact believe what he was seeing, so he actually lowered his head and tried again. What he saw the second time round was the same as the first.

The laboratory was more or less as Myles remembered it – an open-plan affair that resembled a classroom of sorts, with half a dozen steel islands stretching the width of the space. Each surface hosted half a dozen stations, all occupied by lab equipment. The very latest in gleaming Myishi diagnostic tools stood side by side with Lord Teddy's beloved Victorian and Georgian apparatuses. Myles saw robot-assistant claws clamped to a bench beside a vintage craniometer complete with steel spikes and grinning skull. And a 3-D printer sharing a station with a magneto 'nervous disease' shock box.

On any other day, Myles might have allowed himself the luxury of examining each piece, perhaps lingering over the gleaming steel curves of a Victorian trepanning drill, robustly constructed to bore through the toughest cranium, but today his attention was fully occupied by a piece of equipment that had not been in the laboratory on his last visit. It was a titanium X-frame that was either a torture device or a surgical mount, with a gas canister on each arm and a fishbowl-style helmet of orange gel mounted directly above it, presumably ready to be lowered on to the patient's – or victim's – head.

It was undoubtedly an ominous construction, made even more so by the fact that Beckett was strapped into the device, grinning like a loon.

'Can you believe it, Myles?' he asked, jittering with excitement. 'Proctor let me try out the X-frame. How cool is that?'

Proctor stood beside Beckett. It was obvious from his body language that the diffident young man was gone. No more downcast eyes and hunched shoulders – in their place was an imperiously straight back and a condescending sneer towards the world in general.

'That is, as you say, most cool,' said Myles, walking slowly towards the pair. 'Why don't you climb down from there, Beck?'

Proctor smiled thinly. 'Climb down? Beckett hasn't even tried on the gel helmet yet. What kind of interplanetary adventurer passes up an opportunity to try on a gel helmet?'

'Yes, Myles!' said Beckett. 'I have to try on the helmet.'

'No, Beckett Counterclockwise Fowl,' Myles insisted. 'What you have to do is climb down from there, right now!'

Beckett did not actually have an official middle name. He'd bestowed the middle name Counterclockwise upon himself as he correctly believed that it summed up his personality. Myles rarely used Beckett's made-up name – only when he wanted his twin's complete attention, which he most certainly did now.

'Beckett, listen to me. Get down from there right now! I command you!'

Proctor winked at Beckett. '"I command you", eh, Beckett? You'd better do as you're told.'

Beckett sighed.

Proctor was right, and Myles, too, he supposed. Also, his twin scar was tingling, which meant his brother was agitated. And, as much fun as Beckett was having, he had no wish to upset Myles.

'Okay. Why is it that every single time I get strapped to a dangerous piece of equipment you tell me to get down?'

Myles came closer, speaking calmly in case there was the tiniest chance that Lord Teddy didn't know he had been found out. 'Hardly every time, Beck. Remember when you went wing-walking on that Tiger Moth? I was the one who applauded. It was Mum who got so upset.'

Beckett was suddenly very focused. Myles had used the endearment *Mum*, which was also an abbreviation. Myles loathed both endearments and abbreviations. Indeed, he had once felt physically ill when a rocket scientist from New Zealand had included a joke in a correspondence and then ended with *Lol, Mylesy. Your bud, Doc JB*. There was so much wrong with that sign-off that Myles had sent the man a three-page letter and then never spoken to him again.

So Beckett knew there was something wrong here. Myles had seemed a little out of sorts since the mortuary, but this was more than simply *out of sorts*. His brother was out of breath, too, which meant he must have run up the stairs.

Running up stairs and endearments!

For Myles, this was the equivalent of all-out panic.

I need to get down from here, thought Beckett, but he could not, strapped in tight as he was. Even someone with Beckett's gifts could not wriggle his way out of simple leather straps he had volunteered to be buckled into.

'Let me down, Proctor,' he said. 'I've had enough.'

Proctor smiled but made no move to release Beckett. 'I could, I suppose. I was planning to, so I might draw this out a little longer, but it seems to me that Myles has caught on to my game.'

'What game? Are we playing a game?'

'It's not the fun kind of game, brother mine,' said Myles. 'It's one of Lord Teddy's cruel hunting games.'

Beckett was confused. 'You said Teddy was definitely one hundred per cent dead. Were you wrong, Myles?'

Myles winced. '*Wrong* seems a little harsh. I was temporarily mistaken.'

'So Teddy is alive?'

'It would appear so,' Myles admitted.

Proctor grinned broadly. 'Do you know what, boys? I am delighted by this turn of events. One schemes for months, but there is always the danger that the Fowl Twins will find a way to scuttle a fellow's plans. As it turns out, this is as good a time as any to reveal the master plan.'

'I would like that,' said Myles. He actually would have preferred to explain the criminal mastermind's plan to the criminal mastermind, as was his habit, but he reckoned that as long as Proctor was talking he himself could be counter-planning.

Proctor sat on a lab stool and pulled a ridiculously oversized pipe from the depths of his linen smock. He lit the pipe with the blue flame from a handy Bunsen burner and took several puffs before continuing.

'I began to scheme in my recovery suite, while my brain, having been removed from the old body, rested in a tub of restorative gel, very much like the gel you see in the helmet above Beckett's head. When I was eventually plopped into my new cranium, I was prompted by a question from old Ishi Myishi. "What would you like me to do with this body?" he asked. A simple enough question, but it got me thinking that it would be a pity to waste the corpse. I asked myself, Teddy, old bean, wouldn't it be marvellous if an old cadaver could do a chap one final service?'

Myles couldn't help supplying a detail or two. 'So Myishi put your brain into a cloned body. You bribed the London coroner to ignore the fact that the skull of your old body had been opened. Then you strapped your former body into a remote-controlled Skyblade, impersonated yourself on the smart screen, and *voilà*, everyone believes Lord Teddy is dead.'

Proctor puffed furiously. Myles was ruining his reveal, and he didn't like it.

'I will thank you to keep your deductions to yourself, Fowl. This is my story and I am prepared to suspend the rules of criminal-mastermind behaviour to tell it.'

'I do apologise, Your Grace,' said Myles smoothly. 'The story is, of course, yours to tell. Please proceed.'

And so Proctor-who-was-actually-Teddy did proceed to fill in the twins, as he had recently filled in Lazuli, revealing much of the same information in the same supercilious delivery style. Since we already know this information, let us skip ahead to the climax, where Teddy shows Myles and Beckett the video of Capsule Thirteen's plummet into the Atlantic Ocean on his phone.

'And here we see your dear friend Specialist Heitz sucked out of the capsule at twenty-five thousand feet. The poor dear was completely drained of power and magic, so I feel confident in saying that she is fish food by now.'

Teddy, as we shall refer to him from now on, had told his story well, with plenty of variation in tone and a gradual build-up to the climax, and he was right to be pleased with himself.

A little too pleased, thought Myles. *There is perhaps something Teddy has forgotten about from our very first meeting. I would not count Lazuli out just yet.*

But for appearance's sake he shouted, 'That was cruel and unnecessary, Lord Teddy! Specialist Heitz was simply doing her job.'

Beckett did not add in one of his typically colourful comments because the blond twin was crying.

'Come now, brother mine,' said Myles. 'We must bear up for the time being.'

'"The time being" being perhaps all the time you have left, Beckett,' quipped Teddy merrily. 'Myles, on the other hand, has all the time in the world.'

Myles scowled. It seemed as though Teddy intended to reveal his plan one detail at a time. And even though Myles should've been glad of this, because it would afford him more time to think, he could not help but be irritated by the duke's grandstanding.

'Really, Your Grace?' he snapped. 'You're reduced to teasing children now? Where is your character?'

'Myles, as my murdered relatives might attest, my character comes and goes. There are very few rules I will not bend, unless I have given my word, which a fellow does try not to break.'

'Of course, the famous Bleedham-Drye word.'

At this point, Beckett growled a little and followed this with a sniffle. Teddy misinterpreted these sounds, as most people probably would.

'It seems your brother has regressed, Myles,' he said.

Myles did not enlighten the duke. 'Who can blame him? You do have my twin hooked up to a macabre operating table.'

'That X-frame may be macabre in your eyes,' said the duke, 'but it saved my life, and the little fellow begged to, as he said, "have a go on it". I simply obliged him.'

Beckett growled some more and added a whistle at the end.

'Oh, dear,' said Teddy. 'I fear the news of Specialist Heitz's demise has rattled your brother, Myles, old fellow.'

'Release him, Your Grace,' demanded Myles. 'You have me.'

The duke tugged his linen smock over his head and tossed it aside. Underneath he wore one of his customary pressed white shirts and a tweed jacket, and holstered at his hip was a cowboy-style Colt .45. On the other hip sat a plastic electric pistol.

'That's better. I'm actually glad you caught on to my ruse. Proctor was becoming intolerable, even to me, and I invented him. How did I slip up, by the way? I truly believed that you were blinded by my flattery and your own ambition.'

Myles tried some flattery of his own. 'You didn't slip up, Your Grace. Myishi left a tag on the fake brain. A nice big *M*. It took me a while to find it.'

Teddy chuckled. 'Ishi, you old rascal. I might have known. We shall laugh about that over a glass of Scotch.'

Myles couldn't help adding, 'And also you were lucky. I had an encounter in the mortuary that clouded my mind. Otherwise, I never would have fallen for any of this.'

The duke was not in the least bothered by Myles's veiled insult about his plan. 'All's well that ends well, at least. I have a Fowl on a frame.'

'*I* am the prize here,' insisted Myles. 'Surely that was your endgame?'

'It was,' admitted the duke. 'But there is one more step required to make it perfect.'

Myles could guess what that was. 'I must surrender myself?'

'Precisely,' said Teddy, his eyes glittering with malice, which is not an easy look to achieve. 'You must walk up here and voluntarily climb into the other side of this double-sided frame.' The duke swivelled the X-frame to reveal a second set of straps on the reverse side. 'This is where my clone body was strapped so the brain wouldn't have far to go. I want you to experience exactly what I did. To feel what it's like to imagine that the world is possibly about to lose a great man.'

Myles shuddered. He could imagine that. Indeed, there was no need to imagine it, as he was feeling it right now.

'And, if I do that, you will release Beckett?'

'I will release him *from the frame*,' said Teddy, qualifying the offer. 'That is all I am prepared to grant you, my dear Fowl. He will have a few moments to orchestrate some form of escape. Will that be enough, do you think?'

It could be enough, Myles knew. Beckett had squeaked out of tighter spots. And he had an ace in the hole, or, more accurately, a troll in the pocket. It was a chance, at least, which was more than he had now.

'I suppose I have no choice but to accept your meagre offer.'

Teddy disagreed. 'You do have a choice. You can watch while I slice off your twin's head and preserve it in the helmet, or you can take his place. Only one head is getting preserved, and I would really rather it be yours.'

Beckett seemed to come round. 'Did he say Lazuli was dead?'

Myles could not bear the quiver in his brother's voice. 'It is not certain, Beck. Nothing is certain.'

'I can't get down,' said Beckett. 'These straps are too tight.'

'You'll be down in a twinkle, Beck,' said Myles. 'I'm coming to release you.'

'Twinkles are not accurate units of measurement,' said Beckett. 'You taught me that.'

'They will do for today,' said Myles.

As he walked towards what would effectively become his guillotine, Myles remembered a quote from *A Tale of Two Cities* – *It is a far, far better thing that I do, than I have ever done* – and he tried to summon the same strength of purpose as Dickens's hero, but he could not.

I will, of course, take Beckett's place, but I don't have to feel good about it.

Also, there was the fact that if one Fowl could be loose to cause chaos then that Fowl should be Beckett. All Myles could do in situations like this was trip over his own feet and possibly give himself a concussion. Beckett could rip through this room like a human cyclone.

Lord Teddy had apparently grown tired of Myles's dilly-dallying because he sideswiped Myles's backside with his boot.

'Up you go, Fowl,' he said. 'Time's a-wastin', as our American cousins might say.'

The X-frame was mounted on a central pole that was itself slotted into a metal stand block. The helmet above was dotted with dozens of adhesive monitors that broadcast via Bluetooth to banks of waiting computers in a stack by the wall. Myles knew that if his head went into that orange gel, it would never come back out, and he was reasonably certain that this operation had never been successfully performed, as it would be a tough sell to any ethics committee.

I am sure the duke is not overly concerned with ethics, thought Myles now as he climbed on to the low iron step and backed into the frame.

'Arms up, there's a good chap,' said the duke, leaning in to tighten the straps. 'I had a welder chappie adjust the beams for you tykes. I'd say he did a smashing job, wouldn't you?'

Myles had to agree that the duke's workman had made a neat job of it, as the straps were situated perfectly for the twins' wrists and ankles. He was slightly more worried about the gleaming circle of wire hooked up to a small dynamo motor over his head, between him and the gel helmet seal.

'Oh, that,' said the duke, noticing the direction Myles's peepers were pointed. 'That wire is your best friend because it's the difference between a painless death and an extremely messy botched experiment should it not reach the correct temperature. Which would be hilarious but a waste of an adequate brain.'

'*Adequate!*' said Myles, irate. 'That really is the last straw, Lord Teddy. Now, release Beckett, if you please. That was our agreement.'

'I shall release him as per the agreement,' said Lord Teddy. 'But first I must admit our audience.'

'Audience?' asked Myles.

Lord Teddy tugged an oversized phone from the pocket of his tweeds and tapped in a few commands, no doubt summoning said audience. 'Of course. This is a historic moment, Myles. It will be the first time a human will suffer decapitation and survive intellectually – to some degree, at least. I can't say how smart you'll be in that helmet, but imagine my satisfaction at having you floating around me all day, appreciating my work and wishing to high heaven that our paths had never crossed.'

Myles had to admit, 'That is indeed the ultimate pay-off for a revenge scheme. I couldn't have planned anything sweeter myself, although, if we do manage to get out of this, I may put my mind to it. Especially if dear Lazuli has been injured in any way.'

Lord Teddy tightened the final strap. 'If I were you, I'd worry about myself.'

Myles could not see the entrance to the laboratory, as he was faced towards the rear wall, but he did hear the door scrape open and several sets of feet march down the aisles between the workstations.

'I must be dreaming,' said Beckett. 'I hope I'm dreaming.'

'Ah,' said Teddy, beaming. 'My audience. Aren't they a handsome bunch of fellows?'

And Myles knew then what Teddy had done, even before the duke spun the frame round.

'Look,' he said. 'What do you think of them?'

The room was jam-packed with identical Teddy clones, and Myles realised instantly that, even with Beckett and Whistle Blower in absolutely top form, there was no chance they would prevail in a fight.

Things always look darkest before the dawn, he thought. But it was not dark, and dawn seemed a long way off.

9
IMPENETRABLE SHADOWS

LAZULI WAS FALLING FAST, AND SHE KNEW THAT stabilising herself was imperative because, if she deployed her equipment while corkscrewing, her only lifeline would be plucked from its frame by the wind like the wings of a tortured fly.

Of course, she did not make these observations rationally, as the wind spinning her end to end in a gyroscopic whirl made it hard to think straight. Instinct and training took over and, somewhere deep inside the chaos of her mind, Lazuli screamed at herself: *Stabilise, Specialist!*

Lazuli had been trained in how to fall properly, and the desired air-shape was known as the *banana*, which meant pulling the legs and chin up while forcing the torso down, thus forming a rigid frame that could ride the airflow. Further tumbling was prevented by extending both arms like paddles to guide the sky-diver's fall to earth. Lazuli followed these steps now and soon had her descent under some sort of control. She was still falling, of course, but at least the world now made sense visually. Below her, she could see the vastness of a twinkling blue ocean dotted with human vessels, and out of the corner of her eye she could make out the hatch from which she had been pulled, surrounded by the failing camouflage of the plummeting capsule.

Lazuli waited five more seconds and then whipped her body as vertical as possible, praying that this new suit was old enough to feature a particular backup system that the newer model didn't have.

'Activate!' she screamed at her suit, also remembering to press the button in the gloves. 'Activate!'

And, once the suit's mechanical spirit level, altimeter and anemometer assessed Lazuli's altitude and descent rate, and found them compatible with deployment, it did indeed activate. Gossamer-thin wings built into Lazuli's suit slid out and connected to a dynamo that she could power through her own efforts.

Thank goodness for old equipment, she thought.

I don't know if any of you have ever tried pedalling through a free fall, but this is what Lazuli did now. She felt her jumpsuit legs stiffen as the epicyclic gear-and-cog system slotted into place and the soles of her boots effectively became pedals. The efficient gears soon built up enough power to set the wings flapping and slowed her descent.

Everything went reasonably well, even though the air was thin at this altitude and she began panting a lot faster than usual this early into a cardio exercise. Nevertheless, Lazuli persevered and she was even able to take stock of what exactly was beneath her and what her options might be. As a result, when the abandoned capsule impacted on the ocean surface, sending up a plume of water and debris that rose to a height of around a hundred metres, it was nowhere near enough to touch Lazuli. It did cause her to miss a stroke in her pedalling and drop a lurching ten metres, but she soon had the rig under control again. The gigantic splashdown attracted the attention of a passing cargo ship, which ponderously altered its course to come closer for a look.

Lazuli inspected the ship from above and noticed that there were rectangles of impenetrable shadow between the towers of metal containers.

Perfect spots for an LEP officer to hitch a ride without attracting any attention.

The ship was going the wrong way, but her only option was to tread water, or sky, until something came along going in the other direction.

And that something would be too slow.

Lazuli switched into a lower gear and set the clockwork wings' flap to descend.

THE ISLAND OF ST GEORGE, SCILLY ISLES

The Fowl Twins found themselves outnumbered by one person, as it were. To explain, there were a few dozen versions of Lord Teddy at various stages of development, from early twenties to late fifties, positioned strategically in the laboratory, all pointing electric rifles at the Fowl Twins – which seemed a little like overkill, considering the fact that both Irish boys were strapped into operating frames and completely helpless for the moment. The real Lord Teddy, who was the only one with a meticulously shaped Vandyke-style goatee, was running through diagnostics for the upcoming decapitation operation, pinging each one of the helmet sensors to make sure there was solid contact.

'It would be a terrible shame, scientifically speaking, if you woke up with all systems firing except your sense of taste, for example,' said Teddy as he triple-checked the Bluetooth. 'I'd consider it a failure. And it would be especially galling if it was because of something perfectly avoidable, like a low battery charge. Oh, my word, how embarrassed would I be?'

Myles's response was a barely audible grunt, which was unusually rude for him, but, in the boy's defence, he was distracted by the cheese wire's buzzing as a heating charge ran through its coils.

Beckett was also grunting, but in a more complex fashion, almost as if he were communicating. Or trying to. At the moment, it seemed to be a bit of a one-way street.

'Release my brother,' said Myles. 'Give him his chance. You owe me that much.'

'I owe you precisely nothing,' said the duke, testing Myles's straps with more violent tugging than necessary. 'However, I did give my word to free your wild-animal brother to a degree. So I will do that. My word is one of the few things sacred to me.'

Myles hid a smirk.

Wild animal.

Teddy had no idea what he was about to release. When Whistle Blower popped out of Beck's pocket, he would slice through those clones faster than the Osaka 2 Petawatt laser would slice through the atmosphere.

Lord Teddy spun the X-frame so that Beckett faced him. The boy was unusually but understandably glum, and tears slicked his cheeks and dripped from his chin.

'Don't be sad, little Fowl,' said Teddy. 'You're possibly going to survive. Now, here's the game. My lovely clones are programmed to fire at you upon my command. They won't disobey because they have no brains of their own, just computer chips. And their rifles, which I have rather cleverly named Clonoscopy rifles, fire electric shocks that aren't strong enough to kill, just incapacitate.'

Teddy squatted down level with Beckett's face. 'Although, between us two, I imagine four or five direct hits would stop a heart as small as yours,' he said as though sharing a playground secret. 'So, when I undo these straps, I want you to climb on to that shiny table.

I will close my eyes for ten seconds, and you see what you can do. Obviously, my beautiful clones will fire upon you if you make a move towards me or your brother, but aside from that your seconds are your own. Nod if you understand.'

Beckett nodded and Myles called to him.

'Make a run for it, Beck. There's nothing to be done here. Get help and come back for me.'

Even as he said the words, Myles knew it was never going to happen. His twin would no more leave him than he himself would leave Beckett if the roles were reversed.

The duke undid the straps one by one, talking as he did so, trying to put Beckett off his game. 'Use the opportunity you're being given, dear boy,' he said. 'It's your brother I'm after primarily. Specialist Heitz was collateral damage, and you should try to avoid that fate. Survive if you can, and live to climb trees, or whatever it is you do, another day. Believe me, you will be better off without young Myles leading you down all sorts of wrong paths.'

Beckett made no reply to the duke, but he was talking to someone in animalistic grunts and growls.

The straps were thrown aside, and the electric rifles

of the clones swivelled as one to zero in on Beckett's head and torso.

'Slowly, now,' said Teddy, taking a step. 'Up on the table you go. And I should tell you that your famous cluster punch won't work here. I myself am wearing a kneepad under my trousers, and I took the precaution of adding an elongated kneecap to the clones' design. But please knock yourself out trying if you feel there's time to spare.'

Beckett moved in a daze, unable to come to grips with the terrible reality playing out around him. Lazuli was dead, his brother was about to have his head chopped off, and he was being set on a table like a jester on a stage, given a single chance to change the course of the day. Myles was able to do something he called *compartmentalise*, which meant storing unhelpful emotions in a mind box until he had time to deal with them, but Beckett was a creature who ran on emotions and could not shut them off at will. In fact, he rarely put anything in boxes.

He mounted the table in a most untypical fashion, crawling aboard on his hands and knees as though his legendary coordination had deserted him.

'There's a good fellow,' said Teddy most patronisingly,

spinning Myles round to watch his brother's sad escape attempt. 'Steady now. Don't worry, I won't start counting until you are in position.'

Beckett was certainly not in optimal shape for a breakout, and it seemed as though he might not try anything . . . until Myles called to him.

'Beck. The only way we survive is if you use the ten seconds granted. Unleash the beast, if you know what I mean.'

Lord Teddy, surprisingly, agreed. 'Yes, boy. Listen to your brother and unleash the beast.'

Beckett patted his pocket and felt the shape of Whistle Blower in there.

Unleash the beast. Lord Teddy could not know that I've been grunting at Whistle Blower this whole time.

The clones stared at him with their cold eyes and Beckett was certain they would not miss when the time came.

It's hopeless.

But no. Whistle Blower would spring into action and then, Beckett knew, he himself would be inspired to follow suit. He inched his hand towards the pocket in his cargo shorts, like a cowboy preparing to draw his weapon.

Lord Teddy tut-tutted. 'Not yet, old chap. Wait for the countdown.'

Beckett froze, but even the small action of reaching for Whistle Blower had fortified him and he felt the palest ray of hope light up neurons in his brain.

Can I do it? Without Myles?

And perhaps Teddy sensed this renewed hope as well, because he chose that moment to deliver a devastating blow.

'Oh, and by the way, before we kick off, I should say that the little troll fellow in your pocket won't be of any use to you. I gave him a rather fatal dose of deadly nightshade when I was strapping you in. No sense stacking the deck against myself.'

Myles didn't believe it. 'He's bluffing, Beck. Teddy has coveted Whistle Blower's venom for years.'

'Not any more,' said Teddy airily. 'I have an unlimited supply of clones to inhabit. I can grow them at will, don't you know? And slightly different ones, too, thanks to an employee of mine named Jeffluent. Still, there was no need to expose this pristine body to that little mite's teeth and claws, so I stuck him with a hypodermic of belladonna half an hour ago. I'm well practised in the technique. Many of my relatives went that way when they came between me and the title. If only one of them could have led me to the Lionheart ring . . . Eh, no matter. That's a quest for another day.' The duke closed his eyes. 'Anyway, your time begins now. Ten, nine . . .'

Beckett didn't absorb much of this chatter except for one crucial phrase, though Myles automatically filed everything away in case it might come in handy later. Beckett ripped open his shorts pocket and carefully lifted out the limp frame of his little troll friend. Whistle Blower was not quite dead, but he was in bad shape. Any visible skin was grey, and his mohawk, which was his pride and joy and usually kept vertical with blobs of animal fat, had collapsed completely, giving the troll a fringe that made him seem quite bookish. His eyes were dim and jittering in an alarming manner.

'Oh, my friend,' said Beckett. 'What has he done to you?'

'Six,' said Teddy. 'And five . . .'

Whistle Blower breathed with difficulty and spittle fizzed on his lips. He coughed an instruction at Beckett. 'Throw me,' he said.

'What?'

'Throw me at those scentless Teddies or my death will be meaningless.'

'Three,' said Teddy. 'Two . . .'

'Throw me *now!*' ordered Whistle Blower.

It would have seemed incredibly callous had there been witnesses to judge him, but Beckett did as he was told and, against every instinct in every fibre of his young body, he stood and hurled his dying friend directly towards the nearest cluster of impassive clones.

'One,' said Teddy, and he opened his eyes just in time to see the little troll fly past him, mouth opened, poison-laced spit trailing behind him.

It was comical, really.

'Wonderful!' said Teddy, his revenge proving more entertaining than he'd ever imagined.

Six of the clones fired, and three bolts hit Whistle Blower dead centre, momentarily suspending the toy troll in a nimbus of crackling electricity before the energy transfer sent him back the way he'd come. Like a cannonball, he charged directly into Beckett's chest, carrying them both through the window behind them, the frame of which had been weakened by the three electrical bolts that had missed Whistle Blower.

'Well now . . .' breathed the duke as tendrils of fog

snaked in through the window. 'That was unexpected. Most unexpected.'

The fall should kill the boy. Of course it should, but of course it wouldn't. These Fowls never went down easily.

No matter. The clones already abroad on the estate would find him. Find him and execute without prejudice. Or *with* prejudice. It didn't really matter to Teddy, as long as one of the Fowls was dead.

'The boy has flair,' said Teddy to Myles. 'I'll give him that.'

Myles was smiling a mirthless, vicious smile, devoid of all his usual mannerly civility. 'You should remember this moment, Bleedham-Drye. This is the moment when your demented plan went off the rails.'

Teddy didn't laugh exactly, but his smile matched Myles's own for mirthlessness. 'I think we're still on the rails, Myles, old chum,' he said, bonging the X-frame with a knuckle. 'In fact, you're tied to them.'

This was an excellent rejoinder, and the force of it took the wind out of Myles's sails. He slumped in his bonds and waited for the wire to tighten round his neck.

'Oh, don't be despondent yet,' said Teddy cheerfully. 'Buck up, why don't you? I still have several items on my pre-op checklist. And then I plan to gloat for a while.'

Myles thought he might stay slumped for the moment and hope that Beckett would somehow escape the island and not have to see his brother's head in a jar.

10
BECKATRON THE BOLD

SOME MINUTES LATER, BECKETT SAT CROSS-LEGGED on a loft hatch of the Childerblaine estate's barn. He sat there because, as he reasoned, his weight would make the space more difficult to access should Teddy or one of his clones try to investigate. But after several minutes he crawled into a corner because his trembling was making the hatch creak, and it struck him that if someone did try the ceiling-mounted door and find it obstructed, it would make sense for even a dim-witted clone to shoot through the hatch and into the boy who was weighing it down.

And, although Beckett was bodily present and functioning on a basic level in the barn, his mind was replaying the final moments of Whistle Blower's life – moments he could not accept as reality, even though the images were now seared into his memory.

They had tumbled through the window, boy and troll, sharing the lingering sting from the Clonoscopy charges. Whistle Blower was clamped so tightly to Beckett's chest that his claws cut through Beckett's T-shirt to the skin below. There'd been no time for Beckett to strategise or even let instinct find some path to safety, as the electricity was effectively rebooting the airborne boy. Not so with Whistle Blower. The troll was beyond any kind of short-term reboot. Beckett would surely have died had Whistle Blower not flipped them over so they impacted with the boy on top. Even so, the touchdown was not so much a *splat* as a *thump*. Beckett was merely winded, which was several notches down the injury scale from death.

Beckett did not understand and, when he could draw breath, he said as much to the troll. 'What's going on, Whistle Blower?' he asked, tears blurring his eyes. He felt that he couldn't bear to lose another friend.

'Troll magic,' breathed Whistle Blower, the words rasping from his mouth.

Beckett rolled off his friend and saw that Whistle Blower was not himself. His face was still recognisable, but the rest of him seemed to be decomposing as

Beckett watched. His limbs and innards were bursting open in soft blooms of vine and flowers, which intertwined eagerly with the existing flora.

'Our only magic,' said Whistle Blower. 'We keep the secret of our race. You are the only human ever to see our return to the earth. It is a special thing.'

Beckett watched his friend's body expand and bloom with exotic flowers and wriggle with rainbow-coloured worms. 'It's beautiful.'

'And soft,' said Whistle Blower, his eyes becoming the shining carapaces of beetles.

'You saved me,' sobbed Beckett.

Whistle Blower's mohawk stiffened and became a clutch of reeds. 'Now you save the other one. Myles. He's not so bad.'

Whistle Blower smiled and his teeth became salt crystals that dissolved slowly in a pool of Beckett's tears.

And now Beckett was in the loft. He probably wouldn't have moved at all had Whistle Blower's last wish not been to save Myles. That perked up Beckett enough to run away from the approaching clones and hide in the barn. But, now that he was here, he felt the situation close in on him and any spark of purpose fade.

Lazuli gone.

Whistle Blower gone.

This was not how Fowl Adventures were supposed to go.

Beckett noticed a stack of paintings half covered by a yellowed dustsheet. He untucked a corner of the cloth, crept beneath it and draped it over himself, hoping his shivering would not billow the canvas like a sail.

Beckett Fowl shivering? Surely not. Beckett, the indomitable creature of poise and instinct, shivering? How could this be?

First, there was the damp that seemed to infuse every breath of St George air with a ghostly chill. Like many twelve-year-olds, Beckett was generally immune to cold, but he had felt the remorseless tendrils of mist curling round his bare limbs even when he was inside Childerblaine House. Having said that, mere mist would generally be shrugged off by the Fowl boy, but there were other contributing factors too – low blood sugar, stress, dehydration and something else that Beckett usually neither suffered from nor succumbed to: uncertainty.

Beckett didn't know what to do and, worse, he felt

that what he had done so far in this adventure had been all wrong.

I let Lazuli get shot in the Southbank Centre, he thought. *And I didn't know goblins were fireproof. Plus, I brought Whistle Blower to St George. My instincts told me to sneak one of my best friends on to the island, and that was exactly what mean old Teddy had wanted me to do all along. And now Whistle Blower is dead.*

And perhaps worst of all: *I'm sitting in a horrid loft while Myles is in deep trouble.*

Beckett had to do something, but he couldn't for the life of him think what that something might be.

His mottos had always been:

Eat dessert first.

Blame the seagulls.

And . . .

Follow your amazing instincts.

But there were neither desserts nor seagulls in sight, and his amazing instincts had undeniably let him down badly in recent days.

So . . . was it time to actually *think* about something before doing it? Beckett moaned quietly.

Thinking before acting was so tedious and complicated. Myles was always planning before he acted, and look at what was happening to him – hooked up to an X-frame, which although cool was seriously uncool too.

No, decided Beckett. *I think thinking is not for me. I must do as Lazuli often says:* follow the way of the Beckett. *Something will come up.*

Beckett felt a poke in his thigh and looked down to see what was either a small dog or a large rat bristling in the shadows. On closer inspection, the creature proved to be a rat, which smoothed its whiskers and said, 'Boy, why are you crying?'

Beckett wiped his nose and replied, 'I'm in a bit of trouble.'

The rat was surprised to get an answer. 'Hey, are you the talking kid I've heard about?'

Beckett nodded. 'I am,' he said in the rat's tongue, which was not really a tongue. It was mostly a complicated sign language in which words were formed by complex strummings on certain whiskers, a little like playing classical guitar. As he was devoid of a single whisker himself, Beckett was forced to mime. 'Who told you about me?'

'One of the seagulls,' said the rat. 'Chatty guy with a black ring round his eye.'

Beckett remembered the bird. 'Oh yes. He said to watch out for the giant rats.'

'Watch out for *us*?' said the rat indignantly. 'I'm not the one going around lifting fish straight out of the sea with my razor-sharp bill. I eat rubbish and pass on a plague or two. That's it. You could say I'm good for the environment.'

'Maybe, if you cut out the plague bit,' said Beckett.

'We don't do it on purpose,' strummed the rat. 'I'd rather not spread any plagues, to be honest. The last one killed more Bleedham-Dryes than Lord Teddy, who isn't fooling anyone with that new body, by the way.'

This was interesting. 'Teddy kills his relatives?'

The rat confirmed it. 'Oh, sure. He's been at it for a long time. Anyone who might have a claim on the ducal seat is bumped off. I heard that one time he had a garden party and poisoned all the guests. Can you imagine? Humans are the worst. No offence.'

'No,' said Beckett, 'you're right. We *are* the worst. Teddy is trying to murder me and my brother right now.'

'That's my cue to go,' said the Gambian rat, waddling away. 'I try to distance myself from Teddy's targets. He tends to cause a lot of collateral damage.'

'That's okay,' said Beckett. 'I don't blame you. Go easy on the plague-spreading, will you?'

The rat felt bad about leaving on such a downer and so paused to strum his whiskers one more time with something a little more optimistic. 'At least you won't be lonely after you're dead. My gran is sensitive and she told me that this place is overrun by the ghosts of Teddy's victims.'

Ghosts, thought Beckett. And then, in spite of all his determination to follow his instincts, he had an idea.

A scary idea.

Myles had vowed never to do it again, in spite of the fact that he might learn something from the experience, when learning from experience was one of his main objectives. He'd sworn off it, even though the experience was one Artemis hadn't yet had, and doing things before Artemis was most certainly a prime life goal for Myles Fowl.

'One thing you must swear, brother mine,' he'd said back in London. 'Artemis must never know that my discovery was accidental. When he asks, you must tell him that my peek into the spirit realm was planned.'

At the time, Beckett had called Myles a big fat liar,

but his brother had assured him that nearly all scientists were big fat liars, none more so than that charlatan Einstein, so he intended to take that as a compliment.

And now Beckett was preparing to go where Myles had vowed never to return (at least until he got back to his laboratory), and this scared him.

I would prefer to fight a million voles, he thought now, and voles are notoriously dirty fighters – just ask any snail.

Beckett pulled back the dustsheet and crawled over to the circular stained-glass window so he might take advantage of the late-evening light pouring through. Any other day, the window would have fascinated him, as it depicted the battle between the island's namesake and a red-scaled dragon, but today there was no room in his brain for distractions.

Beckett rooted in his pocket until he located the spectacles containing the intravitreal injections. Myles had adapted the glasses so that each lens could accommodate one of the injection pods, and thirty teeny-tiny micro-needles would dump their antibodies into his eyeballs at the press of a button. And even Beckett, who was usually game for anything, the grosser the better, had cringed the first time he'd witnessed the procedure, asking, 'Brother, is there anything in the world important enough to make you want to stick needles in your eyes?'

'There are several things,' Myles had replied, blinking away tears. 'Posterity, the advancement of humanity, red gummies, the envy of other scientists . . . I would do it for you, of course, and Mater and Pater, and, under certain circumstances, Artemis.'

Myles would do it for me, thought Beckett now. *And I must do it for him. It's the law of twins everywhere.*

Beckett put on the glasses and ran a finger across one arm, searching for a plunger button. He found it and, after a moment's tense hesitation, pressed, activating both a mist puffer and the twin pads of micro-needles. Besides a slight fright from the puffer, Beckett felt nothing.

It didn't work, thought Beckett and, with typical boy-child impatience, he pressed the plunger again.

Still nothing but a puff of mist.

Four more times Beckett pressed the plunger, not realising that the puff was a shot of local anaesthetic that numbed his eyeballs and he had just self-administered six doses of Myles's antibody injection. One dose usually took several hours to activate, but

Myles had never tested more than one dose. Nobody had.

Until now.

Beckett packed away the SPOOK apparatus, grumbling, 'Stupid science never works properly. I'll just have to do things the Beckett way.'

The Beckett way was to run directly into the middle of whatever trouble was brewing and see what happened. Usually what happened was cluster-punching on an epic scale. But cluster-punching would not work on these clones, so Beckett would have to use some of the other tools in his arsenal, like the fairy art of *Cos T'apa*, or what he called the Windy Elbow. This move was the classic sharp elbow to the solar plexus, causing a diaphragm spasm that drove every breath of air from the victim. Beckett was, of course, very adept at landing these elbows, but he had on more than one occasion forgotten to remove himself from the strike zone and so, when the winded victim threw up a previous meal, it often landed on the twin.

'Remember to get out of the way,' he told himself now.

'Out of the way of what?' asked a voice behind him.

'People throw up when I give them the old Windy

Elbow,' said Beckett, answering automatically. 'Sometimes worse. So I like to strike and move on. Which is against the natural law. Usually creatures strike, then eat their prey, but I don't want to eat clones. In fact, I don't eat animals at all because I know what they're saying.'

Beckett guessed what was happening about halfway through this speech, but he kept jabbering on to buy himself a few seconds during which he could come to terms with it.

Myles's injectacles worked *and I am about to see ghosts*, he thought.

As little as a week earlier, that would have been an exciting proposition, but, having seen the experience's effect on Myles, Beckett was more apprehensive than he'd ever been in his life. He felt his heart play a frenetic drum solo in his chest and a flush creep up from the neck of his T-shirt to lodge in his cheeks.

'You don't eat animals?' asked another voice, this time mocking. 'What do you survive on, boy? Grass?'

This comment annoyed Beckett slightly, as it was the same tired and lazy criticism that people always threw at vegans, and so he spun to face this judgmental ghost, but he kept his eyes down for the moment.

'Actually, you can eat loads of grasses, smarty-pants,' he said a little crossly, which was not like him. 'Or drink them, at least. Crabgrass, for example, and one called bristle. Just grind them up and swallow the juice. Don't eat the fibre, though – it's too tough.'

The lady who had spoken was embarrassed. 'I'm so sorry, young man. That was very rude of me.'

'That's no problem,' said Beckett. 'I'm sorry for snapping.'

Then he took a breath and raised his gaze to take in the room, expecting several nightmare columns to beam themselves directly into his brain as Myles had described.

It didn't happen.

Because of his multiple presses on what he had dubbed the *injectacles'* plunger, Beckett had skipped over several months of trials and happened on the correct dosage. Yet another accidental discovery.

Even though there were no phantom nightmare memories zooming around, the loft had completely changed. Where there had been gradients of shadow, there were now various sections – different environments that overlapped like the bleeding edges of a watercolour painting. Inside each area was a spirit who seemed to travel complete with their own special location. There were several rooms from Childerblaine House that Beckett recognised from his quick race-through earlier. Also, meadows and forests at all times of day and night. Fancy apartments with city skylines in the background. One lady reclined in a deckchair with the lacquered deck of a cruise liner stretching off behind her. Clamped to the wall of a cliff was a young, heroic-looking chap with the Bleedham-Drye head of jet-black hair. Someone wearing a Victorian swimming costume stood under the nozzle of a beach shower. And, to continue the watery theme, there was a figure in diving gear, floating in their very own slice of ocean. Altogether there were perhaps a dozen spirits, though Beckett didn't count them, as he was not the sort of person inclined to count.

The old man who had spoken originally was surrounded by a lamplit library with towering shelves that should not have been able to fit in the cramped loft. The fellow had a look of Teddy about his face, especially around the wide brow and sharp eyes. He was wearing a blue uniform with gold piping down the sleeves, and his chest was weighed down by three rows of medals.

'Who are you?' Beckett asked the man.

'I am Brigadier General Ronald Bleedham-Drye. Teddy's cousin. And this –' he pointed to a girl in a sparkling ball gown and powdered wig – 'is my niece, the Princess Daphne.'

'Not one of the important princesses,' said the girl, and Beckett realised she was the anti-vegan. 'Just important enough for Teddy to murder.'

'Can I call you Daffy?' asked Beckett.

The ghost smiled. 'That would be very nice, young man,' she said. 'And what might I call you?'

Seeing as they were playing this game, Beckett thought he might as well give himself a heroic moniker. 'I am Sir Beckatron the Bold of Dalkey Island. The High Mage of Communicado. But you can call me Beck.'

Princess Daphne dipped her chin slightly, which was her version of a deep curtsy. 'Beck. Delighted, I am sure.'

She extended her hand and, when Beckett leaned in to kiss it, he saw an oversized ghost ring on her finger with a lion motif embossed on the head.

The Lionheart ring, he guessed.

At this point, all the other ghosts realised that

Beckett could see beyond the nightmarish level to the revenants beyond, and they all began speaking at the same time. Beckett, overwhelmed by the visceral emotion that ghosts could inject into their voices, actually pressed himself back against the hard stone wall until the princess took charge.

'Silence!' commanded Daphne. 'I am the ranking royal here and will lead the negotiations.'

The other spectres, being of royal heritage themselves, had protocol bred into them and so were immediately, if reluctantly, quiet.

'I do apologise, Sir Beck,' said the princess. 'Please forgive my family. They are excited. I, too, am excited to have an audience with a living person, but I do wonder how it is that you can see us on this occasion when on your previous visit you could not?'

'My brother is a genius,' said Beckett. 'He invented an injection.'

The brigadier interjected from his library. 'Is this the brother who is currently hooked up to Teddy's mechanical doodah?'

'That's the one,' confirmed Beckett. 'He's only a *brain* genius, not a fighting one like me.'

Princess Daphne sat on a fancy golden chair that materialised behind her. 'It appears that you need our help, Sir Beck.'

'I do,' said Beck. 'I thought you might help me save my brother. I have an idea, which is not my strong point, but it might work.'

Daphne's eyes narrowed. 'I do instinctively like you, Sir Beck, but why would we help you? We have our own struggle here.'

Beck frowned. 'Are we negotiating now?'

'We are, Sir Beck,' said the princess.

'That's not my strong point, either. Can you tell me what I should say?'

Daphne smiled. 'You might point out, Sir Beck, that your brother is a scientific genius and, should we assist you with his rescue, then you in turn could guarantee his help with our problem.'

Beck thought he'd better ask. 'What is your problem, Daffy?'

The princess and, in fact, all the spirits were immediately sad, and their environments dimmed considerably.

'It is a problem easily explained but extremely difficult

to solve,' said Daphne. 'We wish to move on. To ascend. We have seen others rise towards the light and pass through. But we, consumed as we once were by hatred for Lord Teddy, seem to have expended all our energy on that emotion. And now, when a Bleedham-Drye tunnel appears, we can only go so high before we plummet to this cursed island prison once more. For decades, we have wrestled with this problem.' She stamped a royal foot. 'The whole thing is simply impossible.'

And this was when Beckett knew his twin brother would accept the challenge.

'Impossible! You should have mentioned that straightaway,' he said. 'Myles loves the impossible.'

THE LABORATORY, CHILDERBLAINE HOUSE

Lord Teddy Bleedham-Drye was finally getting round to some criminal-mastermind monologuing – or he would have, if Myles hadn't kept interrupting.

'And so I said to myself, Teddy, old boy, isn't there a way you can make Myles Fowl come to you . . . ?'

'Interesting,' noted Myles, still spread-eagled on Teddy's upright operating X-frame. 'You talk to yourself.

I could help you there, you know, with a few counselling sessions. Free of charge, of course.'

Teddy barked a derisive laugh. 'Oh, you will be helping me, Fowl, with all sorts of things. Or at least your head will be, if you don't want your nutrient juice drained through a plughole.'

The truth was Myles could think of worse fates than being a wise head floating in nutrient juice with all the time in the world to concentrate on big issues. But he suspected that Lord Teddy would be more interested in the small issues, like how to make his beard more luxuriant, or how to become king of the world, which might be entertaining but would hardly add to Myles's legacy as a great thinker.

'At least allow me to work on my own so-called nutrient juice,' said Myles. 'My first suggestion would be to change the ludicrous name. It's not a fruit smoothie, for heaven's sake.'

'My juice, Fowl, my name,' said Teddy, stroking his beard. 'When you have *my* head in a jar, you can name the preservative.'

Myles's tummy rumbled ominously, something he really should have taken note of, but he was too concerned with his head being sliced off, etc.

'Anyway, Lord Teddy,' he said, 'you were about to explain your plan, I think. I should very much like to hear that explanation in its entirety.'

Teddy relaxed into an exquisite Edwardian club chair with intricately carved lion's-paw legs, which Myles remembered nestling his own posterior in on his previous visit to Childerblaine. Having wiggled into a comfortable position, the duke relit his ivory-rimmed pipe, which was so oversized it might also have functioned as a French horn.

Both the chair and the pipe irritated Myles, for they were out of place and, quite frankly, dangerous in a sterile environment. The pipe for obvious reasons, and the chair because most antique furniture pieces harboured veritable legions of various mites in their upholstery. But Myles could admit the real reason the club chair annoyed him was that he would never have the sensation of sitting in one again, and he realised he would miss feeling stuff.

Teddy blew a noxious cloud that smelled of a factory smokestack towards Myles and then said, 'I would have loved to continue sharing the details of my plan, Fowl, but I have no wish to bear your constant interruptions. The fact of the matter is, here you are, so my plan worked.'

Myles conceded this fact with a nod. 'And it was such a convoluted plan, which, as we both know, is the most satisfying kind.'

Teddy was drawn in, in spite of his reservations. 'Yes, you are right, Fowl. Any idiot can kill someone. All an idiot needs is the will to succeed and a crude weapon of some kind. After all, I could have easily killed you in London.'

'You could have, but instead you decided to strip me of more than just my life.'

Teddy exhaled with obvious satisfaction. 'I needed to beat you, comprehensively and undeniably. I needed you to come here of your own free will and deliver the troll to me. And I needed you to remain somewhat alive so you would spend eternity at my side with the full knowledge that I can pull your plug at any moment.'

Myles was impressed. 'It is as diabolical a plan as I have ever heard. Bravo, Lord Teddy.'

'I know you're just playing along, Fowl, hoping that your twin will come up with something.' Teddy laughed. 'Well, let me tell you, my fine young scamp, Master Beckett Fowl would have to come up with something simply out of this world to put one over on the Duke of Scilly at this stage in the game.'

Don't do it, Beck, Myles broadcast. *Don't come in here.*

But he knew that, in all likelihood, his brother was already on the way to save him.

For we are twins, he thought. *And that is what twins do.*

PORT NOLA, LOUISIANA, USA

THE PIXIE SPECIALIST LAZULI HEITZ, LEP ambassador to the house of Fowl, had been put through the wringer on what humans might call a wild-goose chase, but what her fellow inmates in the orphanage used to call a *lithograph hunt*. This was because the sprite administrator of the Haven Family Facilitator Facility was actually a treasure hunter who'd spent years climbing the social-service ladder simply to gain control of the orphanage. He made his charges dig up the grounds in search of famed lithographic limestones depicting San D'Klass, the third king of the Frond Elfin dynasty, otherwise known as Father Christmas. The facility was believed to be the site where the limestones were buried, but the orphans came away from their searches with nothing but calluses and a code phrase for a massive waste of time.

Lazuli had managed to touch down on a cargo ship

bound for the port of New Orleans. It was more of a crash landing than a touchdown, as her pedalling gears had seized up when she was still six metres above the craft. Luckily, Lazuli was able to glide the rest of the way and reach a shady corner without breaking any bones.

Now Lazuli found herself depleted of magic after a failed Ritual attempt, and without HQ backup, and with limited weapons and technology. She knew there were LEP safe houses all over the world, but she also knew that should she show up at one, protocol dictated that she be taken into custody for a debriefing. And, by the time the top brass concluded that it was probably best to keep the Fowl Twins alive, the Fowl Twins would be comprehensively dead with no sneaky retractions or workarounds. And so Lazuli decided that she should make an attempt to reach her human friends before Lord Teddy dispatched them both to the afterlife, which she now knew existed, because she could no more desert her friends than her friends could desert her. The Regrettables were a real team now. What had started as a joke name had developed a deep significance, and Lazuli knew that, if either of the twins were to be injured, she would feel responsible for the rest of her life. Which for a fairy could be a very long time indeed.

In a way, Commodore Holly Short had set the precedent for this kind of behaviour when she'd regularly flouted LEP regulations to protect the twins' brother, Artemis, though Lazuli doubted mentioning this in her defence would buy any lenience from her mentor. In fact, ex-rebels often became the strictest members of the establishment, and Commodore Short had matured into one of the most by-the-book senior officers in the force.

All of which is a long way of explaining why Specialist Heitz had spent the last twenty minutes perched on an iron gargoyle on top of a gantry crane overlooking the Port of New Orleans at the bottom of the mighty Mississippi River. It was an unusual place to put a gargoyle, but that was New Orleans for you. The port of NOLA was a mini-state unto itself. It was bigger than both the major fairy cities combined, and it shipped almost a million deep-draught containers per year.

But Lazuli was not interested in these statistics. She was watching an internal canal in the heart of the complex that could be drained for dry-dock work, but, as the LEP had discovered, it very rarely was. Lazuli happened to know this because one of her fellow Recon agents had been dispatched to New Orleans the previous year on the trail of a dragon sighting, of all things. The dragon had turned out to be a bigfootesque hoax, but in the course of his investigation the agent had got wind of a smuggling operation being run out of the port, and he'd done some preliminary recon before presenting his findings to Police Plaza. A full operation was approved and, though the smugglers didn't know it, they would have an entire surveillance team up in their business before the month's end.

There were dozens of rogue fairy teams smuggling contraband from the surface, and they didn't all merit a bells-and-whistles operation, but this mob – dubbed the Nola Network – had been caught on spy satellite using one very special piece of missing LEP equipment. (Technically, it wasn't LEP equipment, but something the LEP had confiscated from a goblin triad several years previously that had apparently avoided the recycler.)

Lazuli watched the Network's office, a repurposed shipping container on the bank of the canal, through emergency-issue goggles she had liberated from an

LEP locker on the dock. There were thousands of those lockers in the US alone, but Lazuli knew that the moment she opened that door to retrieve the emergency pack she'd be on the clock. The fingerprint scanner on the lock would have triggered an alert in Police Plaza, and a team would already be on the way. Lazuli reckoned that she had an hour at most before the cavalry arrived to stitch her up in a shielded transport sack and whisk her off to Haven City. So, when the office emptied of customers as far as she could tell from her perch, Lazuli finished up her recon following an absurdly short observation period and, in the absence of time to concoct a better plan, she applied a coat of spray skin from the pack to her blue face and hands, pulled up the hood of her toddler's SpongeBob SquarePants sweatshirt, climbed down from the gantry and strode through the front door.

Lazuli wasn't sure what she had been expecting, but it certainly wasn't a young red-headed human lady covered in beautiful Gnommish swirl tattoos – although that wasn't the most surprising thing about her. She stood behind a glass security screen, which also wasn't terribly surprising. The surprising part was the baseball cap struggling to contain the human's unruly hair, which bore not a Gnommish symbol but the SpongeBob logo.

Coincidence?

Maybe.

Lazuli knew that SpongeBob was a human cultural phenomenon, but still the serendipity set a flame licking her toes (which is the fairy way of saying *set her teeth on edge* and makes about as much sense when you think about it).

The office was empty except for the two SpongeBob devotees, and the one behind the screen raised an eyebrow at the *little girl* who had just strolled unattended into her office. 'You looking for someone, honey? Your mother, maybe?'

Now that she was here, facing the woman, Lazuli wasn't sure exactly how to play this.

What would Myles do? she asked herself.

He would probably browbeat this person with irrefutable facts until she broke down weeping.

But that was not her way, Lazuli decided. If this human was in fact a go-between for the outlaw fairies behind the scenes, antagonising her would not help the situation.

'I *am* looking for someone,' she said. 'But not my mother.'

'Really?' said the woman with no change of expression. 'And who might that be?'

'The proprietor,' said Lazuli carefully. 'I'm searching for the person running this operation.'

The lady took a drink from a large iced coffee on her desk. '*Proprietor*, you say. That's a long word for a short girl.'

Lazuli took both a step forward and a risk. 'Maybe there's more to me than meets the eye.'

'Maybe there is at that,' said the lady. Lazuli could see now that the brass plate behind the desk read:

MINERVA PARADISO

DIRECTOR

'I like your name,' said Lazuli. It seemed familiar to her, but she couldn't place it.

'It means *heavenly*,' explained Minerva. 'Paradiso. *Minerva* means *squasher of bugs*. Are you a bug, kid?'

'I'm no bug,' said Lazuli, stepping closer. 'So, if I were you, I wouldn't try to step on me.'

The woman did not answer this. 'Noted. At least

you know my name. I don't know anything about you, except that you're an unsupervised toddler with a big vocabulary. You *are* unsupervised, if you know what I mean?'

'I am,' confirmed Lazuli. 'Completely unsupervised for once. But, if you're worried about that, you could always call the NOPD.'

Minerva smiled broadly. 'Oh no, honey. We don't use the local police. We have our own security here. Very effective. Maybe I should call them.'

Lazuli scowled and for a moment did resemble a toddler. This was going nowhere. They could dance round each other all day. It was time to lay her cards on the table.

'Listen, maybe we can help each other out.'

'I doubt it,' said Minerva. 'How are you going to help me?'

'I have things in my bag that maybe you could use.'

'That little bag? Where'd you get that? Probably the same kind of place I got this hat. I'm surprised there are any of those lockers left in the city. Most of them have been found. We left a couple intact – except for the trackers. So, if you think there's someone coming, well, you would be very mistaken.'

This was a lot of info to digest. Nothing explicit had been said, but Lazuli could infer that Minerva knew she was a fairy and was informing her that there was no backup on its way.

'I don't want anyone to come,' said Lazuli. 'I'm colouring outside the lines, if you know what I mean.'

'Kids do that,' said Minerva, peering down at her with some interest.

Lazuli reached up to grip the edge of the counter. 'I've got information,' she said. 'You've got something here – something you shouldn't have. If you give it to me, then when they break down that door you won't have it any more. And they *will* be coming to break down the door. I know that for a fact.'

This was all pretty non-specific unless you knew what was under discussion here, but the lady behind the glass decided to up the specificity of the exchange.

'If you know they're coming, then you're one of them,' said Minerva, glaring at Lazuli. 'And, if you think I'm giving an LEP officer something that could land me in Howler's Peak, then you're dumber than you look in that hoodie.'

Lazuli was suddenly even more nervous than she'd already been. She'd taken a risk coming in here. She had banked on the rogue fairies being scared enough of an LEP investigation to hand over their chute pod, but it looked an awful lot like this woman was not scared of anything, with the exception of the maximum-security prison Howler's Peak, which was mainly a goblin facility but also had a surface traders' module.

'Okay,' Lazuli said, showing her palms, which is the fairy gesture for *I come in peace*.

Minerva mimicked the gesture. 'Okay, sure. You come in peace. It doesn't sound like it, officer. It sounds an awful lot like you're threatening my operation.'

'I'm giving you a chance to reduce your sentence,' protested Lazuli.

'I didn't have a sentence before you walked in here.'

'You're on the LEP's radar, and they're coming for you,' said Lazuli. 'It's only a matter of time. I shouldn't be revealing that much, and I'll probably end up in Howler's Peak with you, but I'm desperate.'

Minerva sighed deeply. 'There's no getting away from the LEP, right? All I want to do is live my life without interference from police forces, fairy or human. That's all any of us want up here. I mind my own business, run a fairly clean shop and don't hurt anybody, but still the mighty LEP feel that they've got to come knocking.'

Lazuli was starting to get the impression that this human had some direct connection to the fairy world. Perhaps she had married a fairy. It had been known to happen. After all, the legendary villain Turnball Root's own brother's partner had been a human.

'I've got things to trade,' Lazuli said. 'Cash.'

Minerva snorted. 'Your standard-issue go bag? I've got a hundred of those in the back. And cash? News flash, officer: no one uses cash any more. You have nothing for me except heartache. Now I have to relocate my daughter again.'

This was not playing out as it had in any of Lazuli's imagined scenarios. She'd expected either abject surrender or a fight against a cardboard criminal. Not this verbal jousting with a genuine three-dimensional human. A mother.

She was snapped out of these thoughts by the clunking of electronic bolts, which were, of course, to secure the door she'd come through.

'You're showing your true colours,' said Lazuli.

'I am,' said the woman. 'You've been scanned a dozen times since you came in here. You're not beaming any images anywhere. So no one will know if you don't walk back out.'

'What are you going to do with me?'

Minerva seemed genuinely irritated by the question. 'Just shut up, won't you? I'm trying to think. Of all the chop shops in all the world, why did you have to walk into mine? We deal in small stuff here. We don't hurt anyone, and no one hurts us.'

'Except the pod. That's what got you tagged. All you have to do is hand it over. My offer is good.'

The lady swore. 'D'Arvit. That cursed pod. I told Nord it would bring bad luck, but dwarves never listen to sense.'

Lazuli had some experience with dwarves, most of it criminal. 'Not if there's a profit to be made.'

Minerva glared sharply at her. 'Don't try to bond with me. So we both know dwarves are impulsive, big deal. I'm still going to do what I need to do.'

Lazuli pressed her impatiently. 'Which is what?'

'I don't know!' exclaimed Minerva. 'Kill you. Tie you up. Put you in a bag and ship you to the moon. Whatever I decide, it won't be to hand over that pod. I can't trust you enough for that. It's as good as handing an LEP captain evidence against me.'

'I'm just a specialist. They might not even listen to my evidence.'

'I can't take that chance,' said Minerva.

Even though Lazuli knew she was in deadly danger, she could not help but vent her frustrations, throwing up her arms and scowling at the woman seated above her. 'Oh, for Danu's sake,' she said. 'Every time I get mixed up with Fowls, things get complicated.'

Minerva's thinking face froze as Lazuli's comment wiped away the years. She stared at Lazuli, then disappeared from sight behind the counter.

Some seconds later, a door opened in the counter and Minerva stepped into the reception area. On the plus side, her expression was confused rather than aggressive. On the negative side, she had a tiny human two-shot derringer in her hand.

'You have five seconds to explain to me what you mean by that Fowl comment,' she said, cocking the pistol.

So, it turned out that Minerva and Artemis Fowl had a history, not all of it bad. Though most of it had indeed been bad, and they hadn't parted on the best of terms. And suddenly Lazuli remembered where she had heard her name before. It was all over an LEP Fowl file detailing the return of the goblin race from Hybras.

'I read about you,' said Lazuli. 'In a file called *The Lost Colony*.'

'I read that file too,' said Minerva. 'And I was seriously unimpressed. I was completely shafted by that file. I come across like a supporting character to the great Artemis Fowl.'

'I know the feeling,' said Lazuli. 'My whole life is Fowlcentric.'

'Did you know Artemis and I were kind of an item for a while?' asked Minerva as she led Lazuli through a connecting tunnel to the port's disused internal canal. 'But then he found his true soulmate.'

Lazuli cut in. 'Don't tell me – himself, right? Myles is the same. Worse, maybe.'

Minerva almost laughed but then reeled it in. 'You better not be messing with me, officer. Playing on our shared connection with the Fowls.'

'No,' said Lazuli. 'I've put in my time with that family. I have the bruises to show for it.'

'Me too,' said Minerva. 'Can I ask you something? Does Myles wear those silly little suits?'

Lazuli nodded. 'Yes. He used to print a new one every day. Now it's every week.'

'Once Artemis took me to a bowling alley. He printed

up a weird suit/tracksuit combo. I thought I'd be mortified, but actually it was kind of endearing.'

This set them both to laughing and their mirth echoed in the curved stone chamber, bouncing back to break over their foreheads and changing the mood completely, something that wouldn't have seemed possible a few minutes ago. The tunnel was an Aladdin's cave of fairy and human contraband, though of course fairies would not use that term. The fairy equivalent was a *Horteknut's Trove*, referring to the famous dwarf raiders who had amassed and lost several bullion fortunes over the past centuries. The tunnel walls were lined with everything from packaged food to personal communicators and even one bio-printer for at-home transplants. The water end of the tunnel was blocked to the waterline by a transparent micron wall that shimmered slightly. Beyond it was suspiciously dark shadow that Lazuli saw was intensified by one of Foaly's inventions: a **Sh**adow-**A**mplifying **D**arkness **E**missions lamp that produced light half a wavelength behind the existing light and cancelled it out. Lazuli rightly suspected that the centaur had chosen the name for his system mostly for the acronym SHADE.

That's one thing Myles and Foaly have in common, she often thought. *They love their acronyms.*

The SHADE lamp made darkness a little blacker than it would normally be – nothing too noticeable if the gradient were set correctly – and a good operator could fade out a crunchball pitch in a way that wouldn't turn heads. Whoever had set this up was an artist and managed to subtly paint out the light until the dock itself was steeped in opaque shadow that, though completely out of place, looked perfectly normal even on a sunny day, which this was.

As they neared the end of the tunnel, the echoes of their own footsteps ran up the walls on either side, and Lazuli commented, 'Is this your work?'

Minerva confirmed it. 'Yep. I hid a pleasure shuttle down here one time. Right out in the open. Nobody looked twice.'

Lazuli nodded in appreciation, but *she* was looking twice now, searching for the giveaway straight edges inside the deep shadow.

'Are you looking for edges?' asked Minerva.

'Yes, but I can't see any.'

'And you won't till you're a metre away,' said Minerva. 'I wrote some new code for the program, smoothed out those edges.'

It was beyond impressive. Even the LEP hadn't managed to produce such a deep level of shadow. Lazuli didn't see the pod until she was close enough to touch the two-metre-diameter orb and, when she did, her fingers sank in a little through a spongy material.

'Stealth paint?' she asked.

Minerva poked in her own finger. 'Are you kidding? That stuff is useless close up. And cam foil can't take any kind of hardship. This is a foam made from a network of reflective beads that we print directly on to the surface. Most of it will shear off during transport, but it'll get you into the air.'

'Shear?' asked Lazuli, not really fond of that word and all it implied. 'Why would it shear off?'

Minerva shrugged. 'The wind, the bouncing. Or if you hit something, like a whale or an island.'

Lazuli suddenly disliked the word *bouncing* even more than she had disliked the word *shear*.

'How did you even get into this line of work?'

Lazuli asked, switching to a less nauseating subject. 'There aren't many humans working with rogue fairies.'

'There are more fringe dwellers than you might think,' said Minerva. 'I like you, Specialist, but excuse me if I don't get into specifics with an LEP officer I just met.'

Lazuli nodded. She understood.

Minerva relented. 'I can give you basics, Specialist. After the Lost Colony incident, I became obsessed with fairies, as a scientist. But, the more I learned about the rogue element on the surface, the more I became interested in them personally. The heart always trumps the head in the end, except maybe with the Fowls. Anyway, long story short, I fell in love and had a hybrid baby. A little girl. We were happy for a while . . . then ACRONYM got my partner in a shoot-out.'

'That's awful,' said Lazuli. 'I am so sorry.'

'Yeah,' said Minerva. 'I've been plotting their downfall ever since, but I heard one of the Fowl boys took them down with the help of a hybrid specialist.' She paused in the tunnel and looked Lazuli in the eye.

'So thank you both, Specialist,' she said. 'And tell

Myles he should let his heart trump his head once in a while.'

Minerva explained some of the pod's mechanics before take-off. Lazuli absorbed as much as she could through the comm of the rudimentary helmet she wore while strapped into a bare-bones, military-style seat harness.

The tattooed human peered in through the craft's one porthole, which was not as transparent as it might have been. 'This window is all scratched up, but that's superficial, mostly.'

'Mostly?' echoed Lazuli weakly.

'You'll be fine,' said Minerva. 'This was going to be the getaway pod for me and my girl, but now I have time to leave through the front door. Thanks to you, I guess.'

Lazuli wondered where Minerva's girl had been supposed to sit. It was already cramped in here with a single passenger, and Minerva was almost twice her size. 'It's a pretty tight squeeze. I don't even see any flight controls.'

Minerva disappeared from the porthole. 'There aren't any in a model this old,' she said in Lazuli's earpiece.

'No controls apart from the hatch. Not on your end, at least.'

'There are definitely supposed to be controls,' said Lazuli, swallowing her panic.

'I didn't say there weren't controls,' said Minerva, and Lazuli could hear thunking noises as the human unscrewed fuel and coolant hoses, dropping them to the ground. 'Just not in there. Everything is controlled by the preprogrammed automatic guidance system.'

'That's not how a pod works,' said Lazuli. 'I'm supposed to have manual override.'

Minerva rapped on the window as she appeared again. 'This is not a pod as you know it, Specialist. I needed something that could get me and my girl to the other side of the world in thirty minutes should your comrades come knocking. This is a one-shot, never-been-tested clean getaway. After I programme in the destination and you take off, ground control eats itself and they never find you. Or they never find your body. As I said, never been tested. Are you sure you don't want to forget the whole thing and leave the Fowls to their own devices?'

'No,' said Lazuli. 'Myles and Beckett need me. We're the Regrettables.'

The tattooed lady laughed. 'A team name? You're doomed, Specialist.'

Then she turned serious. 'This better not get back to me,' warned Minerva, and she opened the porthole from the outside. 'I have a mean side that you don't want to see. Especially when it comes to my daughter's well-being.'

'Don't worry,' said Lazuli. 'You'll never see me again.'

Minerva laughed. 'I better not,' she said. 'Pass on a couple of messages for me, though. Tell N°1 I said hi, and tell Artemis he still owes me a favour.'

'I owe you one too, Minerva,' said Lazuli.

'You owe me several,' said Minerva, then she screwed a pipe to a thread on the porthole and began pumping in a very sloppy-looking green gel.

'Gel?' asked Lazuli, fearing that she'd just strapped herself into an execution chamber. 'Why are you pumping in gel?'

'Can't talk now,' said Minerva. 'We're on a countdown. Flood your helmet one more time for fresh air, then listen to the recording.'

Why would I need to flood my helmet? wondered Lazuli.

The last thing Minerva said specifically to her was,

'Happy bouncing, Specialist.' And Lazuli was reminded how much she detested the word *bouncing*.

The recording the smuggler human had referred to was a preflight rundown she'd made for her daughter, Numi, possibly to keep the girl calm while gel flooded the claustrophobic chamber, and Lazuli had to admit that Minerva's voice did have a soothing quality.

Every mum probably sounds soothing to her little girl, thought Lazuli, wishing she could confirm that from personal experience, but she had zero personal experience with her own mother and so banished that notion and concentrated on listening to the message, which might contain useful information. It went as follows:

'Okay, Numi, sweetie. The impact gel is pouring in now, like we talked about. But no need to worry, because I mixed in a surprise for you. If you look closely, you might see the occasional little foil unicorn floating in there. I know you love unicorns, baby, so once I'm finished speaking why don't you count unicorns and try to take a catnap?'

Lazuli glanced down between her feet to see foil unicorns twinkling in the impact gel, which had risen to knee level.

Mums are great, thought Lazuli, and then: *Impact gel? Why do we need impact gel?*

Recorded Paradiso was ready for that one. 'Now I know I don't have to tell you, my little scholar, why we need impact gel, so why don't I just remind you, okay? We need the gel because, when the pod is on its way to our new home, it can't change course. We travel in long bounces like a flat stone, or a bouncing bomb, or the Incredible Hulk, and each bounce is going to shake us up real good, so the gel prevents our bones from shattering and our brains from being scrambled. The only navigation on board is done by preprogrammed gyroscopes and fins that keep us on target, so we can't avoid anything that might get in the way, like a ship or a mountain. So, even though the pod is pretty much indestructible, some of the impact energy is transferred inside and would go into our bodies if it wasn't for the what?'

'The impact gel, Mummy,' said Lazuli a little impatiently.

To which the real Minerva said, 'I heard that. This tape wasn't meant for you, so have a little respect.'

'Sorry, Mummy,' said Lazuli in a chilly tone, which might have had something to do with the cold green gel that was currently seeping through her suit.

The recording continued. 'The pod is like an old-fashioned rocket missile, except for the bouncing, which does slow us down a little but also charges the engines with every contact, so we might get a few bumps, but we'll also gain a lot of distance to get us even further away from those nasty, smelly, monstrous LEP officers.'

I do know some nasty, smelly officers, thought Lazuli. *But monstrous? That's a bit strong.*

Lazuli realised with a start that not everyone saw the LEP as a force for good and justice, which she would have to think about later when she was not about to be shot across the ocean.

'So remember, Numi, darling, even though the flight might get a little bumpy, how are we supposed to breathe?'

'Through the holes in our faces?' guessed Lazuli, pretty sure that was not the desired answer.

'That's right,' said the recording, which had not registered the passenger's smart-aleckry. 'Slow and deep. Conserve the air in your helmet. Just sit here in my lap and relax while we get shot out of the tunnel like a giant cannonball and, don't you worry, when we land, I'll pop the porthole with the lever. Won't that be fun?'

Lazuli had four responses to that section:

1. So that's where Numi would sit.
2. A giant cannonball? Where's the cannon?
3. What porthole lever?

And finally . . .

4. No, Minerva. That will not be fun.

Lazuli was right. It would not be fun. And the answer to response number two regarding the whereabouts of the cannon was: the pod was already loaded into it, i.e. the channel itself.

Lazuli was submerged in gel now and it seemed as though the sluggishness in her movements had spread to her thought process, but that was probably her imagination. Out of the corner of one eye, she saw the hatch porthole close, and she wondered how secure it could be if a person could simply open and close it so easily.

Too late to back out now.

Minerva spoke in her headset. 'St George is programmed in. You're all set, Specialist. I know you promised I'd never see you again, but the way karma works, I feel sure that I will. Also, you're not so bad for an LEP thug.'

Lazuli smiled inside her helmet. 'You're not so bad for a ruthless outlaw. You should take Numi and get far away from here.'

'I will, as soon as I push this big red button.'

'So push the big red button,' said Lazuli with several hundred per cent more bravado than she felt.

Somewhere, quite a distance from the pod, Minerva pushed the button, and Lazuli's world became a cauldron of roaring engines and compressed gel. In high-pressure situations such as this, where the subconscious perceives a threat to survival, the brain shuts down all minor thought processes and instigates a fight-or-flight reaction. In this most unusual situation, Lazuli found herself doing both.

12
THE WINKING CLONE

NOW WE HAVE ARRIVED AT POTENTIALLY THE MOST disturbing section of the Fowl Chronicles, and not just the most disturbing part of this particular affair, but all the twins' stories. In fact, it may possibly be the most disturbing part of all recorded Fowl history, including the occasion when Artemis kidnapped an elf, an event that is referred to in LEP files as Offence Zero because it initiated the modern cycle of Fowl affairs.

For, in spite of the efforts of the Regrettables, it seemed as though the time had arrived for Myles to endure medical decapitation. The most upsetting aspects of this procedure for Myles were the facts that the laboratory conditions were not up to his own scrupulous standards and that, if this operation truly had to be performed, he would really rather perform it himself. Indeed, he continued to lecture Lord Teddy on the procedure during final prep through the speaker set into his resin helmet.

'Four seconds, Lord Teddy. You have four seconds to equalise my blood pressure and oxygen supply. After that, you'll get nothing out of me but muscle reflexes from my extrapyramidal system, and what a tragedy that would be for the world.'

Lord Teddy was flanked by two clones of himself and completely gowned up, but most infuriatingly, as far as Myles was concerned, he continued to smoke his oversized pipe through a custom slit in his face mask.

'You are not in the Southbank Centre now, Fowl,' he said. 'No one here has been paid to listen to you jabber on. In fact, if you don't stop your chatter, I will simply shut off your speaker.'

Myles's heart sank, figuratively speaking, for it was this *speaker* comment that penetrated his bravado, which was, of course, a coping mechanism. He was about to have his head separated from his body, after all, which was a catastrophic development even for a Fowl. So the boy did in fact *stop his chatter* for a moment while he considered the best way forward for him. It would be so easy, and indeed expected, for him to slip into shock, which would paralyse his mental process, and that was if he survived the operation, which was by no means assured.

I need my faculties intact, Myles told himself. *For the power of my own will, if nothing else.*

There were countless accounts of patients with positive mental attitudes who lived through borderline-fatal injuries by fighting to survive. Myles had theorised that this was due to residual strands of magic in their DNA (left over from the time when humans, too, were magical creatures) that had enabled these patients to heal themselves.

Though it would take more than strands to put a Humpty Dumpty like me back together again, he thought now.

Myles also needed his brainpower operating on all cylinders in order to help Beckett. His twin was out there somewhere, no doubt attempting to mount a breach of the facility, and Myles needed to be alert when his twin came through the door.

And, even though Lord Teddy had instructed Myles to be silent, it seemed as though the duke had taken up the jabbering baton himself.

'You shall be my slave, Fowl. My devoted and useful slave. And should you cease to be useful, or should you perhaps bore me, or irritate me, for that matter, then I shall have your servo motors fly you out to sea and I will take potshots at you with my hunting rifle. How do you like the sound of that, Fowl?'

Myles did not like the sound of that and admitted as much with a shake of his head. He still hoped that Beckett would save the day as he had so many times before, but never had the situation been quite so dire. There is nothing like a motorised cheese wire tightening on a fellow's tender skin to bring him face to face with his own mortality.

'Please, Lord Teddy,' he said quietly. 'What you're doing is monstrous. I am a child, after all.'

Teddy puffed up a storm on his pipe. 'Oh, I've been looking forward to this bit immensely. The begging, I mean. I really thought you might tough it out. Put your best foot forward and all that.' Teddy removed the pipe from his mouth for just long enough to tap the stem against Myles's restrained right leg, and then made a remark that laid bare his cruel heart. 'But it is a well-known fact that poor, clumsy Myles Fowl does not have a best foot, and one supposes that, even if he did, that best foot is never going forward again, eh?'

It was, as Beckett might say, an epic burn.

But not as epic a burn as the heated cheese wire would momentarily inflict upon Myles's tender neck.

Myles felt his Adam's apple bob against the wire and thought he might weep for the planet's impending loss, i.e. himself, but he was afraid that sobbing would only increase the vertical movement of the laryngeal prominence in his thyroid cartilage (Adam's apple to you and me) and get it caught in the cheese wire. So Myles held back the sobs with some considerable effort and determined that he would take comfort in the fact that at least Beckett had got safely away.

But, as is often the case when faced with mortality, people tell themselves what they want to hear, and someone of Myles's intelligence could not make himself believe that Beckett would leave the island.

I feel him nearby in my scar, he thought. *And, even if I could not, I know that my twin would not leave me to my fate. He will concoct some hare-brained plan and come cartwheeling in here, straight into the arms of Bleedham-Drye's cloned goons.*

Myles thought he would like his last piercing stare to be directed at the armed clone nearest to him, and so he tensed his eyelids, which is essential for an effective intimidating stare, and beamed a laser glare at the Teddy lookalike.

And, to his surprise, the clone winked at him in a very unexpectedly jaunty fashion.

Curious, thought Myles. *Perhaps the creature is spasming involuntarily.*

But the clone winked again and then pointed at its own face as if to say, *Look, it's me!*

Myles was surprised to find a tear welling on the lower lid of one eye, for he knew at that moment his twin had somehow put together an actual plan, and he could not have been prouder.

The Barn,
Childerblaine House

A few minutes earlier, Beckett had indeed put something together, but calling it a plan was a tad on the optimistic side. It was more a wish-quilt woven from thought-strands and eternal optimism. The Beckett way, if you recall, was to run directly into the centre of the place where the trouble was and see what happened, and this new venture was a broadening of that life philosophy insofar as Beckett thought he might send an entire group of people to the epicentre of trouble and see what happened. The people he was thinking of sending were the ghosts of Teddy's victims, and the epicentre was the gang of Teddy clones who were guarding the duke. Beckett happened to know that spirits could occupy live hosts, as he himself had been occupied once upon a time, and he reckoned that the ghosts could possess the clones and wreak as much havoc as possible while he unhooked Myles from the cryogenic contraption.

When Beckett had explained his idea to the legion of ghosts in the barn's loft, Ronald Bleedham-Drye had set him straight.

'Sorry, my dear chap,' said the brigadier general, seeming genuinely disappointed. 'It's impossible because that isn't how these pathetic ghostly bodies work.'

This did not dim Beckett's enthusiasm a single watt. He'd had a lifetime's experience of his notions being deemed not worthy, but somehow they often went on to turn out just fine.

'It will work!' he insisted. 'If we want it to work.'

Princess Daphne stepped forward.

'Dearest Sir Beckatron. Beck. We have tried – all of us have tried repeatedly – to possess Lord Teddy and anyone else who came to call, but the willpower of living beings is simply too strong. Even Teddy's electric eels resist us. The brigadier general once managed to infiltrate the brain of a snake, but that only lasted a few minutes.'

Ronald Bleedham-Drye shuddered and his accompanying library shelves looked like they were going to topple over on him. 'Bloomin' reptiles. They lay eggs, you know.'

'I did know that,' said Beckett. 'They told me.' He tried to take Daphne's hand, but his fingers passed through hers. 'You can control the clones because they are not real people. Teddy made them without willpower so they would be his slaves.'

'Do you mean like worker bees?' asked Daphne.

'Oh no, Daffy,' said Beckett. 'Worker bees are no pushovers. They have a union and everything. These clones have computer chips instead of brains. That's what Myles said. He dumbed it down for me, but he meant that their neurons aren't firing effectively. I know that because I can listen when I feel like it. Also, Myles tells me things so often that sometimes they sink in.'

Daphne's smile was dazzling. 'I do like the sound of

this Myles person. But you're certain we could control the clones, Sir Beck?'

'I am always certain of everything,' said Beckett sincerely, allowing his hands to hover over the princess's ghostly fingers so that sparks crackled between them.

'And then Myles will help us ascend?' pressed the brigadier.

'Yes,' said Beckett. 'All I have to do is tell him that it's impossible.'

And so Princess Daphne Constance Gertrude von Stein Bleedham-Drye of the Scilly Isles, as was her full title, ordered that the island's ghosts should attempt a mass possession of Lord Teddy's clones. It was the most unexpected decree she had made thus far in her royal career – although there was one more to come that was so bizarre it could be considered Fowlish.

Contrary to what one might expect, no sparkle clusters or puffs of phantasmal disintegrations accompanied this command, just a mundane packing-up of whatever business the spirits were engaged in and an ordered trudging down a ghostly stairway that presumably had been removed in renovations. Daphne stayed behind for a moment, as she had something special to discuss with Beckett.

'Speak honestly now, Beck,' she said gravely. 'Are you truly a knight of the realm?'

'No, Daff,' said Beck. 'I'm not even Beckatron, just Beckett, and I'm not anything of the realm. I was playing a game, and making myself brave too. Knights are always brave and true in the storybooks. Do you know something? I believe books are more real than people know. Sometimes there's more truth in a story than in the truth, which Myles would say is typical of the kind of nonsense I spout on a daily basis.'

Daphne did that hybrid pursed-lips smile that people do when they are trying not to cry. Apparently, ghosts get emotional easily, and she was not one hundred per cent successful in holding back tears as a single glitter-infused drop traced her cheek. 'One wishes you had been at court in the nineteen hundreds, Beck.'

'I probably will be,' said Beckett. 'Time travel is only a matter of time.'

Daphne held out one silk-gloved hand and a spectral sword sparkled into existence. 'I was King George's favourite princess. And on my tenth birthday he gave me the Lionheart ring and permission to knight my true love so that I might marry him when the time came. It's too large for my delicate finger, so I had a knob of silver stuck inside the ring to keep it on. I never grew up, thanks to Lord Teddy, but I believe a royal decree transcends even death itself, and I would dearly like to confer that honour on you now, if you would have it.'

Beckett nodded. Of course he would have it. This was exactly the kind of impulsive grand gesture that he loved. And also he instinctively liked any princess who liked to be called Daffy, even if he suspected he was not, in fact, her true love.

'Daff, I would love to be a knight, if we can do it quickly before my brother gets beheaded.'

The princess shrugged. 'In my family, you grow accustomed to relatives being beheaded, but as you wish. Bow your head, Beck.'

Beckett did so and felt a shimmering fizz on his shoulders as the ghostly blade touched them one after the other.

'Dearest Beck, in recognition of your service, I knight thee. Arise, Sir Beckett, knight of the realm.'

Beckett did arise and studied his own arms. 'You know something, Daff? I feel different. Definitely more courageous.'

Princess Daphne wiggled her fingers and the slender sword disappeared. 'I am glad to hear it, Sir Beck, because you will need all your courage, and perhaps some good fortune, too, if you are to rescue your brother.'

'At least I am not alone. I have you, Princess.'

'You do indeed,' said Daphne. 'And, if your idea works, I will give Uncle Teddy a piece of my mind, and he will have to listen for as long as I wear the Lionheart ring.'

This was the second time this ring had been mentioned and so Beckett asked, 'What's so special about this Lionheart ring?'

'Nothing, really. It's just a beautiful ring. King George gave it to me as a joke. He said that whoever wore it would never be interrupted, and someday they would be king or queen. It's silly, really, but we royals love that kind of whimsy.'

Beckett silently hoped that Myles would never get his hands on a Lionheart ring. He was bad enough now without a licence to speak uninterrupted.

And so, a few minutes later, one of Lord Teddy's clones was winking at the restrained twin. Myles could see instantly that this fellow was different somehow from his brethren, who were mindless sheeple, but he couldn't tell exactly how many degrees off the party line the winking clone was.

Has he come to save me, or to laugh at my downfall? he wondered as the cheese wire grated ever tighter against his neck.

Teddy waffled on, oblivious to this latest development, if it even was a development. 'Keep your chin up, won't you, Fowl?' he said. 'As I'm sure you're aware, the cut must be precise and clean. It will not be precise and clean if you insist on dragging your flesh across a wire that has not yet reached the correct temperature. If the wire is too cold, it will destroy your trachea, and should it be too hot then—'

'Then it will cauterise my wound,' said Myles. 'Which will make it impossible to regulate blood flow and pressure.'

'Precisely,' said Lord Teddy, who had finally laid down his ridiculous pipe, which Myles found ominous.

'I must say, it is impressive how you maintain a clinical calm under the circumstances. Most people would have given up the ghost.'

At the word *ghost*, the clone wiggled its eyebrows, and Myles thought, *Oh*.

And then, as the light bulb went on, *Ooh*.

Beckett has weaponised the island's ghosts.

This realisation had multiple significances, but the top three would be as follows:

1. There was, if not a spark of hope that he might survive this intact, then at least a flicker.
2. Beckett must have subjected himself to the horror of what he insisted on calling the *injectacles*, even though Myles had not sensed any signs of significant psychological trauma through his scar. And . . .
3. There would soon come an opportunity to escape, and he must seize this chance when it presented itself, as much as he could seize anything, trussed up as he was.

The chance was on the horizon, as they say, but when it arrived it would take a form that Myles could never have foreseen, let alone embraced, and, if Beckett's life had not also been in danger, there was a tiny chance that Myles would have been too stunned and indeed consumed by disgust to take advantage of the opportunity handed to him.

To recap, Myles and Beckett had been inhabited by magical creatures as youngsters, and these creatures had left some magic residue behind, resulting in Beckett being blessed with the gift of tongues. Myles had, unbeknownst to him, also been imbued with a gift – or curse, depending on how a person viewed it – that was usually associated with a certain species of fairy, but the dominant nature of his personality had subjugated that power, as it was incompatible with his highbrow notions. But, as he found himself now with zero hope of navigating an intellectual exit, especially with Beckett on planning duty, this power began to assert itself. Even so, Myles's subconscious might have overridden the instinct, but Lazuli's special magical touch on the banks of the River Thames had awoken the power from years of dormancy, and now it was coming out any way it could. And there were only so many ways it could come out.

Myles's tummy rumbled again. It sounded like there

was a far-off thunderstorm in there and felt like maybe a few lightning bolts too.

Myles automatically opened his mouth to apologise for the volume of his tummy gurgles, but what came out was an extended and multi-tiered burp that ran up and down at least two octaves.

'Sick tummy?' asked Teddy with extremely fake concern. 'Why don't I remove that problem?'

Myles understood this gibe well enough – Teddy intended to separate the twin's head from his body as fast as he could wind the crank connected to the wire round Myles's neck. The crank handle had a dual purpose: first, the act of cranking generated energy that powered a cell to heat the wire; then, when the wire reached the correct temperature, it automatically engaged and tightened round the object to be severed, in this case Myles's neck. Teddy adored the crank because it was his own design and not Myishi's, and its manual design reminded him of the Georgian laboratories where he had first tinkered with experimentation.

The cranking began with Lord Teddy enthusiastically whirling the crank handle round and round, enjoying the strength in his young limbs. The gear-and-cog system could have been more effectively sealed, and it spewed forth a stream of sparks that cascaded against Myles's helmet, which was very distracting and, in fact, the final factor in the activation of his magic. Had Myles been completely focused on the gastric symphony playing in his tummy, he might have held the magic behind gritted teeth and clenched butt cheeks. But the sparks drew his eye, and out popped Myles's gift.

As is often the case in Fowl misadventures, critical turning points unfold in seconds rather than hours, so let us check in on each protagonist in turn so we might clearly visualise the vectors:

Lord Teddy was gleefully cranking a charge into the heating unit while singing the disco classic 'Hot Stuff'.

Myles was distracted by the sparks cascading against the glass of his soon-to-be prison helmet and either did not or could not see that his stomach was actually distended by whatever forces were brewing within.

And the mysterious clone with unclear motivations was slowly turning his Clonoscopy gun on the oblivious clone next to him.

Now that the scene is set, we may proceed.

The clone spoke. 'Oh, dear,' it said. 'I appear to have shot my fellow guard.'

It did not register with Lord Teddy, in the heat of the moment, that a clone should not be speaking. He simply disagreed with the sentence itself.

'You stupid creature,' he said, still cranking. 'You haven't shot anyone.'

'Oh, but I have,' said the naughty clone, and it shot its fellow guard. The clone who was blasted did an almost perfect backflip, complete with landing, and then crumpled to the floor.

'I told you,' said the outlaw clone, and it quickly shot three more clones, who fell over on each other like skittles.

Teddy was still cranking, but slowly now while he digested this new turn of events.

'Stop shooting my clones, blast you!' he roared.

The outlaw turned his expletive into a question. 'Blast you, Lord Teddy? Don't mind if I do.'

And Princess Daphne, for it was, in fact, Her Royal Highness inside the clone's skin, shot Teddy with one of his own Clonoscopy rifles. It was a trifling charge, just enough to short out a clone's chip, but enough nevertheless to curl Teddy's burgeoning beard and turbocharge his cranking arm. And we all know what the crank was connected to.

While Teddy angrily smouldered and the possessed clone continued to mow down the duke's likenesses, Myles felt the heat of the approaching wire on the pale skin of his young neck and a kind of transmogrification took hold of him.

The various organs in his torso continued to expand alarmingly, as though stuffed with rodents, and his jaw swung open, wider than a human jaw had any right to swing. Myles was startled to hear dual clicks as it unhinged itself altogether and should have by rights lain uselessly on his chest. Instead, the jaw tucked itself underneath the tightening wire.

Oh no, thought Myles, who was far too clever not to realise what was happening to him. *Not this. Why can't I sprout wings? Or cough fireballs? Please not this.*

But it *was* this. And there was no putting the genie back in the bottle now.

Myles's teeth, which felt too large for his jaws, chomped down on the wire, severing it on both sides of his bite. He spat out the glowing section with no dental damage, which was impossible.

Unless he had the teeth and jaws of a dwarf.

And dwarves had other skills too.

The crank lost its tension, and Teddy's arm flailed

momentarily until, after a few revolutions, the duke took control of it.

'Blast you, Fowl!' he cried, and every humiliation Myles had ever visited upon him came rushing back. He saw clearly at that moment what a fool he'd been to toy with such an opponent, but he'd been so sure this time that sweet victory would be his. This form of epiphany concerning one or other of the Fowl boys was to become so common among criminal masterminds over the years that it came to be referred to as a *Fowlisation*, as in: *Doctor Crab Claws thought he could submerge Artemis in a vat of crustaceans, but he was in for a humiliating Fowlisation.*

Putting Fowlisations aside, Lord Teddy saw that there was still a path to victory, if he acted swiftly.

I must finish the boy now! he thought, which on the face of it was simplicity itself, as it only required that he drown Myles in his own nutrient juice.

Fruit smoothie indeed, he thought, and activated the cryo-helmet gel intake with a lever that clanked over several cogs when pulled, which Teddy, a twentieth-century man at heart, found most satisfying.

'Consider yourself juiced, Fowl,' he snarled, and then he turned his attention to the marauding clone.

'And you can consider juiced too, traitor!' he cried, drawing his own Clonoscopy pistol and firing off a shocker shell at the clone who was mowing down its fellows.

Obviously, the *consider yourself juiced* comment did not really apply in this case, but the duke was far too preoccupied to compose an appropriate dispatch quip for every single victim. It was such a shame, really, as there were several more appropriate options, including:

This will stop your cloning around.

Or

This might come as a shock to the system.

But the moment had passed, and so the juiced comment would have to do.

The clone jittered as though dancing frenetically in a cool Parisian nightclub, then toppled over, and Teddy, believing that the malfunctioning-clone issue was solved, turned to watch Myles Fowl finally die.

The problem with Teddy's analysis of the situation was that the clone issue was not really a clone issue. It was a possession issue, and the moment Princess Daphne was ejected from one body she simply slipped into another one and resumed her blasting. The remaining clones, who had not been ordered to fight back, just stood there until they fell down.

Teddy, who had previously been delighted to have slave beings obeying only his commands, now realised there was an obvious disadvantage to so much control.

A chap has to think of everything himself, he thought, and shot the new bad clone, who simply transferred to another body, and so on and so forth until the ranks of sentry clones were whittled down to half a dozen and then, shortly afterwards, just one. And this one turned on Teddy and gave him a look that seemed familiar somehow. Familiar and chilling.

While all this clone-culling was happening, Myles got on with the business of drowning in a gel, which, by some considerable coincidence, was a nanocomposite hydrogel, the same kind of substance currently slopping all over Specialist Lazuli Heitz. More about her later. For the moment, Myles's situation is the most immediately urgent, so we shall keep our focus on him.

By the tender age of twelve, Myles had already been embroiled in many bizarre fixes and would be in hundreds more. But some decades later, in his autobiography, *Myles Fowl: You People Do Not Deserve Me*, he listed the Childerblaine House transformation as the single biggest shock to his system in all the Fowl Adventures. This is hardly surprising, considering what was about to happen.

When Lord Teddy activated the mechanism, the crystal bio-egg began sealing beneath Myles's chin, and a clear preservative gel streamed through a dozen influx valves in the connection collar. But Myles's enlarged mouth managed to wiggle under the seal, and most of the gel went down his gullet and into a stomach that was already churning with stress acid and gas. There were no cheery foil unicorns in this gel and, even if there had been, their sharp edges would only have served to increase his discomfort. Myles tried his old trick of imposing order on the situation by narrating his way through it, but his speaking apparatus was thoroughly slimed, and his jaws were not operating in a way he was familiar with.

Strangely, though, he was not drowning as quickly as one might have expected. It seemed as though his stomach could accommodate the litres of gel pouring into it.

Of course, thought Myles. *This is my magic.*

And, while it was true that his tummy could hold the nutrient juice, that was not to say there were no consequences for his digestive organs. Myles's oesopha-gus, duodenum and intestines were all in revolt, tying themselves in crampy knots or skipping rope with each other. Myles felt as though he might explode, and this feeling was perfectly reasonable, especially since he was restrained by sturdy straps. Myles bent his neck as much as possible and squinted down past his glugging throat to see a torso that was rippling alarmingly and actually bursting through his shirt.

I am literally jumping out of my own skin, he thought.

And he would indeed rupture himself in several places were the straps to hold fast. It would turn out to be a tug of forces. Wind, leather and steel bolts.

None of this made sense at first or even second glance.

Myles knew that dormant magic must have been activated for this to be happening, but dwarf abdominal characteristics were not magical. They were physiological. It was the same with Lazuli's fireballs. Magic should not have been able to turn the specialist temporarily into a goblin, no more than it could have given him the organs of a dwarf.

Unless . . .

There was one theoretical way, which Myles vowed

to investigate at a later time, when his arms were not being wrenched out of their sockets by gastric forces.

While Myles endured his own internal struggles, Lord Teddy was stalking the Princess Daphne clone. In this particular game, he was the clear favourite. Teddy had been stalking prey since the age of five, while Daphne came from a time when hunting was very much the purview of males, and at any rate it was a so-called sport that the princess had never cared for.

Teddy placed his pipe in a sink and then retreated a few paces, concealing himself behind a rolling instruments trolley. Any experienced huntsman would recognise the burning pipe as an obvious lure, but Daphne was not experienced and approached a touch overconfidently, thinking that her cousin must be panic-stricken following the loss of his clone bodyguards.

She pointed her Clonoscopy rifle towards the sink and cried, 'And now, Cousin Teddy, you will pay the price for regicide!'

This was an inaccurate statement for two reasons.

1. The term *regicide* usually referred to kings, not princesses, so, even though it was technically correct, it was a little misleading. And . . .

2. Even if Daphne had managed to shoot Teddy, he would simply have jittered slightly, which was hardly the penalty for murder of any kind.

In any event, Daphne did not manage to shoot Teddy. The moment she leaned over the sink, Teddy took a potshot from his hiding place and dropped her like one of the highland deer whose heads the barbarous man had mounted in the banquet hall.

And then he thought about what the clone had said.

Cousin Teddy?

Regicide?

There was only one way for that to make sense.

As recently as a year previously, Teddy might have exclaimed, *What utter tosh! I don't believe in ghosts.*

But, considering the worlds revealed to him by the Fowl Twins in past months, Lord Teddy found himself willing to believe almost anything.

Daphne was for the moment gone, but she had bought Myles the time he needed to complete his involuntary transformation. The liquid-hydrogen tanks rattled in their housings as the boy's body-shakes increased in violence and Myles's frame blurred with the speed and ferocity of his lurchings. His flesh stretched to an extent that human flesh was not designed to stretch, and Lord Teddy could not ignore the cacophony of creaks and shrieks emanating from his X-frame. Myles, for his part, was consumed entirely by what was happening to him and had no available mind space for concocting a plan of any sort. He would have to literally go with the flow that was very shortly to arrive.

Teddy was not certain how to react. A large part of him was highly amused, as it was clear from the Fowl boy's face that he was not enjoying his ordeal, but beneath the duke's amusement was an undercurrent of dread that all these bodily shenanigans would herald a typical, barely credible Fowl escape.

Best to simply plug the scoundrel, thought Teddy, and he selected a second weapon from his belt. This time a classic Colt .45 revolver shooting good ole traditional bullets. No low-level electrical shocks for Myles. Straight to the afterlife for him!

Afterlife, thought Teddy. *I really must look into that once I have purged every last Fowl from my beloved island.*

And, in the American-cowboy style that he employed occasionally, Teddy shot from the hip.

And missed.

Sort of.

Teddy would not have missed had not a jet of air shot down Myles's trouser leg, rippling it like a car-showroom wind puppet, and tilted the X-frame a few degrees to the left. As a result, Teddy's bullet missed the boy's heart and struck one of the four liquid-oxygen tanks at such an angle that a stream of the cryogenic liquid hit the frame's central bolt. This contact, coupled with the continued vibrations passing through the apparatus, caused the bolt to shatter, thus releasing Myles from the central pole. The entire contraption toppled over so that Myles was left pointing diagonally upwards, his helmeted skull looking like a missile's warhead.

One more shot, thought the duke, but this time he aimed in a less cavalier fashion, supporting his right hand with a cupped left hand.

'Goodbye, Fowl,' he said.

But it was too late, for at that moment, much to Myles's horror and shame, the bottom fell out of his world, or, as tabloid newspapers would undoubtedly have quipped, given the opportunity, the world fell out of his bottom.

Although *fell* is altogether too understated a verb.

Myles felt it coming and, even from inside a helmet half filled with thick globs of nutrient juice, he managed to blurt a heartfelt, 'I'm sorry,' for the mortifying display he felt sure was imminent. The trouser-flapping squib was a mere taster, or *amuse-bouche* as the French might say, for the gargantuan explosion that was to come.

Even Lord Teddy seemed to realise that something even more out of the ordinary was occurring, because he hesitated with his finger on the trigger, which gave Myles's bodily functions a moment to initiate a flaming-Catherine-wheel exit.

For some reason, the entirety of Myles's expulsions continued down the same trouser leg as the first burst, leaving the left leg undisturbed. This was an occurrence that could be used to explain chaos theory, but for now all it meant was that the propulsion provided by the cocktail of gas, gel and magic clunked the X-frame on its side so that Myles was in effect in landscape mode. Momentarily at least, until a further pulse double-clunked him to portrait. On and on it went, sending Myles the hyper-flatulent and his X-frame cartwheeling across the laboratory. Had Beckett been there he would have been so proud, because it was in fact his twin's first formal gymnastics sequence, albeit one assisted by wind and metal. The flaming-Catherine-wheel effect was completed when the X-frame spokes sliced through a row of ancient Bunsen burners' rubber cables, setting loose several gas jets, which were promptly ignited by sparks raining from a cracked strip light. On a normal day for normal people, the orderly row of blue flame jets would have been quite extraordinary, but on this day in Childerblaine House they only merited a mention because the flames would momentarily creep back into the supply lines and cause the laboratory to explode.

Not that Myles would be aware of that fact, or any external facts, really, consumed as he was by the physical trauma of his transformation and the mental trauma this transformation was having on such an ordered mind. In layman's terms, what was happening to Myles was akin to tossing two diametrically opposed personalities into a blender and seeing what came out the other end. *The other end* being the operative phrase.

Somewhere in the back of Myles's mind, a shrill voice was screaming, *Make it stop! Make it stop!*

But he was not gassed out just yet. Myles continued to trace a flaming route around the laboratory, pinballing from wall to wall. At one point, his frame even mounted a workbench that ran the width of the laboratory, crunching its way across a priceless line of equipment. All the while, Myles's distended jaw clunked against the helmet, his teeth scratching the glass until it shattered, releasing the remaining nutrient juice, which proved to be highly flammable itself as it exploded in firework blasts on contact with sparks or gas jets.

In short, the Childerblaine laboratory was in complete and frenetic chaos.

Teddy was remarkably cool under the circumstances. He had always prided himself on his ability to remain calm under fire, and he was certainly under fire here – actual fire. The gas flames had spread to the lines that supplied the laboratory from large tanks bolted to the exterior of the walls. Teddy had been meaning, for perhaps fifty years, to replace the ancient rubber lines, but what with one thing or another (e.g. draining trolls of their venom, kidnapping children and trying to secure eternal life) he had never got round to installing safety valves.

And you'll pay for it now, Tedderick, old boy, he told himself.

But all was not lost. Even though there had seemed to be some form of spooky virus in one of his clones, he still had an ace in the hole. In this case, he had over a hundred aces in a very secret hole.

If I can make it to that hole, he told himself now.

Escape from this blasted laboratory is paramount before the Fowl boy destroys it entirely.

Any other child would destroy himself along with the lab, but Teddy had no illusions that Myles Fowl would bring about his own demise.

The little blighter is charmed, he realised. *He has more lives than a bag of cats.*

But with any luck the twin would lose a couple of limbs at least and live out his life in indescribable agony.

Cheered by this thought, Teddy removed himself from the laboratory at great speed, pausing only to scoop up his beloved pipe on the way past.

Myles was running out of fuel. He could feel himself slowing down, and his intellect quickly reasserted itself as the magic abated. The boy was mightily reassured to feel his own self rising to the conscious level, as a part of him had worried that he might be stuck in dwarf mode forever. However, reasserted intellect or not, there were issues that needed imminent solving, like, for example, how to detach himself from the

X-frame and escape this infernal place before the explosion, which was surely imminent.

I wish Beck were here, he thought. *He is better with explosions.*

But Beckett was not there, which Myles was mostly relieved about, and so his escape was up to him.

It was difficult to orchestrate an escape while cartwheeling with one's head inside a cracked and smeared glass egg, but Myles quickly realised that the only way out was down, so he jerked himself bodily to slightly alter the frame's trajectory and was rewarded with a lurching drop as one of the crossbeams thunked into a sink it otherwise might have missed. And, though it pained Myles both physically and emotionally to do it, he completed the manoeuvre with one final squib, which pole-vaulted the X-frame, and of course the attached boy, through the adjacent window.

The metal frame made short work of the window's glass, and Myles found himself for a brief moment suspended in the air ten metres above the grounds. His view was obscured by the shards from the shattered helmet glass and the habitual dense wreath of island cloud known as dragon's breath, but he got the impression of a pitched battle below.

What on earth is happening down there? Myles wondered as he hung in the air, perfectly framed by the setting sun if viewed from a certain vantage point.

But then the moment of suspension was over and, as Myles plummeted towards the sound of pitched battle, he had a sudden premonition that he was, as Uncle Foxy might say, jumping from the frying pan directly into the blooming fire.

13
THE TINY SPARK OF HOPE

AT THE PRECISE MOMENT THAT MYLES FOWL WAS plummeting earthward on St George's Island, Specialist Lazuli Heitz was, unbeknownst to herself, saving the world. This is perhaps a little hyperbolic, as the world itself would not have been destroyed, just the many millions of humans living on it, to the great relief, no doubt, of the planet's endangered species and over-stretched resources.

What happened was this: during one of the pod's scheduled bounces just north of the Azores, it crashed through the wall of a submerged volcano, flooding the crater with seawater and delaying a catastrophic eruption by several centuries. As an added bonus, the brief skid along the heated surface supercharged the pod's batteries so that when it ultimately arrived at its destination it would have quite a bit more energy than required, which would prove to be either fortuitous or catastrophic, depending on your point of view.

Inside the pod, Lazuli was enduring a rattling the

likes of which she had never known. If it hadn't been for the impact gel, she doubted there would be much more left of her than blobs on the pod wall. So far, the craft had bounced three times on the surface of the Atlantic, and Lazuli now knew that liquid was very unforgiving when approached at rates in excess of the speed of sound. Even her magical instincts thought she was doomed. Lazuli could feel the healing engine revving up inside her, but it never caught because she was out of fuel like a dry lamp.

If I die, I die, she thought. *I can't bring myself back, and there's nobody to help.*

But she would not die, could not die, because there were humans to save.

I am so fired, she realised. *Unless Myles can come up with something.*

Worst-case scenario: she arrived too late. The twins were dead and she would be thrown into Howler's Peak for her trouble.

Don't think about that, she told herself. *Focus on the tiny spark of hope that things might actually work out for the best.*

Easier thought than done.

Every now and then, when her vision steadied for a

second or two, Lazuli could see chunks of foam whipping past the porthole.

Shearing off, thought Lazuli. Soon the pod would be detectable to anyone who cared to look for it, or indeed at it. But Lazuli had no cause to worry on that front as the foam network would hold up remarkably well for a coating that had not been fully tested. It was the secret army of killer clones waiting for her she should have worried about.

CHILDERBLAINE ESTATE

A FEW MINUTES EARLIER

If we rewind to just before the spirit of Princess Daphne occupied the laboratory clone, we find Beckett in the barn's loft, feeling a little stunned by the recent turn of events. He had always prided himself on being ready for anything adventure-wise, but something had happened in the loft that no one could have foreseen, and the boy was not sure how his parents would feel about the pact he'd entered into.

I'll make a phone call to space later, he decided, *and ask Artemis. He'll know what to do.*

But Beckett had a feeling that even Artemis would

be stumped by this one. It was, as Myles might say, a genuinely unprecedented situation. His brothers were experts on the laws of science but not so great on relationships. They could both probably construct a human from donor cells and sticky tape, but neither brother was proficient at relating to one.

Beckett made a decision not to worry about it for now. Instead, he would follow up on his amazing plan and see if the ghosts he had implanted into the brain space of clones would be able to get Myles out of his prison frame. As plans went, Beckett knew that it was vague, to say the least, and his brother certainly would not approve. But, as Myles was currently strapped into an operating frame, he was in no position to belittle the plan, especially considering the extra-special commitment Beck had made to save his twin.

He should hug me for four days and go on social media to tell everyone how amazing I am.

But Myles wouldn't make any internet declarations, Beckett knew. Apart from his blog, *Myles to Go*, his twin rarely used social media to do anything except infiltrate large corporations that were trying to harvest personal data online.

I should get the hug, at least, thought Beckett now,

and the boy certainly deserved that much, providing Daff could actually get close to Lord Teddy, as she had promised.

The only hiccup with the strategy Beckett could see was that there were many more clones than ghosts. But Brigadier General Bleedham-Drye assured him that inferior numbers should not be an issue as long as the clones proved easy to infiltrate.

'We shall use the same tactics employed by Lawrence against the Turks,' Ronald had told him. 'Strike and move on.' This was a strategy often employed by Beckett himself, and so he gladly agreed to it.

When Beckett emerged from the converted barn through a side window, it did seem that the brigadier general's plan was proving to be a smashing success. The clones were being mown down seemingly by each other. But, with his augmented vision, Beckett could see the ghosts who were flitting from clone to clone, shooting the Teddy likenesses down with considerable gusto, which was understandable given the fact that it had been Teddy who'd murdered them in the first place. The clones had not been specifically instructed to defend themselves against themselves and were slow to respond. For some, this meant that their chips got shorted out and they became nothing more than inert matter once more. Eventually, others caught on and began to fight back, but even then they didn't know which of their brothers to shoot until it was too late. And, even if a clone did manage to get off a shot, their attacker simply skipped into another body. It was, as the brigadier general might say, a rout.

Beckett dropped to the gravel path that ran round the barn, picked up a discarded Clonoscopy rifle and joined the battle. He did not generally like or approve of guns, but he made an exception in this case because Myles was in such terrible danger and the rifles did not shoot fatal bullets but shocker charges. He ran in a zigzag pattern towards the main house, taking potshots as he went. His first few shots went wide, but, after he compensated for the slight kickback, he managed to knock out a few Teddy clones as he ran. Brigadier General Ronald appeared beside him, enjoying the sensation of being encased in flesh and blood after so many decades.

'The field is ours!' he crowed, his true form flickering in and out of dominance inside the clone. 'Teddy ignored the first rule of estate living: defend the castle.'

It all felt a little too easy to Beckett, and he wondered

if perhaps the duke had left a little surprise for any would-be invaders.

As if on cue, Beckett hurtled round the barn's gable end just in time to see the pair of metre-high stone dragons at either side of the door open their stone mouths to reveal pilot lights within.

Flame-throwers, thought Beckett. *That explains the long snouts.*

The flame-throwers may have proved formidable on any other day, but on the occasion of the Fowl twins' attack neither weapon had the chance to scorch so much as a blade of grass.

The first was blown to bits by Princess Daphne, who kicked open the front door and emerged on to the grounds wearing a clone she had found guarding the laboratory door and also a real dress and wig that matched her ghostly versions. In addition, she hefted a blunderbuss, which she used to blast the left-hand dragon to smithereens, releasing a jet of gas that burst into a blue-hot vertical flame.

'I'm starting to see the attraction of the hunt,' said Princess Daphne, turning the blunderbuss's flared muzzle on flame-thrower number two. Unfortunately for Beckett, who was squarely in the right-hand dragon's sights, this particular blunderbuss housed but a single shell, and all Daphne could produce from pulling the trigger again was a click, which was amplified by the conical barrel.

But not to worry because, as quickly as Beckett's luck had turned bad, it turned good again. The dragon barely had time to spurt a measly two-metre gout when it was skewered from above by a falling steel girder. The impact was so severe that Beckett winced, even though a stone dragon could not feel anything.

When the dust cleared, Beckett saw that there was a second girder attached to the first, and a figure was strapped into the frame.

That's Myles, he thought after maybe a second. *At least I think it's Myles.*

It took him another second to be absolutely sure because, even though the person was recognisably his twin, Myles didn't look like his usual buttoned-up self. In fact, his features were wearing an expression Beckett hadn't seen since a boy called Gumbo Marbles had force-fed Myles a beetle in nursery school.

He is totally panicked.

Beckett rushed to his brother's side. 'Myles,' he said. 'It's all right. I'm here.'

Myles's jaw was a little flappy, but he managed to put a sentence together. 'Get me down from here, Beck,' he said, and then, as if Beckett needed more proof that his brother was not altogether himself, Myles added, 'please.'

Please? thought Beckett, tugging on the leather straps. *What is going on here?*

14
THE WORLD'S MOST VERSATILE MATERIAL

IT TURNED OUT THAT THE ANSWER TO THE question *What is going on here?* was *Quite a lot, actually.*

Myles Fowl, a boy who was usually two steps ahead of the game, intellectually speaking, was forced to play catch-up, which did not sit well with him. In fact, he tried several times to butt in during Beckett's account, which he felt jumped to all sorts of ridiculously unscientific conclusions. And, while Beckett's account was indeed unscientific, it proved more accurate than Myles's efforts, which included the most errors he'd ever opined in a single conversation.

The first boo-boo was proposed as Beckett carried him from the front lawn to the barn. 'Beck, you have found a shoal of flying fish to ferry us to the mainland, and that is where we are going?'

In fairness to Myles, he was still a little woozy from the earth-shattering flatulence he had recently expelled, not to mention the litres of nutrient juice he'd ingested, which had been full of various chemicals.

'No, brother,' said Beckett while he jogged. 'We were trying to storm the main house, but steel shutters have clanged down inside.'

'Steel shutters made of flying-fish scales,' said Myles, holding on to the flying-fish theme with some determination.

'Exactly,' said Beckett, who was a kind boy. 'All stitched together by an octopus seamstress.'

'I knew it,' said Myles with satisfaction. 'A flying-fish scale is the world's most versatile material.'

This was also wrong. Seaweed is the world's most versatile material, as the twins would shortly find out to their detriment.

Beckett decided the rest of the catch-up could wait until they were safely tucked away in the barn. He shifted his grip on Myles, slinging him over one shoulder, and carried his brother up the ladder to the loft. Meanwhile, Brigadier General Ronald and his ghostly clone troops marched sentry below, in case Lord Teddy still had a few tricks up the sleeves of his lab coat.

Princess Daphne followed Beckett to the upper level and found a *chaise longue* under one of the many dustsheets. Beckett deposited his brother on its brocaded velvet and watched with some concern as his brother's tummy slowly contracted.

Princess Daphne spread the skirt of her beautiful, intricate gown. 'I found this in my old room, can you believe it? Teddy – the swine – kept my belongings even as he tossed my poor body from the clifftop.'

'It's shiny and gorgeous,' said Beckett. 'Though useless for climbing trees. Also, Teddy totally is a swine. He gets more swiney each time I bump into him. But I should stand up for real swine because pigs are actually pretty cool, though they don't share well.'

Daphne smiled. 'You are indeed wondrous strange, Sir Beck. You must think me strange too. A princess who walks, talks and speaks like a duke.'

Beckett took the Daphne clone's hand for real on this occasion. 'Daff. Maybe people would think you strange back in the olden days, but kids these days don't care about stuff like insides and outsides matching. And, even if I couldn't actually see the person inside with my ghost vision, I could still see the person inside, if you know what I mean. Anyway, as far as I can tell, no one's insides match their outsides, and anyone who says they do is pretending. Myles could probably explain all that better than me.'

'No one could explain it better, Sir Beck,' said Daphne. 'That was indeed well said. Close to a perfect speech, one would think.'

Beckett's speech may have been close to perfect, but Myles's words were not. The sweet moment between princess and knight was shattered by Myles's babbling about his own recent bodily functions in an explicit manner that was quite shocking for someone who had not been off the island in a hundred years.

'Dear me, Sir Beck,' she said in the voice of a young Lord Teddy. 'Is that what passes for polite subject matter these days, within earshot of a princess, no less?'

'Not in our house, Daff,' said Beckett, wondering precisely what had happened to his brother and why one leg of his trousers was shredded but not the other. 'I do enjoy a good fart joke, but I will swear off that sort of childish behaviour now, of course. Now that I'm a—'

Myles interrupted him. 'Now that you're a ghost whisperer.' Which was the first accurate or at least coherent statement he'd made in a while.

Beckett considered this. 'Yes. That's a good way to put it, brother.'

Myles's wits appeared to be returning along with his usual shape. Before Beckett's eyes his brother's distended belly shrank to its normal size and his eyes regained their focus.

'Beckett, I imagine your gift of tongues helped you connect with the spirits.'

Beckett did not want to tell the recovering Myles that he was wrong yet *again* because it might traumatise him, so instead he said, 'You are nearly right, brother. It was your injections that did it, but I pressed the plunger six times.'

Myles sat up. 'Of course! You stumbled on the correct dosage! Quick, brother, hand me my spectacles.'

Beckett pulled them out of his pocket and asked questions while he did so. 'How did you escape, brother? Did you turn the nitrous oxide into jet fuel? Is Teddy dead? I don't want him to be dead, but it would be a relief, so is he dead? Can we go home now? Mum and Dad need to meet Daphne.'

Myles refused to answer any questions until he had dosed himself with the injectacles. He spoke as he waited for the drops to take effect. 'My magic was activated, and that is how I escaped,' he said, blinking.

This was big news.

'Your magic!' exclaimed Beckett. 'That is huge. Was it cool, your magic?'

Myles blinked some more. 'If by *cool* you mean *impressive* or *in vogue* as opposed to *at a low temperature*, then no, it was not cool. I was, in effect, transformed into a dwarf, as far as my digestive system was concerned. Somehow, my expulsions provided propulsion, if you see what I mean.'

Beckett could have cried with envy. 'Do you mean to say you farted yourself out of a window? Because, if that is what you meant to say, then, brother, you are so wrong, because that's the coolest thing I have ever heard. What do you think, Daff?'

Myles's ghost vision kicked in just then and he saw the princess inside the clone.

'I am not sure if all this talk of farts is cool, dear Sir Beck,' she said, 'but perhaps this word *cool* has more than one meaning.'

'Curious,' said Myles, who seemed altogether himself now. 'I can not only see the spirit, I can also hear her. Whether I can actually hear her or whether my mind is interpreting is something that warrants further investigation.'

Daphne was a little put out by Myles's impersonal

style of conversation. 'I, too, can hear, boy. I can hear you talking about me as though I were not in fact here.' She turned to Beckett. 'Is he always like this?'

'Oh no,' Beckett assured her. 'He's usually worse.'

'The really strange thing,' continued Myles, eager to assert his brainpower over his fartpower, 'is that the resident revenant seems to be aping the appearance of the host body, perhaps subconsciously, if ectoplasm can indeed have a subconscious.'

Beckett winked at the princess. 'You see? I told you he was smart. Myles will solve your problem.'

But Daphne was not at all happy with Myles's theory. 'I assure you, silly boy, that I am not aping anyone. These are the very clothes I was poisoned in. I found them in my bedchamber, undisturbed for a hundred years.'

Beckett felt that now he should stick up for apes, which were being cast in a poor light. 'But if you were aping someone, Daff, and it was pointed out, then the pointer-outer would be actually paying you a great compliment because apes have amazing instincts and they can hang from a branch by one finger, which is something any sensible person wishes they could do.'

Myles, who could never read a room, held up three

fingers in front of Daphne's face. 'Speaking of fingers, how many fingers can you see, spirit?'

'How many fingers?!' the princess fumed, unaccustomed to such familiarity. 'I should have you executed. Sir Beck, are you sure this insolent commoner can solve our ascension problem?'

Beckett winked at her and said slowly, 'I doubt it, Daff. It's a really tough problem. Probably impossible even for apes. In fact, I'm not sure even Artemis, who is the smart one in our family, could solve that brain-busting problem.'

Myles may have been emerging from trauma, but he knew reverse psychology when he heard it. 'I know what you're doing, Beck,' he said. And then: 'Nevertheless, tell me a little more about this ascension problem.'

'Sir Ronald should tell you about it,' said Beckett. 'He has a theory. I'll fetch him when he's finished guard duty. Teddy might launch a counterattack.'

Myles, with typical brash overconfidence in spite of his recent brush with decapitation, pooh-poohed this idea.

'Fetch him now,' he said. 'Trust me, Teddy's days of launching counter-attacks are over. A chap can only withstand so many humiliations before he throws in the towel. Take my word for it, the next time we see Teddy, he will be grovelling for forgiveness.'

Poor Myles. Wrong again, for Teddy was already setting up his counter-attack and, what's more, he would die before grovelling for forgiveness. But, given his preference, he would kill before grovelling in front of a Fowl twin.

As wrong as Myles was, he went on to commit his biggest blunder of all. 'And have Whistle Blower see if he can track the duke,' he said. 'No one alive has more acute senses than that troll.'

Beckett's face told Myles that he had said precisely the wrong thing.

The Island of St George, the Scilly Isles

There was a hidden cave on St George that once upon a time could only be accessed by crawling under a rock shelf on the south-western corner of the island, and even then only during the lowest quarter of the tide. Teddy's cousin Rafe had shown it to him one summer afternoon. Naturally, Teddy had orchestrated Rafe's drowning in that very same cave tunnel some years later, reasoning that his cousin could hardly expect to reveal the existence of a secret lair and then live to tell someone else about it. All it had required was mixing several drops of a home-made potion into Rafe's hot chocolate so that the boy dropped off to sleep halfway through the tunnel.

Over the years, the duke had commissioned successive teams of engineers to excavate the space and dig a tunnel from the main house so that he would not have to use the sea door he'd also installed. The engineers' boats invariably developed explosive steam-engine problems on their return journeys to the mainland, so the existence of the cave had remained a secret, and it would remain a secret now that he had collapsed it behind him.

Teddy's father had not taught him many lessons worth learning. Respect for the monarchy was drummed into him, of course – which was why he had coveted the Lionheart ring and mourned its loss still – but the most important lesson his father, an inveterate con man, had hammered into him was: *Always have a fallback position.*

'If a fellow is forced to sound the retreat,' he'd often

told Teddy, usually after a thrashing for some offence or another, 'respect has been lost, so that fellow must return forthwith, wielding the hammer of vengeance to take back what is, by gift of God and King, rightfully his.'

Thank you, Father, thought Teddy now as he surveyed the legion of seaweed-based goblin clones he had grown in his secret cave lab. *Finally, your meaning is clear, and I have my hammer of vengeance. A legion of hammers, in fact.*

Teddy was being somewhat melodramatic, he knew. After all, even though the term *legion* was simply another word for *many*, there were traditionally up to five thousand soldiers in a legion.

I certainly don't have five thousand soldiers, Teddy had to admit as he sliced through rows of fluid sacs, dumping the immature seaweed goblins on to the cave floor. *But I do have many.*

THE BARN'S LOFT, CHILDERBLAINE HOUSE

Meanwhile, oblivious to the seaweed-goblin-clone threat, Princess Daphne and Sir Ronald were bringing the twins up to speed on Teddy's sordid century of avunculicide, familicide, matricide, patricide, nepoticide and sororicide. Thankfully, there was no prolicide, but this was only because Teddy had committed uxoricide.

Princess Daphne was just finishing the tragic story of her death as less than five hundred metres away the goblin clones were having their hearts pierced with adrenalin shots to wake them up.

'And so that beastly Teddy poisoned my hot chocolate,' she explained to the twins. 'Which I have since found out was one of his favourite tricks. He searched my possessions for the Lionheart ring, which would literally have handed him the seal of power, then tossed my body into the ocean. He kept my things, though, in case the ring turned up, but he never found it. I'd hidden it too well, you see.'

'Permission to speak, Your Highness?' asked Ronald, twitching his magnificent ghostly moustache.

'Permission granted,' said Beckett, and for some reason this made Daphne giggle.

'Poison was certainly a favourite method of Teddy's,' he said. 'He used it on me too. A few drops in my evening sherry. We'd all heard the stories of relatives going missing, but I let my guard down for a glass of amontillado. I knew after the first sip that the rich, nutty flavour had been corrupted. *That's it for you, Ronald, old boy*, I told myself, and it was. The worst part of the entire sorry affair was watching Teddy feed my body piece by piece to his blasted eels.'

Myles had recovered himself completely by now and straightened his distressed suit as best he could. *Why is it*, he wondered, *that our adventures always play havoc with a person's wardrobe?*

Myles was perfectly aware that he was focusing on his semi-shredded trousers to subdue the little voice that was screaming, *Some genius you turned out to be! Whistle Blower is dead. You have let Beckett down, you have let your family name down and, worst of all, Artemis might hear about it. Not to mention the fact that you almost had your own head pickled and only escaped because your posterior exploded.*

Myles made a concerted effort to turn down the volume on this little voice, something he knew would not be healthy in the long term.

I will do some mirror therapy later, when we leave this accursed island, he decided. But for now he knew he should probably turn his brainpower towards fulfilling the bargain Beckett had entered into with these spirits.

'So,' he said, steepling his fingers in classic brainy-person fashion. 'You wish to ascend?'

'We do, Master Fowl,' said Princess Daphne, who was still holding Beckett's hand.

'Sir Beck assured us that you were the fellow for the job,' the brigadier general added. 'And, should your rescue be successful, you would see to our ascension.'

Myles felt a point should be made. 'Technically, I did rescue myself.'

Sir Ronald's clone guffawed, as did the ghost inside it. 'Rescued yourself? I think you'll find, my boy, that your so-called rescue was woefully incomplete. It would have left you surrounded by armed clones.'

That was a good point, and Myles conceded it with a nod. 'In that case, you have my thanks,' he said. 'Now, to your issue. It seems to me that the problem is one of energy, or lack thereof.'

Beckett squeezed Daphne's fingers. 'There, you see? Myles said "thereof". Only science brainiacs say *thereof*. Sometimes he says *thus* too. And occasionally *ergo*. He can definitely get you ascended.'

'There is another problem,' said Sir Ronald. 'Our

family tunnel only appears when there is a Bleedham-Drye death, and we have no desire to sacrifice a living person. Except perhaps Teddy.'

Myles stood and paced, the floorboards squeaking with each step. 'The universe is composed of energy,' he said. 'And by resisting ascension for so long you have drained your batteries, so to speak. What you need is a boost while you are airborne, to get you over the final hurdle. A boost that is compatible with your own energy signature, which would seem to be spectral and DNA-coded. There would be little point in showering you with the wrong kind of energy. It would be like trying to power a solar battery with avocados.'

'What's a solar battery?' asked Daphne.

'And what the deuce is an avocado?' added Sir Ronald.

Myles saw his mistake. 'Never mind. Anachronistic examples from your perspective. Let's stick with the facts. I have, by considerable coincidence, been studying this precise form of energy for my current project, which is why we can see you. To summarise, human beings secrete many things, among them ectoplasm. This gauzy substance is inert and perfectly safe without a detonator, as it were. Sometimes it can be resentment that allows the spirits to imprint their likeness on the ectoplasm. Until recently, fairies had been using ectoplasm to power many devices – their Moonbelts, for example, using magic as a detonator – but ectoplasm is difficult to contain, and the devices were actually disrupting the wearers' magnetic fields . . .'

Myles glanced up from his packing and realised he had lost the room. Nothing but blank stares.

He sighed.

It was the fate of the genius to be misunderstood. What he was explaining now would be common knowledge in a hundred years, but, looking at the confused faces in the loft, Myles had to accept the fact that he might have been better off sticking with the avocado imagery.

'Haven't you been eavesdropping on Teddy at all?' he asked. 'The duke is a first-rate scientist. Not on my level, of course, but certainly better than my brother Artemis.'

'One has not been in the laboratory much until this very day,' admitted the princess. 'Science is so very tedious.'

'Finally,' said Beckett. 'I've been saying that for years.'

Myles sighed once more. A sigh that he hoped, along with his highfalutin lecturing, would cement an impression of him as a frustrated genius rather than a cartwheeling flatulence juggernaut.

'Very well. Here is what I propose. Once we have confirmed that Teddy is no longer a threat, I will adapt his spectrometer so that I may study your energy signatures and see if we can't replicate the Moonbelt effect while you are attempting, as a group, to ascend. The operation itself would have to be timed to the millisecond, which I will leave to Beckett, as he is a master of split-second timing.'

'I am!' said Beckett. 'You should see my pizzas.'

'I would love to see your pizzas,' said Daphne, who, having somehow not heard of pizzas, mistakenly suspected that Sir Beckett must own property in Italy.

'It will require quite a feat of engineering,' continued Myles, 'but, if we start immediately, I am confident that after several weeks of intense trials we can move every spirit on to the next plane of existence using some kind of superlight ectoplasm-detonation network.'

'Several weeks?' said Sir Ronald, rising to his feet. He was initially crestfallen but quickly reasserted his stiff upper lip. 'I suppose we have waited this long. What's another month in the grand scheme, eh?'

'Exactly,' said Beckett. 'And Daphne can hang out with me. After all, we're friends now.'

Ronald glanced out of the window. 'I think that perhaps Lord Teddy's tail is not as far down between his legs as we might like.'

Myles was unconvinced. 'Really, Sir Ronald? That scoundrel has been thrashed one too many times. The psychology of bullies dictates that somewhere inside the main house Teddy is weeping uncontrollably and regretting every decision he ever made.'

Ronald's head bonked against the barn wall as he tried to pass through it, forgetting he wore a cloak of skin and bone. 'Pardon me,' he said, embarrassed. 'I'm such a blithering fool. It's been so long, you see.' The brigadier general adjusted his course and peered through the stained-glass window. 'I fear you may be mistaken, Master Fowl, for Rafe has returned, you see.'

Daphne sighed. 'Poor Rafe, the youngest of us. Drugged and drowned.'

Myles joined Ronald at the window. 'So this chap Rafe has returned. What of it?'

'Rafe is one of my scouts,' explained Sir Ronald. 'I sent a couple of them to the main house, and Rafe to search the island. No one knows it like him, especially the underwater cave where Teddy has his secret laboratory.'

Now Myles was interested. *Of course* Teddy had an underwater cave laboratory. What kind of criminal mastermind worth the title would not have an underwater laboratory? His own father had several subaquatic lairs dotted around the world's oceans.

'Secret laboratory!' he snapped at Ronald. 'You didn't think that was worth mentioning earlier?'

The brigadier general's clone blushed. 'I'm sorry, young fella. This is all happening so blooming fast.'

Beckett was quicker on the uptake when it came to matters of combat, caves and outdoorsy stuff in general. 'Is Rafe still inside a clone body?'

To answer this, Rafe himself shimmered into view, bowing to the princess. 'Your Highness,' he said. 'I am sorry to say that my lovely new body was blasted into pieces by Teddy's monsters. The duke has awoken his devils' army, and they are about to storm the barn. They are impervious to possession and, what's more, we are both outnumbered and outgunned.'

There was not a single good-news item in this collection of sentences. The twins had barely had time to draw breath and now they were under attack once more.

'I wish Laz was here,' said Beckett. 'She's nearly as good at fighting as I am. She knows all about battles.'

Sir Ronald's face was grim and determined. 'I didn't get these medals for cricket,' he said. 'I know a thing or two about battles myself.'

Beckett saluted. 'Of course, Brigadier General. What do you need me to do?'

'You protect the princess,' Ronald replied, and then to Rafe, 'and you assemble the troops.'

'And me?' asked Myles, actually prepared to take guidance in the face of a monster-army attack.

'You put your brain to work,' said the brigadier general. 'When Teddy gets in here – and he will get in here – we need a brilliant plan. And your brother tells me you're an actual genius.'

'That I most certainly am,' said Myles, attempting a crisp salute, which, because of his coordination issues, ended up being a slap on his own nose.

Ronald huffed. 'Genius indeed. Heaven help us.'

And he hurried down the ladder to address his soldiers.

Lord Teddy was jubilant. Like a phoenix, he had risen from the ashes. In fact, he had done more than simply rise. He was surging to victory with his home-grown legion of seaweed clones. If he could not be king of England, then at least he could be king of his own secret army. Not so secret any more, of course, but they had been grown in absolute secrecy. Even Ishi Myishi, his arms dealer, was ignorant of these boyos – of course he was. Only a complete dunce revealed all his plans, and Teddy was many things, but he was no dunce. In fact, though someone not so far away might have disputed this, he was a scientist to rival Myles Fowl himself – not with the same level of instinct, granted, but Teddy had been at this game a long time and had forgotten more than Myles had had time to learn. So, when he'd come by cloning technology from a rogue dwarf and a goblin skin shed by one of his mercenary team, it seemed downright wasteful not to combine the two with seaweed and grow a secret army of goblin clones. Frankly it was, as the youngsters would say, a no-brainer. Not that the clones would have their own brains per se, inasmuch as they could make independent decisions. He had imprinted their orders on them upon activation, and now they would follow those orders until they died. *Protect the duke. Kill his enemies.*

Whatever virus had spread through the original clones could not have infected these chaps.

I will wipe the Fowls off my island, thought the duke now as he followed his phalanx of two hundred seaweed-based goblins up from the sea door towards the barn. *And I will have my warriors burn those Teddy clones to ashes no matter how dashed handsome they may be.*

SOMEWHERE OVER THE ATLANTIC

It had been several years since there'd been a helmet-vomit episode during a Fowl Chronicle. The most well-known ones being when the LEP had attempted to storm Fowl Manor following the infamous siege. Several LEP officers had thrown up in their helmets thanks to magical nausea brought on by a ten-thousand-year-old hex that prevented them entering a human dwelling uninvited. The enigmatic demon warlock known only as N°1 had subsequentially lifted this anachronistic hex, among others, but not before leaked helmet-cam footage of decorated officers coating the insides of their visors with the insides of their tummies spread across fairy social media.

Specialist Heitz could not help but flash on those video clips now as she felt her own stomach flip while the bouncing pod sped towards its fourth touchdown of the trip. She had been travelling now for what seemed like an age, and it felt as though there was a kitchen blender turned up to the max churning her last meal into a chunky fizz.

Don't do it, she told herself. *Hold it down.*

Lazuli couldn't even remember what she'd had for her last meal, but she had the feeling she would find out soon enough.

The pixel wasn't particularly squeamish. If she did throw up, it wouldn't be the first time by any means, but there were consequences to puking in a helmet beyond embarrassment. The new LEP models could perform a purge and complete air change in under a second, but this was not a new model by a long shot. This model was so old that Lazuli had never even seen one outside a training exercise, where obsolete equipment was routinely trotted out for cadets to play around with.

The main consequence was the fact that should she lose her lunch, or whatever meal it had been, she would have to hold her breath for as long as possible and then pop her visor or not, depending on what she preferred to drown in, vomit or gel.

What a way to go. If Mother could see me now.

But Mother would not see her die any more than she had seen her live, and Lazuli realised at this moment of concentrated crisis that this was the biggest regret of her life: She had never found her mother.

I will find her, she thought now with her usual determination. *I will keep my insides inside and try again.*

But the pod had other ideas, and ten seconds later the impact emptied both her lungs and stomach.

Which was a real problem, as Lazuli still had four hundred miles to go.

Beckett had been instructed to protect the princess, but it was a flawed order because he could not protect a ghost, and in any event the princess had no desire to hang back and be protected. It was the first time in so long that Daphne had been involved with something real that she wished with all her heart to be fully engaged with it.

'I must enter the fray, Sir Beckett,' said the princess. 'My family needs me.'

Beckett did not argue. When someone's family needs them, they go. Simple as that. Everyone knows that rule.

'I'll go too,' he said. 'Perhaps these monster guys can be cluster-punched. There's only one way to find out.'

Something had been bothering Myles. 'Princess, why do you refer to my brother as *Sir* Beck? We are not from a royal family.'

Beckett had the answer to that one. 'I'm a knight now. King George gave Daff one knight card, and she played it on me.'

Daphne elaborated. 'I was the king's favourite. His Majesty was concerned that I would be ignored at court and forced to marry someone I did not love. And so he gave me the Lionheart ring so I would not be interrupted and made a royal decree that I could knight a single suitor in his place, so that I might marry for love.'

At that moment, something in Daphne's expression reminded Beckett of his twin, who was coincidentally wearing a similar expression. 'I bet you two have a plan,' he said. 'Is it the same one?'

'I do have a plan, Sir Beck,' said Daphne. 'It may sound a little ludicrous, but it might just give Teddy pause long enough for you and your brother to leave this island alive.'

'I think I know what you have in mind, Princess,' said Myles. 'It may be ludicrous, but no more ludicrous than this day has been so far.'

'I love ludicrous plans,' said Beckett. 'They are without doubt my absolute favourite.'

Daphne's eyes twinkled with ectoplasm. 'So, does Sir Beckett wish to proceed with my plan even without details?'

'I do,' said Beckett, and this response made the princess smile, which should have given the boy a hint as to where this was going.

Daphne removed one glove and clicked her royal thumb and forefinger, summoning a dour-faced Bleedham-Drye spectre from the ether who was clad entirely in black except for a white ring collar at his wattled neck.

'Oh,' said Beckett.

And then, when the light bulb turned on: 'Ooh.'

And, though Myles subsequently denied this, it did appear that, during the rite that followed, he cried just a little bit.

They all went downstairs to the battleground, even Myles, who might not be of much practical use but had at least studied Scipio and Napoleon, among other military strategists. He quickly discovered that the brigadier general was every bit the equal of these campaigners and would doubtless have made the history books had not Teddy ended his career prematurely. Sir Ronald had stationed two clones at every window with extra Clonoscopy rifles stacked at their feet, and had sent his finest pair of marksmen to the roof to pick off any goblins who made sorties up the approach path.

It was obvious, however, that this was a battle they were doomed to lose. The odds were overwhelming. Generally, these exact kind of odds worked out well for the twins, but in battle a cohort could not triumph over a legion. It simply wasn't possible. All Sir Ronald could hope to do was keep Teddy and his troops at bay until there was a natural disaster of some kind. A tsunami or perhaps a cyclone that only swept up green-skinned monsters.

And, given the track record of the twins, perhaps that might have happened had not the monsters begun to spit fireballs at the barn.

Sir Ronald squinted through a gap in the shutters and began swearing at length and with some invention, finishing off with: '. . . blooming balls of fire now! It is just one thing after another on this campaign.'

Beckett appeared at his shoulder. 'It's always like this on our adventures.'

Sir Ronald kicked the wall and it clanged. 'At least the barn is not wooden like it used to be. That should slow the blighters down.'

'No,' said Myles. 'This barn was rebuilt with steel cladding. We will be cooked as though we were in an oven, which we are, effectively.'

This theory was quickly proven when a clone standing too close to the main door, where the fire was concentrated, collapsed to the ground, its head running like tallow, leaving the previous occupant staring down at it.

'There are no more bodies to enter,' said the ghost, who had once upon a time been Princess Daphne's cousin and lady-in-waiting.

Fireballs struck the walls like cannonballs, buckling

the steel and conducting thunderous sound waves along its grooves. The noise was phenomenal. The twins felt as though they were in the eye of a storm, and several ghosts vacated their hosts out of sheer shock.

'Stand firm!' roared Sir Ronald. 'These monsters can't do anything to you! They can't even see you.'

The Bleedham-Drye spectres repossessed their hosts and fought on under Sir Ronald's direction. The snipers continued to take potshots from the roof, and, though they soon found range with their Clonoscopy rifles, there were always more goblins to step into the holes in the ranks. More ghost clones switched rapidly from one wing of the barn to the other, taking shots at the goblin flanks, trying to sow confusion and chaos. Perhaps these tactics might have worked on emotional beings, but the clones had zero regard for their own lives. As for Lord Teddy, he kept himself safely shielded by ranks of seaweed-goblin-clone slaves, even though his own brain function could have withstood several direct Clonoscopy hits.

The reptilian goblins were not fully cooked, so to speak, and trailed strands of seaweed behind them as they literally unravelled while they marched. This led to some slippings and tanglings that might have been comical from a perspective other than the one inside the boiling barn.

The goblins' rolling side-mounted eyes were not historically evolution's finest moment, as goblins were forced to lick their own eyes for moisture, but these seaweed clones found that their tongues were little more than desiccated leathery flaps, and, when embedded instinct commanded them to lick their eyes, their raspy, sandpaper tongues plucked their eyeballs right out of their sockets. And still they kept loosing fireballs, often doing more damage to their own ranks than the ghost clones could ever do, because even though actual goblins were to a certain extent fireproof the seaweed versions certainly were not. Their seaweed popped like bubble wrap as they went up in flames, and more often than not the clone who spat the fireball went up in flames itself as a result. All in all, they were a most imperfect creation.

If the battle could have been extended, then perhaps the mindless seaweed goblins would have whittled themselves down to manageable numbers, but all this was part of Teddy's plan. He was prepared to sacrifice as many clones as he needed to. After all, he could always grow more.

Inside the barn, the temperature rose rapidly, and in places rivets popped from their housings like bullets.

The twins had no choice but to retreat to the centre of the barn and from there up to the loft, even though that was exactly the path the superheated air would shortly follow.

'Please go with them, Your Highness,' Sir Ronald begged Daphne. 'I can't allow Teddy to kill you again, even if you're not exactly you.'

'I do have a trick up my sleeve, Uncle,' said the princess. 'Or in my wig, to be more precise, but only if I can confront Teddy.'

'Go,' said Ronald, moustache quivering. 'I'll hold them as long as I can. After that, it's up to the Fowl boy to see us through to the other side.'

'I thank you for your sacrifice, Uncle,' said Daphne. 'And His Majesty thanks you.'

'*Her* Majesty at the moment,' corrected the brigadier general, then he turned back to his troops.

And bravely he continued to command even as his soldiers were melted out of their bodies and Sir Ronald himself was the last man standing.

Might as well go out in style, he thought and, taking a Clonoscopy rifle in both hands, he charged straight out the front door, firing as he went, hoping against hope that he would manage to hit Teddy. And – will wonders never cease? – one slug ricocheted off a particularly crusty seaweed scale and clipped the duke's ear, an impact that caused minor burns but major irritation.

'Torch that clone!' the duke commanded, though there was no need to verbalise the command, as the seaweed goblins were programmed to protect the duke from assailants and this pale lookalike was definitely that.

At any rate, whichever command the goblins followed, follow it they did, and Sir Ronald's clone was consumed instantly. The clones themselves felt no pain, but the brigadier general experienced plenty of emotional anguish as he hovered above his recent vessel.

I miss it already, he thought glumly. And then he realised: *I was cold! I had forgotten how smashing it is for a fellow to feel cold.*

Sir Ronald made one final fruitless attempt to occupy a seaweed goblin, then jogged through mid-air to the loft, where the others waited nervously.

To be fair, the mood was more grim than nervous. The Fowl Twins were reasonably certain that this was the end of the line. After all, who could have predicted seaweed-goblin-clone slaves? *Absolutely no one* was the answer to that, but still Myles could not help berating himself.

'I can't believe I didn't anticipate this,' he said, mopping his streaming brow with a ragged Gloop tie. 'Of course there would be seaweed-based goblin clones. If I had a goblin skin lying around, that's exactly what I would do.'

Beckett tugged his own Gloop tie. 'I'm glad we didn't clone Gloop, even though we could've had an army of special-forces goldfish. It would have been wrong to clone a friend.'

'Absolutely,' said Myles and, if Beckett had been watching his brother's face, he might have noticed a flush that had nothing to do with the heat. 'That would be terrible. Who would try something like that while his twin was visiting Uncle Foxy in Norfolk last year? Not Dr Myles Fowl, that's for certain.'

Beckett used the Gloop tie to cover his mouth, but that didn't help his breathing much. So he dropped it and said, 'Are you going to say your last words, brother?'

Myles was shocked. Beckett was the eternal optimist of the two, but apparently not so eternal if he was asking Myles to quote his own *last words*, which of course Myles had practised for years.

Weep not for me; weep for a world without me.

The idea that Beckett, the human ray of sunshine, was feeling defeated gave Myles the little shot of determination he needed to set his final delaying tactic in motion. It might buy them only a few minutes, but who knew what could happen in a few minutes? Whole galaxies had collapsed in less time.

'No final words, brother mine,' he said. 'It's time for one last roll of the dice. We need to get Teddy up here.'

Teddy had zero intention of going into the barn. He was done toying with the Fowl Twins. He'd done that before, not a hundred metres from this very spot, and all it had got him was a skull-cracking eviction from his own body. So on this occasion he was more than content to keep his distance and let his seaweed goblins fry the twins in the giant makeshift pizza oven the barn had become.

Just a few minutes more, Teddy, old boy, he told himself, *and the Fowl chapter in your life will be up in smoke.*

It certainly seemed hopeless for the twins, though those among us who have studied Fowl history know that the family in general does some of their best work when hopelessness rears its head. But not this time, even if Myles's little delaying tactic did actually delay the inevitable. Inevitable was still inevitable.

Teddy surveyed the devastation he had wrought and saw that it was not bad. Yes, his clones were unravelling and would hardly last much longer than the barn, and in truth the loss of the barn bothered him a bit more than the loss of the clones, as he'd had it refurbished recently. But in the end, all things considered, both were a small price to pay for the final and comprehensive death of the Irish devil spawn.

'Irish devil spawn!' he said aloud, enjoying the sound of it.

Tomorrow things could get back to something approaching normal. He would have any surviving clones tidy up the remains of their brothers before tossing themselves into the ocean, all under the cover of the ethereal concentric rings of fog that shrouded St George for an average of two hundred days per year, due to a combination of its particular positioning on the southern tip of the Scilly Isles, the prevailing winds and the unusually high temperature of the landmass itself. So, as far as any spy satellites were concerned, it was mystery as usual on the island of St George, thanks to the ever-present dragon's breath.

Mentally, the duke was already enjoying the tremendous feeling of relief that would come with dispatching the twins, which as everyone knows tempts fate almost as much as mastermind monologuing. In fact, the fairy Hey Hey Monks, who are very much in tune with the universe and make lists about such things, have written in their scrolls that the only activity that is almost guaranteed to provoke a response from fate, destiny or the cosmos – whatever you wanted to call it – was a criminal mastermind on the brink of achieving his or her goals making a definitive statement about something he or she would or would not do.

So, when the duke stepped to the front of his legion and shouted over the sound of buckling metal, 'Burn in hell, Fowl Twins. There will be no reprieve this time. Nothing in the world could make me stop this assault and come in there,' it was almost inevitable that the clone occupied by Princess Daphne would stick her upper body through the only window frame not glowing red and call out:

'If I melt, Cousin Teddy, the Lionheart ring melts with me.'

The duke thought about this for a moment, weighed the pros and cons and then, having stroked the air where his luxuriant beard used to be, said to his seaweed clones, 'Stop the assault! I'm going in there.'

TEDDY DID NOT SIMPLY WALTZ INTO A BOILING building. Instead, he ran through the various possibilities and scenarios while the twins sensibly took advantage of the ceasefire to throw open the various hatches and windows, allowing the barn to cool down to a bearable temperature.

The duke, who was taking absolutely no chances with his own safety, was more than willing to take chances with that of his clones. To that end, he sent an occasional seaweed-based biped to stand near the barn's main door and, if the goblin's bubbles popped, essentially tearing the clone apart, Teddy would remark thoughtfully, 'Still too hot,' and go back to his musings.

It would seem as though the clone wearing Princess Daphne's dress and wig had somehow become convinced it was indeed Daphne. And, if that were somehow true, then by extension that clone could conceivably know where the Lionheart ring was.

To possess the ring after all this time would give me a claim to the throne, the duke thought.

It might seem ridiculous, Teddy knew, to think that way. It was just a ring, after all, but his was a family of traditions. And the most established tradition in any noble family was to marry or murder your way as high up the royal ladder as possible. For Teddy, the duchy had been as high as he could ever hope to climb and he had resigned himself to that, but, with the Lionheart ring on his finger, he'd have a claim to the crown itself. Perhaps not a legitimate claim that would bear a stress test, but the world was in such turmoil that the famous Lionheart ring and well-documented inscription would certainly be enough to rally some of the more traditionalist royals around.

'King Teddy the First,' murmured the duke now. And he certainly liked the sound of that.

Teddy glanced towards the barn and saw that the latest clone sacrifice had not exploded from boiling bubbles, and so it was safe to enter. He knew that this was in all likelihood a delaying tactic, and he also knew that Myles Fowl would use every extra second of life to plot against him, so, if he was to actually do this, it was now or never.

'Form up, slaves,' he said to his home-grown goblins. 'We are going in.'

The seaweed clones, like the mindless servants they were, did as they were told.

When I am king, thought Teddy as they marched towards the barn, *my entire army shall be made of seaweed goblins.*

Many of the goblins were falling apart so quickly that they didn't even make it to the barn, instead unravelling to form a sort of path that their comrades marched across without any emotion whatsoever. Their brethren's demise had little to do with their prime directive of *Protect the creator*, so it didn't factor into their thought process, inasmuch as they had one.

Inside the barn, the floor was covered with a layer of particulate ash, which was all that was left of the construction and insulation materials that had yet to be tidied up following the renovation, besides a few pieces of still-smouldering furniture that had not yet made the trip upstairs into storage. Teddy had been planning to have the clones of himself do that, but now they were all melted to slop . . . except the wig-wearing one, who was gazing down imperiously from the hatch.

'Cousin Teddy,' she said, tapping her toe on the hatch

frame, an impatient gesture the duke remembered seeing a hundred times before.

Good heavens, he thought. *That's uncanny. What is this madness?*

'Up you come if you want the ring,' said the princess pretender. 'But I will need some assurances.'

The duke ran through some possible retorts in his head.

I am certainly not going up there. You come down.

What assurances?

I'm in charge here.

Show me the ring.

And so on and so forth, but Teddy knew that at the end of the day he would have to listen to her offer and then make his choice, and to hear the offer he would have to climb the ladder.

'Blast and bother,' he swore, and then called to his cousin, 'Move back. I'm sending a few sentries your way.'

By a *few* Teddy meant a *few dozen*, which he figured was about all that could fit in the attic with all the old furniture stored there. The goblins climbed up, and it took an infuriatingly long time for them to pack the loft, what with all their unravelling and tumbling back down. Apparently, rungs were tough on seaweed.

I need to keep the upper hand, thought Teddy. *And I can't do that from the lower deck. Take the high ground, Tedderick, old chap.*

And so he tackled the ladder, taking care to take care, but also to maintain the legendary Bleedham-Drye swagger. Teddy did manage to maintain his casually menacing demeanour, using a ladder technique passed down from his cousin Brigadier General Ronald Bleedham-Drye: 'A fellow should never crane his head back while going up steps, ladders or any kind of rising conveyance,' he'd said. 'Your average head-craner has no panache and looks soft in the noggin, which he probably is. Eyes front at all times, young Ted.'

It was good advice and Teddy was almost sorry to have poisoned the old duffer, but necessity compels and so on. Teddy maintained the eyes-front strategy now, which was just as well, as the ladder was a little rickety, having not been updated with the barn itself.

Even if I do fall, thought Teddy, *being on the lower level of this barn is better than being on top at the moment.*

In this, he was dead wrong. And, when the time came, almost actually dead.

* * *

Teddy counted three loft occupants, but he was off by over two dozen, as the ghosts of Bleedham-Dryes past glared at him from glowing eyes. That accounted for the sudden mild discomfort the duke was feeling, but he put it down to the nervousness many people experienced just from being in the presence of a Fowl. Empath elves actually use the term *Fowlprehension* for this form of anxiety.

'We meet again, my boys,' said Teddy as he climbed into the loft. 'I must say, you fellows have the resilience of those tigers that simply refuse to be wiped out.'

Teddy stepped off the ladder and straightened his commando beret. He was beginning to look more and more like the duke of old. His beard was growing back at an accelerated rate thanks to the course of amino acids he'd just started.

In contrast, Myles was certainly not looking his best. The so-called nutrient juice had dried on his head, shaping his hair into rock-hard spikes that glowed faintly orange, as did his teeth, and his beautiful suit was ripped beyond repair.

He stepped forward. 'It seems, Your Grace, that every time I visit your island you destroy one of my suits. Do you suffer from sartorial envy, I wonder?'

Teddy begged to differ. 'You destroyed that suit yourself, Fowl. I don't know how you did it, but I will thank you to keep your distance in case you start popping off again.'

Myles winced. He did not like being thought of as a person who *popped off*.

'Rest assured, Your Grace, there shall be no more, as you put it, "popping off". At any rate, I prefer the phrase **Bum**per **R**elease of **U**ndigested **S**ugars and **H**igh-sulphur food waste.'

The duke had to ask, 'No clever acronym, Myles?'

'I did think BUMRUSH, but that's a bit on the nose, don't you think?'

'I do,' said the duke. 'In fact, the entire affair was very much on the nose.'

Banter out of the way, Teddy got down to business. 'Now, tell me your terms, Fowl!'

The Daphne clone stepped forward. '*I* will be setting the terms, cousin. You may remember I was quite the negotiator. If it wasn't for me, you would have sold off one of the Scilly Isles to France, remember?'

Teddy did remember this lost opportunity, but so did the history books. This was not proof positive that Daphne's ghost had somehow possessed this clone.

'I do not negotiate with clones,' he said.

Daphne's royal composure evaporated. 'You will address me by my title, cousin. I am Princess Daphne of the royal house, and the Lionheart ring is mine by right. If you would have it, Tedderick, then you will agree to my terms.'

Teddy was shaken. No one had known the Tedderick endearment except Daphne, who had bestowed it upon him. The duke was uncertain as to how this had happened, or indeed the implications of having a dead relative living in a clone, but now he knew in his gut that this was somehow Daphne.

'Forgive me, Your Highness,' he said smoothly. 'My manners are rusty. And my apologies for poisoning you. A family tradition, you understand? And now the ring. Please hand it over if you would?'

'I would not,' said Daphne. 'What I would do is command you to have your monsters lay down their arms.'

Teddy was already beginning to regret agreeing to this meeting. 'Can we skip over the horse trading, Highness? What is it you actually expect me to do for the Lionheart ring? If indeed you do have it.'

'I have it, Tedderick,' said Daphne, rummaging inside

her wig for several moments before drawing a shining ring from its depths. 'I have it right here, and I expect you to let the twins go free, unharmed.'

Teddy groaned. The wig. Of course. For nigh on a hundred years, it had sat in his very own wardrobe.

'And why should I not simply take it?'

Daphne was ready for that. 'Because, dear cousin, it is a thing of nothing for me to drop this trinket between the floorboards into the hot ash below. Silver is delicate, and it would not take much to erase the king's dedication.' The princess read George's words aloud: '"To a future monarch. Twist the ring and become the king."'

In the duke's peripheral vision, Beckett Fowl moved. Nothing significant or threatening, but Teddy realised that he could not tell *dangerous* from *harmless* with these infernal children.

'Cover the boy,' he said to his goblins, and several of the seaweed clones aimed their snouts at Beckett.

'I'm just fidgety,' explained Beckett. 'I've been standing still for ages.'

Teddy ignored Beckett's explanation and delivered his counter-offer to Daphne. 'I shall kill the twins, but I shall allow you to hold on to that new body so you may keep me company in the evenings. You might well live forever inside a clone, which must be better than whatever existence you have now.'

Myles had warned Daphne to expect this offer. 'I doubt I would live forever, Tedderick. I expect you'd dispose of me the moment you had the ring in your sweaty grasp.'

'You have my word that I will not dispose of you,' said Teddy smoothly, so smoothly that Daphne appeared to consider the offer. After all, the duke famously prided himself on his word and had boasted in the press that he never gave it unless he intended to stick to it. Occasionally, he had broken his promises to a commoner, but never to a member of his or the wider royal family. It was a royal trait generally to pretend that keeping one's word was the same as being a good person and, as long as one didn't give one's word to do or not do a very specific thing, then one didn't have to keep one's word, so to speak.

'Do I have your word as a Bleedham-Drye that you will never kill me as I currently exist, or anyone else in our family?' asked Daphne, gesturing around the room to spaces where presumably more ghosts hovered.

Teddy baulked at this. After all, one never knew

when a long-lost nephew was going to turn up with a claim to a slice of the royal pie, so he amended this proposition somewhat. 'I give my word to never kill you as you currently exist or anyone *here present* in our family,' said Teddy, as he cared not a jot for ghosts and would not know how to dispose of one if he did.

'Don't do it, Daff,' said Beckett. 'That means Teddy will kill Myles and me.'

Teddy smoothed the nap of his tweed jacket and twisted the brass buttons so that the dragon crests embossed upon them aligned. 'I *will* kill them,' he said, drawing his Colt .45 pistol. 'That is non-negotiable.'

'I am sorry, Sir Beck,' said Daphne, hugging her own torso. 'It's just that this body, it's so real. I can smell things – and taste, too, I'll wager. I would so like to have an ice cream. Perhaps with some strawberries.'

'Of course you would,' said Teddy. 'I have both in the main house. And, as you saw, your old bedchamber awaits.'

Daphne shrugged. 'I never believed that Teddy would agree not to kill you boys. I'm dreadfully sorry.'

Myles was furious. 'We had an agreement!' he said. 'You help us and we help you. This is indeed a betrayal worthy of a Bleedham-Drye.'

Daphne took a few steps towards Teddy. 'At the end of the day, that is what I am. And if Teddy becomes king, which he indeed could with my help on the more subtle matters in court, then I become the king's ward. And in our clone bodies we will rule for a hundred years.'

'It is merely a ceremonial monarchy,' said Myles. 'You won't have any real power.'

Daphne considered this. 'Perhaps not initially, but I think there are many people in this country who are ready for the monarchy to take back what is theirs. After all, we can hardly do any worse than Parliament and, when the Lionheart ring returns like Excalibur itself, there will be a groundswell of support for the Bleedham-Dryes.'

Teddy was sold. He had not even considered *real* power, but everything Daphne had said was true. It made him almost regret killing her in the first place.

But, if I hadn't, she would be queen and I would never be king.

So, all in all, murdering his cousin had probably been for the best.

'You have my word, Daphne,' he said. 'Now give me the blasted ring and let me get on with killing these accursed Fowls.'

Beckett lunged at Daphne but was easily restrained by a bunch of clones. 'No, Daff!' he cried, his voice muffled by seaweed. 'You are being a total meanie.'

'I suppose I am,' said Daphne, holding the ring tantalisingly between thumb and forefinger. 'It's a family trait.'

And with that she slid the ring on to Lord Teddy's outstretched middle finger. It was a little tight due to the welded nub inside the band, but nevertheless it went on and the whole thing seemed meant to be.

Teddy enjoyed the sensation of cold silver on his digit for the briefest moment and then decided he could revel in satisfaction post Fowlicide as he floated in his bath of electric eels.

Perhaps the twins, too, can float – around the island as ghosts, that is, he thought. *How wonderful would that be?*

'Stand behind me, Daphne,' he said. 'Time to fry the boys.'

Daphne did not move. 'But, Tedderick, have you forgotten your vow so soon?'

'Of course not, cousin,' snapped Teddy, eager to be about his murderous business. 'I shall not kill you or any of our family here present, although I might point out that ghosts are already dead. The only people I plan to kill are those twins, and I must get to it, for they are slippery blighters.'

'More than you know, cousin,' said Myles, who did not seem as furious as he had been moments before.

Teddy felt the old familiar dread that one felt in the aftermath of a hoodwinking by the Fowls.

'Cousin? What does he mean, cousin"?' And something else occurred to him. 'And why did you call the other brat *Sir Beck?*'

'He is a sir,' said Daphne. 'I knighted him.'

Teddy was almost speechless. 'You . . . You knighted a *Fowl?* But you cannot knight anyone.'

Daphne begged to differ. 'King George granted me a royal warrant.'

'That was a joke!' spluttered the duke. 'A jape for the court.'

'It was signed and sealed,' argued Daphne. 'And witnessed by yourself. In fact, you, too, signed the warrant. So, joke or not, it is perfectly legal.'

'But you are *dead!*' said the duke. 'You cannot exercise a warrant. That is a contract.'

Myles had primed Daphne for that one. 'And yet you yourself just now entered into a contract with me by giving me your word, so obviously I can exercise a warrant.'

Teddy had heard quite enough of this legal twaddle. 'Now I remember why I poisoned you, Daphne. Anyway, this is all immaterial. Let's say I accept that the Fowl boy is indeed a knight of the realm. That doesn't make him a part of my family.'

At this point, Myles took over because the big reveal was his wheelhouse and he did so enjoy it. 'It is a pity, Your Grace, that you cannot see the ghosts who hover above you, because, if you could, you might notice one wearing a black robe.'

Black robe, thought Teddy. *Who was wearing a black robe when I murdered them?*

And then it hit him.

'No!' he said to Daphne, horror sweeping over him. 'Tell me you didn't!'

Daphne delighted in her cousin's horror. 'I *did*!' she said. 'I did with the greatest of pleasure.'

'I did too,' said Beckett from underneath a press of seaweed. 'We both did.'

Myles added his affirmation. 'They did indeed, Lord Teddy,' he said, enjoying this *coup de grâce* more than any other that had come before it. 'Sir Beckett Fowl

355

and Princess Daphne Constance Gertrude von Stein Bleedham-Drye were lawfully married not fifteen minutes ago, which makes us part of your family.'

The duke thought he might be ill. The Fowls part of his family. It was an utter disaster.

'No!' he said. 'I will not accept this. It's highly irregular. A ghost cannot marry a twelve-year-old boy. There must be a million grounds for objection.'

Myles had no problem with this. 'Dozens, at least, but by the rules of your own monarchy any marriage disputes must be adjudicated in the House of Lords. We are happy to abide by their ruling in a year or so. In fact, we will await their communications from Dalkey Island. Shall we go, Prince Beckett?'

This was too much for Lord Teddy to bear. 'He is not *Prince* Beckett. Even if this ludicrous union is somehow given the royal seal of approval, he would not be Prince Beckett. At best, he would be *Sir* Beckett, prince of the realm.'

Beckett was not hung up on titles. 'Sir Beckett is fine, cousin.'

'Do not call me cousin!' Teddy shrieked. 'Never refer to me as that. We do not belong to, or indeed in, the same kingdom.'

Daphne was theatrically shocked. 'Tedderick, how dare you speak to our cousins in this manner? Especially my husband, who is not exactly beloved, I grant you, but I am certainly very fond of him, for he, unlike *some* people, has never murdered me!'

This hammer blow brought it home to Teddy just how comprehensively he had been blinded by the lure of the crown. He should have known that Daphne would never forgive him. She would do anything to spite him just because he'd killed her one single time back in the previous century.

Teddy had been in tight spots and tough corners before. He'd spent four days between a rock, a hard place and a shark. Once, he'd been forced to weave a lasso from his own hand-plucked beard hair in order to escape a lion pit, which the lion was none too happy about. But, in all his close calls and near misses, he had never felt the way he did now, which was totally and utterly defeated and dejected on every level. On previous occasions, Teddy had used his hatred towards pretty much anyone who was not a member of the royal family as fuel to see him past the point where most people would have lain down and died, but now, somehow, his mortal enemies had become his relatives by way of a supernatural covenant with the ghost of his cousin. It was too much to take in, and Teddy felt the will to live forever drain out of him.

That's it, old man, he thought. *You are beaten. Time to hang up the old hunting rifle and learn how to play draughts.*

Without another word to either Fowl or to the princess who had stabbed him in the back, Teddy climbed down the ladder and walked in a daze towards the main house. The seaweed clones, still on anti-Fowl orders, stayed where they were and Teddy pushed through the rustling forest of their ranks.

The moon was a blurred ivory disc through the rings of dragon's breath, and though Teddy had always enjoyed this sight, and the feeling of privacy it brought, tonight he did not so much as glance upwards. His old life was over, that vital career of hunting and taking his due from the world. Now he would accept whatever indignities were piled upon him by the foul Fowls. No doubt there would be a legal battle for his very research since he had willed it to Myles.

It is even possible that I will be evicted from the family pile.

Not so long ago, this thought would have elicited a

cry of, 'Never!' But now it was just another humiliation to add to the list. It was amazing how quickly it had happened. One moment he was the Teddy of old, prepared to give the order to attack, and moments later the fire in his belly had burned out and he had become this shell of a man.

Defeated, demoralised, depressed.

Perhaps what Myles had said in London was true: 'When are you going to realise that you can never beat me and it would be easier on your self-esteem if you simply stopped trying?'

That is what I shall do, the duke decided. *I shall simply stop trying.*

Teddy trudged along the gravel towards the front door, finding no comfort in the touchstones of his youth. The flowery borders that old Higgins the groundsman had planted. The adjacent humped mound where Higgins had requested to be buried. Actually, truth be told, Higgins had requested a burial in the borders themselves, but the duke's mother hadn't wanted to ruin the flowerbed. The scurrying of the indigenous rabbits at the edges of his vision brought on no desire to draw his Colt .45 for a casual potshot. Even the looming house itself inspired no heart-swelling pride in his own dynasty. Why would he be proud of a family that contained Fowls?

Teddy paused before the main doorway, a sandstone-and-redbrick affair that had been modelled after the entrance to the prime minister's country house of Chequers. Pre-PM, however, Chequers was where Queen Elizabeth I had ordered Lady Mary Grey confined when the latter married without permission.

Those were the days, thought Teddy gloomily. His eyes drifted upwards to a tapestry that hung on the wall depicting, as one might expect, Saint George slaying the dragon. Teddy had travelled the world and knew only too well that Saint George had never even been to England, but the duchy needed a strong symbol to believe in, and the Bleedham-Dryes were prepared to appropriate a dragon and a saint if it meant rallying the people behind them. As Teddy's grandfather had confided to the teenage Teddy, 'We knew. We've always known. But sometimes a lie is necessary to preserve the family.' And so there were pictures and indeed statues of dragons all over an island that bore the name of a saint who had never so much as placed a foot on the beach.

Teddy had never agreed with pretending that Saint

George was English, seeing himself as a keeper of the Bleedham-Drye word, but now it was suddenly so clear.

Sometimes a lie is necessary.

And, just like that, a switch in Teddy's mind was flipped and he realised that one broken word today would be so much better than a lifetime spent jousting with Fowls.

You were right, Grandfather, he thought. *And today is the day for my one lie.*

And, thus heartened, he turned and strode right back the way he had come. You might think that Myles and company had put in an awful lot of work for such a brief stay of execution, but sometimes a brief stay is all you need.

Princess Daphne was dancing in jubilation, twirling as though at a ball.

'We did it, my boys!' she said. 'We tricked him. I can't believe that Teddy took the bait, but he always coveted the crown. As if a ring could ever make a man king.'

Myles held up a warning hand. 'It is not yet time for celebrating,' he said. 'I thought him beaten before, and I was wrong.'

Beckett had wiggled out from under a pile of seaweed goblins who made no move to stop him, frozen as they were by a lack of orders from their leader.

'Those goblins are tied up in knots,' he said. 'Without skin, they are basically held together by a few stitches.'

Daphne took his hands and spun him round. 'I duped Tedderick, husband. Did you see?'

'I did, Daff,' replied Beckett. 'Most of it, anyway, from under a pile of seaweed goblins. I was letting them hold me down.'

Myles lost a little of his legendary cool. 'Silence, brother! I think I can hear something.'

Daphne stopped spinning. 'Silence?' she said, outraged. Her anger was a little comical due to the fact that she was quite dizzy. 'You dare to shush your prince?'

Myles did not have time to debate royal etiquette and so amended his command to: 'I beg a moment of quiet, Your Highness. Methinks thine enemy approaches.'

There was no need for *methinks* or indeed *thine*, but Princess Daphne appreciated the effort.

'In that case, Myles, mum is most certainly the word.'

And so, among the crackling seaweed goblins, the three stood stock-still, their heads cocked like deer, waiting for confirmation that the duke was, in fact, returning.

They did not have long to wait, as within moments they heard the dry sweep of his boots through the ashes below and then the *clunkity-clunk* of his rise up the ladder. Teddy began speaking even before he cleared the hatch.

'I cannot believe I find myself in this position once again!' he cried as he climbed into the attic. 'On the very cusp of pulling the trigger, and stymied once more. This will not stand. I will not allow it to stand.'

And on that pronouncement he stamped the attic floor with one riding boot and the entire structure shook slightly. Teddy stamped again and the shake was even more evident, and a rumble accompanied it on this occasion.

I will not allow it to stand, thought Teddy, and he made a decision about how this would be done.

'I have had enough of this charade,' he announced. 'And so I will once again take my leave, *cousins.*'

'We, too, shall leave,' said Myles. 'Perhaps you would be so good as to lend us your spare Skyblade for the trip home?'

'Certainly I will lend it to you,' said Teddy. 'I would be delighted, cousin.'

With that unlikely offer, Myles knew for certain that

Teddy had zero intention of allowing them to leave. Myles blamed himself. He had pushed the duke so far that Teddy was prepared to sacrifice his honour, his very soul, to put an end to the Fowl Twins.

Myles decided to call the duke on it. 'So I see you intend to go back on our deal, Your Grace. To break your word, in fact.'

'Oh no,' said Teddy with a great show of innocence. 'My word is sacred to me, and I wouldn't dream of breaking it. I plan to turn round and leave this building once again. Simple as that. You are free to do as you wish, and I *personally* will not stop you.'

'*Personally*, Tedderick?' said Daphne. 'Personally? Speak plainly, if you have the courage to do so. You plan to have your minions finish off the twins.'

'Far from it,' said Teddy. 'No one is finishing off anyone. In fact, I plan to have my so-called minions climb this ladder and bow to their new prince. I cannot be any more welcoming to my new family members than that, can I, Your Royal Highness?'

Beckett was best with balance and structure, so he understood instinctively what this would mean. 'But the barn will collapse!' he said. 'It's already teetering and tottering.'

'You seem tense, boy,' noted the duke. 'Be careful not to become aggressive, or my clones will defend their master. I'd hate to see you injured in any way.'

'Don't worry, Your Grace,' said Daphne. 'You won't see it. I'm sure you'll be far away from this building before it falls.'

'I plan to be,' said Teddy, and he took one step down the ladder, then stopped. 'I don't understand exactly what has happened here, but be assured I will investigate. Perhaps my chum Myishi and I can somehow weaponise the spirits that appear to infest the island. So I thank you for that gift of knowledge, Fowl.'

Teddy could not know this, but he and Myishi would not be weaponising anything together ever again, and the person responsible for that was fast approaching.

The duke continued down the ladder, speaking to his seaweed minions on the ground floor as he descended. 'And now, faithful clones, I command you to bow to your prince. In fact, give both Fowl Twins exactly what they deserve. Up the steps, my boys, as lively as you can. Get nice and close now.'

Beckett raised an eyebrow towards Myles, asking to be let off his leash.

'Go, brother,' said Myles. 'Do what you can.'

Beckett did not need to be told twice. In fairness, he only waited to be told once so that Myles would think he was in charge, a belief his twin enjoyed. He spun away from his new bride and towards the nearest cluster of seaweed goblins, who stood dumbly and watched him come until they realised they were being attacked.

While Beckett had been restrained by the clones, he'd noticed that they seemed to be held together by knotted strands of seaweed. Obviously, once their scales grew in, they wouldn't be so fragile, but for now it seemed to Beckett, who prided himself on his ability to untie even the most hopelessly tangled charging cable, that a well-placed Windy Elbow in the solar plexus could unravel a clone completely.

He hit the first guy a little high, which only made the clone burp, but on the second try Beckett adjusted his strike angle a few centimetres and, with a noise like a party popper, the clone exploded into streamers of seaweed confetti. All except the startled eyes, which rolled across the floor, dropping through the hatch.

They must have bonked Lord Teddy on the head, for he called to his minions, 'Defend yourselves, idiots!'

The clones were slow to act, which gave Beckett

ample time to unravel the half dozen more goblins who were strewn round the loft space. One managed to hawk up a fireball, but it zoomed harmlessly out through the open window, followed by most of the clone himself as Beckett's Windy Elbow untangled his tendons.

As Beckett dealt with the clones already on the upper level, Daphne attacked the ones clambering up the ladder. It was a Spartans-at-the-pass situation, as no matter how many clones there were, only one could come up the ladder at a time. Daphne stomped on their fingers and heads, which proved very effective, since both fingers and heads crumpled under the slightest pressure.

Even so, the situation grew increasingly hopeless as the goblins proved themselves adept climbers and began scaling the walls and finding cracks in the flooring to wriggle through. It was only a matter of time before their weight would cause the stressed floor to fall altogether. The groans of steel girders and cracks of floorboards heralded the total collapse that was surely imminent, and Myles knew that they had arrived at the very nexus of crisis. If something was going to happen, it would surely happen now, because that's when things traditionally happened in Fowl Adventures for some reason, at the moment known in common parlance as *just in time*.

But who would care enough to risk everything to make that thing happen?

16
INCOMING

LAZULI HAD ALREADY POPPED THE HATCH WHILE the pod was on its final approach because, as you may recall, she had been forced to purge her helmet. So there was nothing in it but a vacuum, and while vacuums are the perfect places to be if you want to deaden sounds or avoid spoilers, they are not-so-great places if you want to do other things, like, for example, breathe. Lazuli had been forced to pull the lever between her feet and drain the pod while it was still in mid-air, which had all sorts of ramifications, the most immediate being that the hatch itself acted as a kind of fin and threw the pod off course ever so slightly. As a result, it would miss the water splashdown and impact instead on St George itself, which would be considerably more traumatic for anyone inside the pod, especially after the gel had been drained.

Lazuli caught a break with the spin caused by the protruding hatch. The tumble of the pod and the swirl of the turgid gel inside lined up in such a way that her head was actually in an air pocket for two seconds out of every five, and she was able to take a number of breaths before a touchdown that was really more of a crash landing.

Lazuli saw the ocean speed by below her in a blur of moonlit wavelets, which was worrying, as hitting water at this speed was like hitting solid ground, but only metaphorically – hitting actual solid ground was much more like hitting solid ground. When Specialist Heitz registered actual earth on her next spin, she tensed, even though all her crash training said to loosen up on impact in order to minimise trauma. Again, Lazuli was lucky with the spin because, when the pod ploughed into the earth in front of Childerblaine House, she was completely submerged in the remaining impact gel, and, although the air was driven from her chest in bubbles, at least she did not suffer any broken bones.

The pod completely destroyed the flowerbeds, which would have exasperated Teddy's mother, who'd spent her lifetime instructing Higgins the groundsman in how to tend them in the vain hope that someday the king would visit St George. To add insult to injury, the pod disinterred Higgins's remains and deposited them smack-bang in the middle of the plantings, where Lady Bleedham-Drye had most specifically not wanted them buried.

The pod managed one last bounce before careening to the left directly along the seaweed path laid down by the unravelled clones, scooping sheaves of the green stuff into the pod itself, which padded the space enough to keep Lazuli alive at least. From the path, it rolled into the metal sheeting of the barn, which had already been weakened considerably by several rounds of fireballs. The pod dragged the sheeting's bolts from their mounts and punched through the barn, wielding the corrugated steel like a double-sided scythe, which wreaked absolute havoc among the seaweed clones packed into the confined space. The goblins were mown down like so many stalks of corn, and the air was quickly thick with seaweed particles, most of which would settle on the Childerblaine grounds and effectively rejuvenate the salty soil with their concentrated nutrients.

But, while both soil rejuvenation and exhumation followed by reburial are important, they are not really our primary concern. What's important here is the turning of the battle tide caused by the cavalry's arrival in the form of a spinning-scythe pod. Where seconds before any pundits would have tipped Lord Teddy for the victory, it seemed that now his forces had been summarily destroyed and he was left alone on the ground floor of a barn, miraculously untouched but up to his ankles in the remains of his legion and breathing in the particulate remains of his soldiers, which, while excellent for the soil, are not ideal to suck down the lungs. And so it appeared that in the twinkling of an eye Lord Teddy had gone from conquering hero (in his own mind) to defeated general on his knees (metaphorically) at the feet of his foes.

The pod spun in place for several seconds, whirring like an entire swarm of bees and shedding its cowl of sheet steel, then wore itself out digging a crater in the barn's concrete floor until it came to a full stop, one rear burner still flaming.

Inside, Lazuli was having trouble believing she was still alive and, what's more, not broken into a million tiny pieces.

That impact gel is good stuff, she thought, punching the release button on her harness several times until the straps opened and she was deposited into a puddle of gel that slopped directly into her mouth for one final indignity.

Lazuli spat out a foil unicorn and thought, *I need to exit this pod and find out what's happening. Did I just save everyone or kill everyone?*

Lazuli took ten seconds to catch her breath and then scrambled up the pod's curved interior wall. It took her several tries to get a few fingers over the lip of the porthole because the gel slickened every surface it touched. This delay probably saved her life, as it wasn't likely the universe would spare two people in such an unlikely manner as it was about to spare Lord Teddy Bleedham-Drye.

The barn had a paper certificate pasted to the inside of the main door (which was now floating in the small harbour, by the way) that read THIS BUILDING IS CERTIFIED AND BONDED FOR TWENTY YEARS BY J. B. HOYT AND ASSOCIATES, ARCHITECTS AND ENGINEERS. In all fairness to Hoyt and Associates, they could never have foreseen either seaweed clones or fairy pods before issuing their guarantee. In any event, no one would ever attempt to sue J. B. Hoyt or his associates, because no humans outside the Fowl family would know what had transpired here for certain.

Events post-pod impact clipped along at such a pace

that it will take much longer to describe them than they actually took to transpire, unless a person reads at double speed and skips over conjunctions and pronouns. The entire island seemed to hold its breath while the pod spun on its nose, burrowing through the poured-concrete foundation and sending a spiderweb of cracks running from the impact point to the edges of the building. There was a single moment of relative peace when the pod creaked to a halt and everyone living checked to see if they were indeed alive, and then all hell broke loose.

The barn decided that enough was enough and began a graceless slump. Its supporting girders bent at the knees like a collapsing camel, and the upper level was deposited on to the lower level. It must have seemed to the Fowl Twins that they were being sucked down into hell itself. Entire sections of the floor opened up beneath them and a *whoosh* of blistering air rushed upwards, bearing with it sharp slivers of brittle seaweed. Bubbles popped like automatic gunfire, and metal panels sang like infernal saw fiddles.

The drop, though, was strangely slow as the girders held on to some of their elasticity and, amazingly, there was not even enough impact to shock Princess Daphne out of her clone body. The twins survived with no more hairs out of place than had already been out of place, and Lazuli was safe inside the pod that had punched through the wooden floorboards. It seemed that Lord Teddy would be the odd man out and not survive, but in fact he did when the loft hatch framed him perfectly on its way down, saving the duke from a squishing.

'I say,' he said, which was all he did say.

Imagine the scene: the Fowl Twins, one princess ghost inside a clone and a duke all on the same level now, and Specialist Lazuli Heitz, still wearing a SpongeBob hoodie, crawling from a gunge-smeared pod that had just wiped out Teddy's army. And, just in case the participants were under the impression that the madness was past, the barn itself provided an encore when the roof panels parted and slid from their fixings and floated away gracefully on the currents of warm air, landing several metres from the collapsed outbuilding with a noise like faraway applause.

In future fairy postgraduate crime-studies courses, some would attempt to diminish Specialist Lazuli Heitz's part in the resolution of the Childerblaine affair. They would argue that her contributions were by and large accidental. She certainly had not intended to crash into the barn, and she had no way of knowing that the pod would pick up some handy corrugated steel on the way in. While these points are accurate, it is on Specialist Heitz's final gambit that she should be judged, and this was very much a proactive and purposeful ploy with a rather macabre endgame, as we shall see forthwith.

What happened was as follows:

Lord Teddy Bleedham-Drye, Duke of the Scilly Isles, was livid. He had cycled through all the emotional extremities in the past few seconds and settled on a blend of outrage and fury. It seemed to the duke as though the universe itself had it in for him and, every single time he was convinced that the game was won, something ludicrous happened to turn the cosmic tables. First, the ghost of his dead cousin, and now some class of flying craft annihilating not only his soldiers but also his barn, which he'd just had renovated, for heaven's sake.

This white-hot anger obliterated his higher brain functions and regressed the duke to his teen years, when he had been a creature of rash impulse. The problem, his little voice told him, was all his grand machinations.

There was only one way to deal with upstarts like these – shoot them dead with a sidearm.

It would be nothing for a crack shot like the duke to plug the two Irish boys. After all, they stood two metres away, still shaky on their feet after the unexpected collapse of the upper level.

'Very well then,' snarled the duke. 'Cold steel it is.'

Not as classy as he would have liked, but it would do in a pinch.

Princess Daphne intervened. 'Cousin, please. Spare the boys.'

'Shut your yap, Daff,' said Teddy. 'Or you'll be next.'

Daphne showed tremendous gumption by placing herself between the boys and the duke, declaring: 'I shall be first, cousin.'

Teddy shrugged and cocked the revolver. 'Very well, cousin dearest. First it is.'

The duke summarily shot the Daphne clone in the shoulder, which was more than enough to eject the princess from her host body.

Daphne rose to join the ring of spirits circling above Teddy's head and wept silvery tears at her own powerlessness. 'I am sorry, husband,' she called to Beckett. 'I could not save you.'

'Don't worry, Daff,' said Beckett, to the air, it seemed. 'Something will turn up.'

And it was at this precise moment that Lazuli presented her ruse, calculating that Lord Teddy would not be able to resist the notion.

She flopped, sopping wet, spray skin streaked and generally bedraggled, on the upper curve of the pod's hull. 'Stupid duke with his stupid Lionheart ring,' she said, then laughed for a few seconds to make sure Teddy's attention was on her. 'It's not even activated.'

Luckily for the Regrettables, the duke was particularly susceptible to mockery at this precise moment, presenting, as he was, like a truculent teenager.

'Not activated, you say, fairy?' he said, looking down at the ring. 'Why, dash it all if you ain't right. Well, that's an easy one to remedy.'

And, thinking it an insult to add to the injury he was just about to inflict in the form of bullet holes, Teddy grasped the Lionheart ring between the finger and thumb of his left hand and, without ever letting up the pressure on his trigger finger, twisted the ring twice. He had meant to twist it three times, but twice was enough for the nub – soldered there so that the ring would stay on Daphne's finger, if you remember –

to double-click Ishi Myishi's knuckle switch and pop the top of Teddy's skull open like an escape hatch.

The top flipped through the air, and Myles grabbed it with both hands. 'Amazing,' he said.

'I know,' said Beckett. 'You caught something.'

The last words Teddy spoke as a creature of flesh and blood were: 'I say, Fowl, is that the crown of one's head?'

'I'm afraid so,' said Myles, and he deduced the truth. 'I imagine that, technically, it's an access port.'

Lord Teddy seemed on the verge of saying more, but at that moment his ghostly likeness floated perhaps fifteen centimetres out of his body.

And yet the duke, not quite ready to sever ties with the mortal world, forbade himself to die. 'No, Teddy,' his ghost told itself, wiggling back down into his body. 'It is not yet your time.'

But the next life seemed to think it *was* Teddy's time, for a hole opened in the rings of fog above the island, and through it poked what could only be described as an enormous ribbed ice-cream straw. The opening of this straw pulsed with a pure bright light.

'He's ascending,' breathed Daphne. 'We can go with him!'

Upon hearing this and realising that here was a real opportunity to at long last access the afterlife, the ghosts of Teddy's murdered relatives formed a kind of inverted multicoloured ectoplasmic cyclone and dived into the duke's open cranium.

'That is disgusting,' said Beckett, who could not look away.

'What is disgusting?' said Lazuli, who was squatting atop the pod, tugging off a bucket helmet.

'You, Laz,' said Beckett, waving at her without averting his gaze from the ghosts rummaging in Teddy's head. 'And also the murdered Bleedham-Dryes in the duke's open skull.'

'Murdered Bleedham-Dryes,' said Lazuli. 'I'm not even surprised any more.'

Myles did not join in the Regrettables' reunion conversation. He could thank Lazuli for saving them later. For now, it was his duty as a scientist to observe every second of the evolving spectral tussle. His only regret at that moment was that he had not yet devised some method of recording ghostly interactions.

He decided to use that old observer's trick of narrating events aloud. This would help both to reinforce events in his memory and keep Lazuli up to speed. Also, if he sprinkled in endearments and used a singsong tone, he could disguise his lecture as communication so Specialist Heitz would know he was glad to see her.

'Currently, there are several ghosts – which are composed mostly of ectoplasm imprinted with the pain of lost souls, by the way – who have spotted an opportunity to wreak their revenge on Lord Teddy, the person responsible for all their deaths, Lazuli, my dear.'

Lazuli knew what Myles was doing and totally appreciated both the updates and the effort he was making to be warm towards her.

'What can the lost souls achieve, Myles?' she asked.

Myles, in turn, appreciated the pertinent question. Beckett would most likely have asked something irrelevant, like 'What colour are Teddy's ghost trousers?'

And so Myles was surprised when his twin asked, 'Is the giant tube the conduit to the afterlife, brother?'

Conduit? thought Myles. *My twin is full of surprises.*

He did his best to answer both questions. 'The lost souls hope to ascend to the afterlife through the tunnel, which I do believe is the *conduit* – well done, Beck – to the aforementioned afterlife.'

The Bleedham-Drye ghost conglomerate pounced on Teddy's soul and tugged, hauled and wriggled him out of his body like a reluctant cork from a bottle. The ascensionists were determined, but the duke was at least as strong, and he fought back with arms, legs and even teeth, fending off the bunch as best he could.

Myles translated this into science-speak. 'The duke is proving himself resistant to the idea of ascension. Judging by his spectral glow, which is many lumens brighter than his assailants', I would say that he has considerably more energy than the historic ghosts.'

It was true: this was no easy battle for the ascensionists, and the further up they went, the more their own glow faded. The tunnel was still there, but it was flickering in and out of existence.

'It would seem, Lazuli, my dear,' said Myles, 'that there is a time limit on this exercise. The ascensionists appear bound to miss their chance.'

'Go on!' Beckett called to Daphne. 'Get in there and be happy.'

Daphne twisted her head from the floating mass of writhing limbs and Beckett saw glittering tears on her cheeks. 'We are trying, husband. We are trying so very hard, but he resists.'

Myles filled in Lazuli. 'My brother exhorts his wife to enter the conduit,' he said. 'But she worries that their combined efforts will not be enough to transport them.'

Lazuli took one word from that statement. '*Wife?* Beck got married?' And then something else occurred to her. 'Beck got married to a *ghost?*'

This was surprising even by Fowl standards.

'It was a brief union,' said Myles. 'And a separation could be imminent.'

Beck was on tiptoes, shouting at the translucent tangle of airborne ghosts. 'Let him go, Daff!' he said. 'Just go through. It's a Bleedham-Drye tunnel.'

Ronald's face separated from the bunch. 'No,' he said firmly. 'Teddy must pay for what he has done. He must be punished.'

This made no sense to Beckett. 'Trying to punish Teddy is what got you stuck here in the first place. And, anyway, the afterlife could be amazing – what kind of punishment is that?'

Ronald was startled.

It hadn't occurred to him or the group that they were yet again wasting valuable and limited energy on the exact thing that had resulted in them being earthbound in the first place. The tunnel was here and they were voluntarily generating negative energy that would only drive it further away.

Daphne added her voice to the discussion. 'Prince Beckett is right. We must ascend now, my fellow Bleedham-Dryes. That is our goal.'

'Don't worry about Teddy,' Beckett assured them. 'We'll take care of him.'

Myles kept Lazuli up to speed. 'Currently, dear Specialist, Beckett is attempting to persuade the hovering revenants that they should release Teddy, who is impeding their ascension, and simply pass through to the afterlife, which in my opinion is more than likely a parallel dimension.'

The ghosts reached some kind of unspoken group decision and suddenly Teddy was ejected from the amorphous huddle. The newly excreted ghost wandered on the air currents, trying to make sense of what was happening, and it was a credit to his strength of purpose that he began clawing his way almost immediately towards the open cranium of his clone, swimming against the tide of attraction between him and the tunnel of white light.

Daphne and her group were not affected by this tide of attraction as this tunnel was not coded to their auras, and they approached the tunnel as if trying to move through a powerful gale, which literally cut into their huddle, stripping the colour and vibrancy from their ectoplasm.

'The collective has expelled Lord Teddy,' Myles explained to Lazuli. 'I think that was a wise move emotionally and practically. They do not have the strength to both fight him and traverse the tunnel. Teddy is attempting to re-enter his clone body while the ascensionists are, quite frankly, being torn apart. They simply don't have the energy.'

Beckett called up to his wife. 'Keep going, Daff! You're nearly there.'

But Beckett was simply offering encouragement. The truth was the Bleedham-Drye collective was not *nearly there*, and it was becoming more obvious by the second they were not going to succeed.

'Okay, Myles,' said Beckett, rubbing his hands together. 'Your turn.'

Myles was aghast. '*My* turn! My turn? Beck, this is not a turn-taking situation. I have no equipment. We have not run any tests, and these are hardly laboratory conditions. The suggestion that someone might be able to somehow give these unfortunate trapped souls a boost is ludicrous.'

Beckett was not about to give up with his wife's soul at stake. 'Not someone, brother. Myles Fowl.'

Myles was understandably reluctant to take on this task. There was a reasonable chance that he would fail, and the news of his failure was not something he wanted making its way to Artemis's spaceship.

But still . . . there was a challenge here to do something historic.

Lazuli stood upright on the pod, ribbons of gel dribbling from her fingers. 'Come on, Myles. I just did two things. I flew here in an ancient pod, and I did the ring bit. And I was already ahead on rescues this adventure.'

This was infuriatingly true, and Myles was at the point of suggesting that they calculated rescues on aggregate, i.e. take the Regrettables' adventures as a whole rather than individually, as he was certain that he would be ahead then. He was about to make this rather pathetic suggestion when his intellect saved him from embarrassment.

'Just how old is that pod?' he asked.

Myles had good reason for asking this question. If we cast our minds back to earlier mentions of Moonbelts, they had been standard LEP issue in the days when

Commodore Short was still a captain and gallivanting around the planet with Artemis Fowl. The Moonbelt, like many LEP gadgets and gizmos, had been partially powered by ectoplasm. It was considered to be the best possible fuel, as it was excreted by every living being and, if not taken advantage of, it tended to gather over population centres and decay over time, eventually contributing to a sky glow that interfered with magnetic fields. So the experts in the LEP figured using it as a power source had the double advantage of producing energy and cleaning up the atmosphere. Unfortunately, the eco-conscious fairies were horrified to find that the scrubbed ectoplasmic energy developed a resistance to staying clean, almost as if it were somehow alive, and was reasserting itself over population centres and becoming more disruptive than ever. The ectoplasm pollution became quite the scandal, forcing the resignation of two Council members and inspiring an in-depth documentary series that those Council members felt was rather unfairly classified as *true crime*. The long and short of it was that ectoplasm was finished as a fuel and all ectoplasm-powered pods were retired.

Except this one, which had been stolen from the

LEP yard by smugglers and had an ectoplasmic booster still burning not two metres from Myles Fowl's gaze.

Myles knew all this because it was old news. He'd read about it in the files Artemis had hacked from Foaly, which Myles in turn had hacked from Artemis, which were now being re-hacked, or hacked back, by Foaly in Haven City.

The important thing was that Myles was now standing adjacent to a source of ectoplasmic energy. And, if his theory was correct, then if he could activate that energy as an airborne vapour it could disrupt the spirits' magnetic fields and shunt them to the next level.

'If only I could see the raw ectoplasm,' he said, thinking aloud, not really expecting a solution from anyone.

'Maybe if I did *this*,' said Beckett, and he pressed the plunger on Myles's spectacles a number of times.

Myles was horrified with this break from scientific incremental dosage experimentation. 'Beck! What have you done? My brain could turn to mush, or—'

He stopped complaining because, as his eyes adjusted to the new dosage, Myles realised that he could now, in fact, see the ectoplasm drifting from them all in sparkling gossamer folds that slowed down momentarily when they hit solid matter but then quickly drifted through. The strongest currents were emanating from the pod's hatch but most intensely from the still-flaming pod booster that was bent out of whack and was turned back towards the pod itself, scorching a hole in the pod foam.

'I bet that worked, Myles,' said Beckett. 'Did it work?'

Myles didn't answer. He was cobbling together an ad hoc plan.

Beckett grew excited. 'Look at that face, Daff!' he called up to his spirit wife, who was a little occupied. 'Here it comes. The big plan.'

Princess Daphne's face appeared in the ghost muddle. She was obviously exhausted. 'Quickly, my husband. We are so very tired.'

Lazuli didn't see how a big plan could be coming. Surely even Myles could not pull an ectoplasmic rabbit out of the hat at this late stage . . . but, then again, the Fowl boy had surprised her before.

Overhead, the spirit cooperative was beginning to moan. They were almost completely translucent now and devoid of all but the barest lick of colour. They could not have more than seconds left before they fell spent to earth and were stuck here until the next

Bleedham-Drye died right here on the island, which would be never, as Teddy was the last in the line.

Myles could see ectoplasm mushrooming from the pod's hatch. 'The battery is leaking,' he said. 'And the burner is overheating the interior.'

Lazuli climbed down. 'We should move away.'

Myles was thinking fast. 'Yes. No. In a moment. What I need, you see, is a delivery system. Some way to get the ectoplasm up there and then disperse it as a superfine mist. Also, a detonator.'

He lay on his back and calculated the angles, using his outstretched arms as a gauge.

'Close the hatch,' he told Lazuli.

Lazuli objected, for the record, even as she did what she was told. 'You know there's a leaking battery in there and a ton of seaweed, and the burner is heating the chassis now, so if you want an explosion you're going about it the right way. Are you trying to open a tunnel for us too? If there even *is* a tunnel.'

Myles handed his spectacles to his twin. 'Beck, do the honours, would you?'

Clamping the spectacles between his teeth, Beckett cartwheeled unnecessarily to Lazuli (although he would argue that there was no such thing as an unnecessary cartwheel) and, ten presses on the plunger later, the pixel's eyes had been opened regarding the ghost situation.

'Teddy doesn't look happy,' she noted.

It was true. While the other ghosts struggled vainly, it would seem, to reach a tunnel that appeared to be growing both dimmer and further away, Teddy was hauling himself down as though dragging on an invisible rope.

'Here I come, Fowls,' he said grimly. 'This ain't over yet.'

Lazuli was momentarily lost in the sky drama playing out above her when Myles called from his place on the ground.

'Specialist Heitz, I need more heat. Turn that booster round even further.'

Lazuli nodded. She wasn't sure what Myles was doing, but she had to trust that he knew. The ecto-boosters did not radiate much heat – it was all in the flame. And so she was able to put her boot to the hinge, thumping it even more back on itself.

I am kicking a rocket, she thought, *which is probably not a great idea in general.*

Myles issued a second command to Beckett. 'Beck, I need you to pop the hatch.'

Beckett scrambled on to the pod. 'When, brother?'

Myles considered this. No one was better at timing than Beckett as long as he knew what the parameters were. Telling his brother that he needed maximum temperature and pressure-build before the roiling energy seeped completely through the hull might not penetrate, so he couched it in Beckettian terms.

'Pop it just before it pops itself.'

'Gotcha,' said Beckett, placing his forehead against the glass so he could feel the thrum.

A noise floated down from above. The Irish would call it a keening sound, as the ghosts realised their struggle was hopeless. They were swimming against a current that was too strong. The tunnel was coded to the Bleedham-Drye DNA but not theirs specifically, so perhaps they could have forced themselves in, but only if they had been in top form, plasmically speaking, and, after a hundred years dedicated to revenge, these spirits were far from top form. Indeed, they were now translucent with only their sharpest features being picked out by the starlight.

Lazuli gave the booster one last kick so that a good eighty per cent of the jet was focused in on the hull, then she stepped back and called up to Beckett. 'Whenever you're ready, Beck.'

Beck felt the vibrations against his forehead and the heat of the roiling energy. Some passed through the pod, peeling off the foam, but most was contained inside in a ghostly soup of ectoplasm, air, dust and seaweed bubbles.

'Just a sec,' he said.

'I agree with Specialist Heitz,' said Myles from his supine position. 'Open the hatch.'

Beckett wrapped his fingers round the handle. 'Nearly there,' he said.

The glass was warm against his head, and the seaweed particles attacked the hatch like hornets. More ectoplasm seeped through the hull, and Beckett knew that if he waited a second too long the pressure would be lost, but he wouldn't open the hatch until he heard the sound he was waiting for.

He heard the sound. A *pop*.

The seaweed bubbles were ready to go. Even half a second more in that cauldron and their explosive energy would be wasted.

Beckett twisted the handle and yanked the hatch open, crying, 'Fly, my pretties. Fly!'

A melodramatic command that Myles thoroughly approved of.

Beckett rolled out of the way and a column of pressurised ectoplasm shot skyward, fuelled by the superheated air and bearing in its depths innumerable seaweed bubbles. The column was attracted to the afterlife tunnel and sped to the mouth with the speed of a laser. Unfortunately, it missed the ghost globule by several metres, which drew forth more keening from the spirits, who were now too weak to stick together and drifted slowly apart.

'Myles!' said Beckett, dismayed.

Myles simply held up an imperious finger. *Wait*, the finger said.

They did not have to wait for long, for barely a single twinkle after the ectoplasm beam reached the tunnel, things began popping inside it. The popping things were seaweed bubbles, which were full of concentrated ectoplasm, distilled and purified by the membrane. The exploding bubbles sent shafts of silver plasma into the night air, several targeting the listless spirits. The effect of these shafts on the Bleedham-Dryes was instantaneous. It was as though they were being electrocuted, which in a way they were. Such concentrated ectoplasm mightn't have been compatible had not Myles contrived to have it delivered at the molecular level by explosion.

Sir Ronald, who had been curled in the foetal position, was suddenly ramrod straight, his moustache quivering majestically, his medals polished and new, his uniform cut from summer sky.

'Onward, my soldiers!' he cried. 'Our new life awaits.' And he marched, double time no less, towards the tunnel mouth that now shone with renewed brightness.

Princess Daphne, who a moment ago had lain dejected in the air, her dress tattered and shabby, was transformed as though by the swish of a painter's brush. She leaped to her feet and pirouetted. As she twirled, gossamer petticoats formed about her legs and a crown grew jewel by jewel upon her dark curls.

'You did it, husband!' she called down. 'You saved us all.'

'Myles helped me a little,' said Beckett, waving goodbye to his bride.

Daphne was happy to go but wistful to leave. 'I feel certain that we would have been in love and happy,' she said, then blew him a kiss and ran after her uncle into the light.

'I know we would have been,' said Beckett. 'And I hope the afterlife is everything you dreamed of.'

Myles watched as, one by one, the Bleedham-Dryes passed through to the next stage of their existence. Most were weeping tears of joy, and Myles fervently hoped that he had sent them to a place where they could be happy, which was what everyone deserved at the end of the day. Myles knew that now, because at this moment *he* was happy, mostly because almost all the Regrettables had survived yet again, but also because he had done something that no other scientist, not even Artemis, and certainly not that deplorable showboat Einstein, had been able to do.

'I hacked the afterlife,' he said aloud, wishing he could see the words float in the air. But, he supposed, he could say it as often as he wished. 'I hacked the afterlife. Professor Myles Fowl hacked the afterlife.'

It sounded almost as good as it felt.

All in all, a good result for everyone.

Except Whistle Blower.

And Teddy.

He doesn't know it yet, thought Myles, *but that clone body is finished.*

The Regrettables gathered by the Lord Teddy clone and watched as ghost Teddy completed his laborious journey to re-enter the body. The fight against ascension had taken everything out of him, and already ghost Teddy was losing his lustre and sweating ectoplasmic droplets as he dragged himself down head first, muttering one word over and over.

'Fowl, Fowl, Fowl . . .'

He seemed almost oblivious to the Regrettables watching him, so determined was he to reach the clone that stood, slumped, its cranium grotesquely bisected, with no spark in its eyes and no beat in its heart.

The machine was broken, and no spirit could reanimate it.

The ghost of Teddy grabbed the skull and crawled down into the body, muttering sentences now. 'I will show them,' he said. 'This time they will see. No mistakes. No more twisty plans, Ted. Simplicity is the key. Kill them all, even the pets, isn't that it?'

Lazuli elbowed Myles. 'Should we say something?'

'No,' said Myles. 'Teddy is in shock. Let's give him a moment to adjust.'

'I'm not afraid of the duke now,' said Beckett.

It was true, he wasn't. In fact, none of them were. If

anything, the Regrettables felt sorry for Lord Teddy. He had fallen so far and would have an eternity to think about what he'd done. The duke had not yet caught on to his plight and still thought he had a chance to actually snatch some kind of victory from the jaws of such monumental defeat.

'Ha!' he said suddenly, glaring out at them, his ghostly eyes nestled approximately inside the clone's eyes.

'Do you see, my boys? You can't kill the duke. Nobody can. I am immortal.'

And with that Teddy made to draw his revolver, but his hand passed straight through, and as if on cue the clone's body toppled over into a bed of seaweed, leaving the duke's ghost behind it watching his corporeal self lying prone in the green flakes. He stood there for the longest time. Flickering. Little by little, the old Bleedham-Drye bravado dropped from his features. It was terrible to watch, even when the watchers were his mortal enemies. The duke's brows changed their arcs, moving his expression from determination to puzzlement. His mouth dropped to a doddery O. And his aquiline, commanding prow of a nose suddenly seemed too much for his face.

'Oh, blast,' he said. 'A chap can't accomplish much with his blooming body out of commission, I suppose.'

'That is true, Your Grace,' said Myles. 'You are at a considerable disadvantage.'

Teddy wiggled his fingers and had just enough spare ectoplasm to magic up a pipe. 'I suppose we should call a truce then, Myles, old chap,' he said, taking a few puffs.

'No surrender even now, Teddy?' asked Myles, amused.

Teddy huffed. 'I'll never surrender, Fowl. I'm a duke of the realm, don't you know?'

'I do know. The last Bleedham-Drye. You could still make it into the tunnel – there's still a glow in the sky.'

Teddy seemed surprised that Myles should even think about the tunnel. 'The tunnel, is it? Oh no, dear boy, no afterlife for me. This is only temporary. I'll find a way back. I'm a scientist, after all. You're not rid of me yet, Myles Fowl.'

'That's the spirit,' said Myles.

'Stiff upper lip, don't you know,' said the duke. 'And, when I do come back, watch out! I'll be coming for you, Myles. And your twin. You won't get away the next time. And, even if you die from old age, there will always be your descendants. I'll make them pay for the sins of the fathers. I have all the time in the world to plot and plan. Mark my word, Myles, one way or another the Fowls will pay dearly for messing with Lord Teddy Bleedham-Drye.'

This would have been a good climax to the speech, but Teddy seemed to be on the point of issuing more threats when a small furry ghost dropped from the sky and latched on to the duke's head.

'Whistle Blower!' said Beckett. 'You're here!'

The toy troll grabbed Teddy by the ears and propelled them both into the air using some kind of leg-kick motion. The duke struggled and screamed, but he was held fast by the little troll, who, even in ghost form, was a lot stronger than he looked.

'No!' shrieked Lord Teddy. 'I will not go! There is so much to do.'

Whistle Blower growled and tightened his grip on Teddy's ears until they stretched cartoon-style.

'Get your paws off me!' howled the duke. 'Don't you know who I am?'

'Ectoplasm seems to be uncommonly malleable,' said Myles, mostly to himself.

It was a macabre and unprecedented event: a toy troll dragging a human duke to his own plasmic tunnel. The remaining Regrettables could not take their eyes off it.

Teddy struggled every inch of the way, screaming till he foamed at the mouth.

'Struggling is actually a big mistake,' commented Myles, though no one was listening. 'He's wasting his own energy and making Whistle Blower's job that much easier.'

As the warring pair ascended towards the shrinking disc of the tunnel mouth, Teddy shrank too, until he was hardly bigger than Whistle Blower. But, even so, when they caught up with the tunnel mouth, it seemed as if the duke's spectre could never fit inside. Yet the regular laws of physics did not apply the same way in ghost space, a fact that Myles made a mental note of, and Whistle Blower rolled Teddy's ectoplasmic frame into a cartoon ball and held him under the tunnel entrance. The duke's own attraction to the afterlife conduit did the rest and Teddy was sucked in, still protesting that the troll had no right to touch the royal person.

'Bitter to the end,' said Lazuli, sinking to the ground as her legs absolutely refused to hold her up for one more minute.

Beckett watched the sky until Whistle Blower drifted back down to earth, riding a ghostly breeze that only he could feel.

'That was awesome,' said Beckett to his deceased

friend. 'You saved us, and our children, and our children's children.'

Whistle Blower sat on an invisible sky shelf. 'I knew that Teddy guy wouldn't let it go. So I hung around.'

'You missed your own tunnel,' said Beckett.

The troll shrugged. 'Sometimes this life is more important than the next one.'

Beckett tried to come up with a plan, even though, as we have learned, planning was not his strong suit. 'All you need to do is wait here until a troll you are related to dies on the island, and then you can hitch a ride on his beam.'

'Yeah, that's what I'm going to do,' said Whistle Blower kindly.

Beckett felt as though he was filled to the brim with sadness. 'I'm so sorry. I let this happen.'

'No, my friend,' said Whistle Blower sternly. 'It was mostly Myles's fault. He's the worst kind of idiot – an idiot who thinks he's smart.'

Myles recognised the growl that meant *Myles*. 'Are you two talking about me?'

Beckett did what came naturally to him: manipulating his brother. 'Whistle Blower says that only you can help him. He called you the King of Geniuses.'

'That is probably true,' admitted Myles. 'But I need to tie up another loose end before I can even begin to think about Whistle Blower.'

The troll growled. 'I'm a loose end?'

Beckett winked at him. 'He didn't say no. That means yes. Soon the Regrettables will be reunited. All you have to do is stay here until we get back, and no jumping into any afterlife tunnels until I return.'

'Very well, Beckett,' said Whistle Blower. 'I shall await your return. Until then, we must perform the parting ritual.'

'Ah yes,' said Beckett. 'The mingling of the winds.' And together they recited the blessed verse:

'Warrior both loyal and true,
The gift of wind I give to you.
The particles inside my tum,
I blow your way from out my bum.'

It was undeniably a beautiful moment, crowned by the mingling of the friends' winds. Whistle Blower's wind emerged as a beautiful cloud of sparkling ectoplasm. Beckett's, unfortunately, did not.

* * *

Beckett, drained by his recent exertions, released a mighty lip-flapping sigh and squatted on his hunkers while Whistle Blower flew off to his special patch on the island, where he felt strongest.

'That was a long day,' Beckett said. 'Are we going to Dalkey now? Mum and Dad will be getting worried. You know Uncle Foxy will crack if he's under pressure. He's not as good at lying as you are.'

Myles rotated his jaw a few times, as it was sore after his recent en-dwarfing. 'We will return to the island soon, brother,' he said. 'First, I want to run a search on my files. I have a theory I need to check out.'

Lazuli was more exhausted than she'd ever been. 'Do you think, Myles, that following your super-important and typically vague search I could go home?'

Myles smiled in a typically vague Mona Lisa fashion and said, 'That could be exactly where you will be going, Specialist.'

EPILOGUE

HO CHI MINH City in the summer. Sweltering by anyone's standards. Myles Fowl would not have been willing to put up with such discomfort had not something extremely important been at stake. Important to his plan. Well, one of the plans. The plan he was concentrating on today.

Sun did not suit Myles. It highlighted the exhaustion that had prompted the migraine behind his eyes. An exhaustion due in no small part to the recent magical ordeal that had heralded the *winds of change*, so to speak.

I must ask Beckett for a slap in the face when we are finished here, he thought.

Myles was as white as a vampire and almost as testy in the light of day, even though it had been his idea to come here in the first place.

'I do hope this is not a wild-goose chase,' he commented to Beckett and Lazuli. The pixel was dressed in her SpongeBob hoodie and had sprayed herself with fake skin from the LEP locker back-pack.

'I haven't seen any geese,' said Beckett. 'Not any live ones, anyway, but I know for a fact that geese do not like being chased. Ducks think it's hilarious, but a goose will have your eye out.'

'It's an expression,' snapped Myles, even though he knew Beckett was winding him up. 'We are, in fact, after a winged creature, but the Regrettables will not be chasing any geese, or ducks, for that matter.'

Lazuli was even more uncomfortable than Myles, despite the fact that she was guiltily enjoying the Asian sunshine on her face. 'Why are we here, Myles? You're being so mysterious about it. I need to turn myself in and explain what happened in London and then St George if I want to stay out of Howler's Peak. There's probably a clean-up crew on the island right now, no doubt wondering why there are seaweed-goblin parts strewn all over the coastline. Not to mention pieces of a chute pod.'

The *why are we here* question posed by Specialist

Heitz was a valid one. Lazuli's very liberty was at stake, and running off to Vietnam with the Fowl Twins could be very easily construed as an attempt to evade justice.

The Regrettables were seated outside a kerbside café on Dong Khoi Street, watching the local teenagers circle the square on mopeds on what the locals called the *Chay Rong Rong*, or Great Ride Around. They had travelled here in Lord Teddy's light aircraft, which the duke would not be needing any more. The plane could never have made the trip until Myles upgraded its engines with the pod's surviving thruster, which still had enough ectoplasm to fly the Myishi Skyblade to eastern Asia with a couple of induction skims on the water along the way – one in the Arabian Sea, and a second on the Thailand side of the Bay of Bengal.

It had been a cramped and uncomfortable journey, but the internet connection had been amazing, as the ectoplasm acted like a lightning rod for radio and broadband signals. That meant Lazuli could put out a coded signal on a monitored frequency, ensuring that the LEP would send a team to St George, and now she was having trouble believing she had agreed to come along on this jaunt instead of waiting on the island.

Especially since the journey had completely crocked the seaplane and there was no chance it could make the trip back to the northern hemisphere.

The on-board internet had also enabled Myles to do a little investigating while he upgraded the Skyblade's engine before takeoff, and a lot more net digging during the flight. He managed to log into the Fowl server in Dalkey Island and run a quick search. There was a single hit on a database that Foaly and the LEP might not have access to, and that hit came from Vietnam, which was why the Regrettables were here and not facing the ire and suspicion of Commodore Holly Short.

Lazuli tugged the SpongeBob hood down over her brow, forgoing the wonderful sunshine. 'Myles, my friend, my fellow Regrettable,' she said. 'I am going to ask you to do something for me, and I want you to do it without giving me the traditional long-winded Fowl runaround version. Do you think you can do that?'

Myles threw an immediate mini-tantrum. 'You have no idea what you're asking, Specialist. None whatsoever. I put on this entire expedition to reveal something wonderful. All for you, by the way, and you would snatch my moment away from me?'

Beckett was finishing what more or less amounted to a bucket of lemonade. 'Myles does like his moments,' he said, before stringing together a series of burps that were calculated to inflate an imaginary balloon giraffe, while also tying the imaginary balloons with his real hands.

'What are you doing with your hands, Beck?' asked Lazuli, because it was distracting.

'He is obviously twisting an imaginary balloon animal,' snapped Myles. 'It's a giraffe, if I'm not mistaken.'

Lazuli was not in the mood for Myles being in a mood. 'I'm here, okay? I came because you swore it was important. Now you tell me right now: what is more important than my future?'

Myles's expression softened somewhat because he knew what was coming, but Myles being Myles he was not prepared to tell all in a single info dump. 'Let me ask you the same question, Specialist. What is more important than your future? Important to you personally, I mean.'

Lazuli scowled. 'This is exactly the sort of thing I'm talking about,' she said. 'I ask you a question, and you answer with a question. Classic Myles. What is more important to me than my future? Oh, I don't know. The environment. Stomach acid. Award shows. I'm sitting out here exposed to any human with a camera, Myles. Give me a break. Show me some mercy for once.' Lazuli rolled her eyes. 'Do you believe this, Beck?'

Beckett smiled at his blue (underneath the skin spray) friend. 'You should answer the question, Laz. My scar is buzzing. This is important.'

Lazuli was experiencing something close to panic. It was very unlike Myles to plonk them all somewhere out in the open like this, and the kaleidoscopic whizz of mopeds and bell-ringing bicycles was making her head spin. She had a feeling that all the various repressed traumas from the past few days had decided to come knocking at the same time.

Specialist Heitz closed her eyes and kneaded her forehead. 'Beck, Myles. I need to get out of here. We're creatures of the shadows. We dig deep and we endure. Remember? How can anything be more important to the world than the future?'

'Not to the world,' said Myles. 'Forget about saving the world just for now. You'll be doing that soon enough, if I'm right. What's more important than the future to *you*? You told me once.'

410

When Lazuli frowned, the spray skin cracked in the grooves in her forehead. '*I* told you? *Me*? When did I . . . ?'

And then Lazuli remembered what she had said. Suddenly her mouth was dry and the implications fell like dominoes inside her head.

Could Myles have done it? she asked herself. *Could Myles have done what the entire LEP could not do?*

The answer to that was simple.

Of course he could. He is a Fowl, after all.

Lazuli's breath came fast and hard and she steadied herself against the table's rim.

'Don't hyperventilate, Specialist,' said Myles. 'Why don't you keep your eyes closed while I explain my thought process?'

Lazuli nodded and felt Beckett's fingers slip between hers. She gripped them tightly.

'I will be brief,' said Myles (snort from Beckett), 'as I know your imagination must be running wild at the moment.'

It was. Running wild through the past decades.

'You said to me that the only thing more important to you than your future was your past,' began Myles. 'And so I gave some serious thought to locating your parents. You should be honoured. But anyway, I asked myself: Myles, if the LEP couldn't find Specialist Heitz's parents, then could *I*, a mere human genius, hope to succeed? The answer to this was, of course, a resounding *absolutely*, because I had figured out something that has not yet occurred to Foaly. I knew that your transformative magic was of a very rare type.

'Throughout recorded fairy history, transformative magic has only ever been exhibited by demon warlocks, who are almost exclusively male. But female warlocks do or did exist. So, I asked myself: Professor Fowl, what if Specialist Heitz's mother was a warlock who passed down her abilities to her daughter?'

Lazuli kept her eyes closed, as requested, but she had to point out, 'I can't be a demon. I'm a pixie-elf hybrid.'

'If you are the daughter of a warlock, you can be whatever fairy species she imprinted on you. It's transformative magic, remember?'

Lazuli nodded. This was all proving to be very close to overwhelming, and she felt like she might dissolve in a puddle of tears, or kick Myles in the backside. One of those.

'Now, if you were a warlock's daughter with trans-formative magic, that would make you the most unique and powerful fairy in the world. And, whatever the LEP decided to do with you, it would not be to lock you up in Howler's Peak.'

Lazuli nodded rapidly, the message being: *Get on with it.*

Myles did so. 'There are more than five hundred genetic loci associated with being a warlock. Obviously, the LEP run continuous searches for those markers, but Beckett, of all people, reminded me that we had access to a single sample that the LEP did not. Some years ago, our older brother, Dr Fowl, visited Ho Chi Minh City on one of his frankly puerile ventures and stuck a needle into a down-and-out sprite, curing her of her alcohol addiction. As a matter of course, he logged the blood sample left on the needle. When I ran my loci check, I got a hit from that needle. To think that all this time Artemis had an invaluable sample in his vault and never thought to check it. What a dope.'

Lazuli heard a thumping noise and correctly guessed that it was indeed a *thump.*

'You never thought to check, either,' said Beckett. 'That was my amazing idea.'

'Ow!' said Myles, and Lazuli imagined him rubbing his thumped shoulder. 'Very well, brother mine. No more Artemis denigrations. I shall proceed with my frankly stunning revelations. I set about tracing this Vietnamese sprite, if indeed she was a sprite, using the ACRONYM files I had downloaded from their server and the message boards frequented by rogue surface fairies, and I very quickly found numerous posts from a sprite living in Ho Chi Minh City who had lost both her partner and female child in an ACRONYM attack on a fairy transport some years previously. The partner's body was recovered but never the child's. Apart from a few years of depression and alcohol dependence, this sprite has spent years searching for her daughter in the hopes that she had survived the attack. There is no doubt, Lazuli, that you are her missing daughter, and that is why we are here.'

'Myles found your mother,' Lazuli heard Beckett say beside her. 'This is the best news.'

Lazuli said nothing. This was because there were so many questions vying for attention that she could not decide which one to ask. Myles, of course, took her silence to mean that she was dumbstruck by awe and gratitude and so kept talking.

'Now, I know, Specialist, that what I have done is amazing and many people might say bordering on impossible, and you will be tempted to hug me, but I must tell you that I have never been comfortable with hugs, and so, though I appreciate the sentiment, I only enjoy hugs from Beckett. You can tell this if you watch my body language during embraces, as I lead with my shoulder, which is a dead giveaway. A simple handshake is all the Fowl Twins need or deserve. And perhaps a statue on Police Plaza.'

'I'll take the hug,' said Beckett, wrapping his arms round Lazuli.

Lazuli returned the squeeze, but there was too much going on internally for her to enjoy the moment.

Is my father dead?

Is my mother alive?

Am I a sprite or a demon or both?

Was I stashed in Haven for my own safety without my mother's knowledge?

Could Myles be wrong?

Even if he's right about everything, am I prepared to go through with this?

And still Myles kept talking. 'There's a lot for you to process, and I'm sure you have many questions, so, while you ask these questions, Beckett and I shall make our way back to the canals where we docked and set about repairing the Skyblade. When you're ready, come and seek us out. You may take some time, but so shall we.'

Lazuli did have questions. So many. Decades of questions, each one threaded with glints of longing and pain. But one question trumped all the rest as the need for an answer was immediate and so very urgent.

She opened her eyes to ask this question and was dismayed to see Myles and Beckett already standing to leave.

'Wait!' she blurted. 'Don't go. I need my Regrettables here with me now, so much more than ever.'

Beckett seemed about a million degrees calmer than she'd ever seen him.

Typical, she thought. *Beck finds his Zen when I'm jumping out of my skin.*

'This is your day for answers, Laz,' he said. 'We don't know what those answers are. You should hear them first.'

Lazuli sniffed. 'I can't believe you've done all this, without even telling me.'

'Neither can I,' said Myles. 'I knew I was brilliant, but to put this together required an extra-special intellect.'

Beckett bowed. 'Thanks, brother. You helped a little.'

Lazuli smiled. 'I owe both of you my future and now perhaps my past. How can I repay you?'

Beckett clapped his hands. 'I have the perfect answer for that – something Artemis learned from Commodore Short. He wrote it down for me.'

'I forbid it!' shouted Myles, startling surrounding diners. 'Unless it is, of course, facile and cheesy.'

Beckett ploughed on. 'Artemis said that the only payment a Fowl shall ever seek from a fairy is the satisfaction of strengthening the bond between them.'

'That's not bad,' admitted Myles.

'So if you smile,' continued Beckett, 'that is all the payment we deserve or want.'

Lazuli smiled through her tears, then shook Myles's hand as requested, was smothered by another hug from Beckett, and while she was in the hug remembered the urgent question she had momentarily forgotten to ask.

'Wait,' she said. 'If you're leaving, who will answer my questions?'

Beckett held her at arm's length. 'You're not going to believe this.'

'I'm not going to believe what?'

Myles pointed towards the traffic island in the

middle of the square where pedestrians waited for the lights to change. 'I took the liberty of reaching out. I was worried we'd miss our chance. I hope you don't mind. But, if you decide to go ahead with this, you're leaving the LEP behind, for now at least. We will, of course, send them on one of those wild-goose chases we talked about, but there is a chance they won't take you back, even if you are a warlock.'

Lazuli nodded. She would reluctantly take off the badge if there was a chance of meeting her mother. The pixel, if she even truly was a pixel, could feel herself sinking into shock. Her senses of smell and hearing seemed to fade while her vision became crystal clear. The clamour of street noise and the smell that had seemed so overpowering mere seconds ago were now dialled down to almost non-existent.

Lazuli turned her gaze to the traffic island that was teeming with pedestrians eager to go about their daily business of getting from A to B. Keeping their families fed and safe. It was said that in Ho Chi Minh City no one stood still for long. But one person was standing still. A small, slight lady dressed in traditional Vietnamese trousers and a two-flap dress. On first glance, this lady was human, but Lazuli knew she was a fairy. She knew it by instinct, but also because tears had worn twin paths in the lady's make-up, revealing a mottled green skin underneath.

Is this happening? thought Lazuli. *Can this be real?*

It *was* happening. It *was* real.

The lady took a step into the road and Lazuli thought she might be run over by the never-ending stream of traffic, but somehow she found a path, disappearing and reappearing between the curve of a chrome mudguard or the strobe of bus windows.

'She's coming,' Lazuli said to the twins, but they were already moving away. The last thing she heard them do was bicker.

'I can't believe you quoted Artemis. He is such an idiot.'

'He is not an idiot. He's our brother. And, anyway, Artemis travelled through time.'

'Any twit can travel through time. You are travelling in time right now, Beck.'

'So are you, Myles. And so is Whistle Blower. Have you finished the clone yet?'

'How could I have finished the clone, Beck? We haven't been home. Did you keep the crisp packet?'

'I did. It's on the plane.'

'Good. Well then, as soon as we get home, I will extract the DNA and begin the process.'

'Can you give him wings? Whistle Blower always wanted wings.'

'I suppose I could, but I don't really want to go meddling with DNA.'

'Could you give *me* wings?'

'Absolutely not.'

'Absolutely?'

'Not *absolutely* absolutely. I'll think about it.'

'That means yes. That's a legal contract.'

'No, it isn't. I could do something about your golden toe.'

'Make it bigger?'

'No, Beck. Not make it bigger.'

The twins' squabbling petered out as they moved further away, and Lazuli remembered a proverb from her Asian studies class: *Khẩu phật tâm xà: A fair face may hide a foul heart.* She realised that, while there were no human faces fairer to her than the twins', they certainly did not hide foul hearts.

She smiled again while the lady with eyes that looked like hers glided across the road magically unhurt by the traffic, arms outstretched now, and Lazuli knew that the hard knot of questions she'd carried around all her life was about to be loosened.

Not *foul hearts*, she thought. Fowl *hearts*.

READ THE FIRST BOOK IN THE BLOCKBUSTING SERIES FROM GLOBAL BESTSELLER EOIN COLFER . . .

Myles and **Beckett Fowl** are twins but the two boys are wildly different. Beckett is blond, messy and sulks whenever he has to wear clothes. Myles is impeccably neat, has an IQ of 170, and 3D prints a fresh suit every day – just like his older brother, **Artemis Fowl**.

A week after their eleventh birthday the twins are left in the care of house security system NANNI for a single night. In that time, they befriend a troll on the run from a nefarious nobleman and an interrogating nun, both of whom need the magical creature for their own gain . . .

Prepare for an epic adventure in which the Fowl Twins and their new troll friend escape, get shot at, kidnapped, buried, arrested, threatened, killed (temporarily) . . . and discover that the strongest bond in the world is not the one forged by covalent electrons in adjacent atoms, but the one that exists between a pair of twins.

The second Fowl Twins adventure starts with a bang – literally.

Artemis's little brothers Myles and Beckett borrow the Fowl jet without permission, and it ends up as a fireball over Florida. The twins plus their fairy minder, the pixie-elf hybrid Lazuli Heitz, are lucky to escape with their lives.

The Fowl parents and fairy police force decide that enough is enough and the twins are placed under house arrest. But Myles has questions, like: who was tracking the Fowl jet? Why would someone want to blow them out of the sky? These questions must infuriate someone, because Myles is abducted and spirited away from his twin.

Now Beckett and Lazuli must collaborate to find Myles and rescue him – not easy when it was Myles who was the brains of the operation. Their chase will take them across continents, deep underground, and into subaquatic supervillain lairs. They will be shot at, covered in spit, and at the receiving end of some quite nasty dwarf sarcasm. But will Beckett be able to come up with a genius plan without a genius on hand . . . ?